LIGHT TO LIGHT

A THORNY WALLACE NOVEL | BOOK 2

BAER CHARLTON

MORDANT MEDIA ™©®
A Division of Charlton Productions

Dedicated to Dr. Bob Denton

*Doc, my friend and spirit guide in the way
of humor and being who you are.*

December 2, 1922 — October 28, 2017

CONTENTS

ALSO BY BAER CHARLTON

The Very Littlest Dragon

Stoneheart
(Pulitzer Nominee 2015)

Angel Flights
What About Marsha?
Pirate's Patch

Southside Hooker Series
Death on a Dime – Book One
Night Vision – Book Two
Unbidden Garden – Book Three
Boomtown – Book Four
One Day Under the Grass – Book Five

Thorny Wallace Series
Death in the Valley – Book One
Light to Light – Book Two

01 FINISH LINE

The few buildings scattered in the desert on the outskirts of the city were a mere blur to the two motorcycles speeding past. The roadway was finally asphalt. The tires rolled smooth. The heat of the sun seared through the shirts of the two riders lying flat over their gas tanks. The long day of racing had started nearly nine hours before.

Roy glanced down at the large white speedometer on his Indian Chief. The slender red needle pointed forward toward the finish line and at the fat side of the eighty. He knew the motorcycle could effortlessly run faster. He also knew the end of the race, a few miles ahead, wasn't a foregone conclusion.

The black, eighty-inch flat-head Harley Davidson ran beside him. His left knee was almost touching his friend's knee. Both sets of boots draped crossed over the rear fenders to reduce air drag, both pair of dungarees worn and faded. Neither man had bought a new pair of anything in over eight years. The depression had been tough, but the rationing and the war had ground on their bones and souls.

The repair shop had gone from fixing motorcycles to also taking in minor repair on cars to now even soldering broken wires in toasters. Anything needing repair the brothers would fix. Anything but the mortgage on their homes and the shop. This race wouldn't fix it, but it would help. This was about helping to fix the town of Bishop and the larger Owens Valley.

Mace glanced at his friend on the red Indian. The night before, the two had cleaned and polished the two motorcycles. The two motorcycle companies had a stake in the race and were given over half of the money needed for the cause. Mace lowered his head to the gas tank, and both men let off the gas and coasted to a stop. There was over a mile left to the city limits. Nobody was close enough to see.

Mace opened his left gas cap and rocked the bike side to side as he listened. He knew the gas was so low, it would be at the bottom end of the tank where he couldn't see—only hear. He rocked the heavy motorcycle again.

Closing the cap, he looked at his brother in life. Their goggles smeared with bugs, mud, and dust, he could see the limpid-blue eyes Roy got from his mother's side of the family. Mace's were the green of both his mother and father. He slowly shook his head. They both knew the rules. There was no more stopping for extra fuel.

Roy bit on his lower lip. "They ain't gonna like it, but we'll just brace it if we have to."

Both men, who had stared down death together, nodded and shook hands.

They stomped on their clutches and pushed their shifters forward as one. The two front tires rolled in unison. The two had become a formidable juggernaut in France. When not flying, they rode two stolen motorcycles in brash, devil-may-care assaults. As they rose up and over the mounds in front of the trenches, the French soldiers became Berserkers behind them. The nerve, flagrancy and inspiring verve de gore led to the Frenchmen in their company to nickname the two men: The Four Horsemen of the Apocalypse. They had never slowed from being forces of nature, but age and the depression had not been gentle.

The two motorcycles roared past the new museum built with the last of the wild money of the 1920s. People lined the street as they approached the gambling blocks, the deafening cheers almost drowned out the sound of the Harley cough.

Roy looked to his brother and then at the traffic light three blocks away.

The Harley backfired and coughed. Mace looked at his friend. The two ear-bashing engines became one. They both rose to a sitting position. Mace slammed the shifting lever forward to the neutral position as the engine died. He looked to his brother in arms with a look of fear and resolve.

Roy threw out his left arm and eased the red Indian closer. Their knees pushed together as Mace gripped his brother's wrist. Their two arms were like a steel bar across from motorcycle to motorcycle. Roy rubbed his face across his right shoulder and arm without letting up on the throttle, his goggles washed from his face and into the street behind them. Mace mirrored the move.

Blue eyes locked onto green, and together they mouthed the word that had bonded them in France. "Brothers."

Two men. Two motorcycles. Two blocks. One engine. One goal. Arms locked, they roared toward the streetlight as they watched it turn red.

The Nevada desert blast furnace—burning their faces and shoulders. The heat was nothing compared to the strain on the shoulders of the two locked arms—dragging the half-ton of men and machines across the finish line.

The tires swept across the brilliant white of the freshly painted lines of the crosswalk. Flashbulbs turned the yellow day white. Their bodies swept the bunting finish line streamer from the two Boy Scout's hands. They looked up at the still red light set in the searing blue sky. Their two smiles were toothy and white. The people lining the street looked to the large clock on the bank. The small black hand stood at the twelve, the longer red hand wouldn't join it for another four minutes.

The two men smiled at each other. From the tension in their arms, they both knew the front tires of both Harley Davidson and the American Indian had crossed the line perfectly lined up. It was a tie.

The two looked forward as they coasted. A single woman stepped into the street. She could pass for the famous pilot. The two who joined her were the men's wives. A tall man in a fedora, open collar, and with rolled up sleeves, stood silently behind the women.

The racer's triumphant smiles washed away. The two older women stood side by side. A glint of silver flashed in the sunshine between the two women. Handcuffs hung condemning between the two arms. With only one motorcycle with gasoline left—there was nowhere to go. Mace squeezed Roy's arm and let go. They glided to a stop in front of the three women. Nobody moved. The big red Indian Chief coughed, backfired, and shuttered to silence. The last of the gasoline was gone.

SIX MONTHS EARLIER

The perfectly polished brown leather dully reflected the mound of yellow ochre pigment. The other shoe reflected the brilliant blue of ground lapis. The large cones of pigment meant little to the man. The seller's piles of every color, produced by thousands of hours of bone-weary labor, were not worth a tenth of the contents the man carried in his small satchel.

Even at the late hour, the medina of Dar es Salaam swirled about the European man. Many shunned the larger grand bazaar for the smaller alleys winding in the medieval part of the city. The sellers were not always what they appeared and sold not what was in their stalls.

The man in the brown suit held his handkerchief to his nose and mouth against the acrid copper smell of blood mixed with the sour odor of putrefied offal, wafting from the butcher stall close by. He closed his eyes to force his mind to think of flower-strewn Alpine hills, instead of the fly-infested carcasses hanging only a few steps away. The square of silk was drenched in lavender and peppermint.

The man hated, with his very fiber, his need to spend any time what so ever in Tanganyika, much less it's port capital. The Schutzstaffel rewarded him handsomely, at home in Berlin and abroad. Not even the tall young Nubian girls in Cairo or the young zaftig Austrian wife to replace his older wife were enough to prevent him from stealing some of the gemstones he couriered for his Nazi masters.

"Masaa'al-khayr, Herr Miller." The man stepped from behind the curtain. His son turned and retreated from watching the pigment seller's stall.

Irritated, the man hissed. "Deutsch. Sprich deutsch, verdammt."

The Arab put his palms together and bowed. "As you wish, Herr Miller. German, it is."

The man glanced about. His eyes darted first past the citric seller and then up the alley past the butcher. His eyes took in every filthy detail of the cramped alley. Much of the alley had been old and crumbling before the Roman's trotted Jesus up the hill with the other two criminals.

Turning on the now half-smiling man in the tattered kaftan, he coughed in his handkerchief. "Must we conduct business out here where the world watches us like common prostitutes on display?"

"Alas, I am but a poor stall keeper. The entire world conducts its business in the street. There is nothing behind the curtain but my small bed and a chair. Even for prayer, I must do so in public."

Miller knew the man was anything but an impoverished shopkeeper. He guessed the man would even lie about what was behind the curtains at the back of his stall. The man's kaftan and the curtains were stained and tattered, but he also knew a vendor was not poor when they sold pigment to the wealthy. The butcher may be poor, the seller of oranges and lemons was most certainly poor, but the man standing before him was as wealthy as any corrupt Berger in Germany.

The man spread his hands in supplication. "Herr Miller, we have but a simple exchange. Nine?"

"Ja, Ja natürlich." He stepped forward between the yellow and blue cones of ochre and lapis. His right hand raised the small brown valise.

The Arab held his gaze as he took the valise. Knowing the man was now on the losing side of the war, he had no more compassion. The valise was light. He weighed it in his left hand as his face cocked and made a face of question.

"It is all there. Twelve-kilograms. The valise has never been opened since Gaborone."

"Shukran, I trust you, Herr Miller. It is my buyers who do not." Two men carrying a rolled carpet approached behind the courier. Their bare feet were as silent as smoke in the night. The slender knife was but a mere flash in the darkness. The two men wrapped the falling German agent in an old carpet as he fell. The fine grindings of pigment cascaded about the carpets they sat on. None of the three men cared about the spilled pigment—the boy would return and straighten the piles. The taller man stooped and took up the carpet-wrapped legs.

The pigment seller stood and watched as the two carpet sellers carried the dirty carpet down the dark alleyway. He stooped and retrieved the bowler hat. His fingers thumbed the fine felt as he thought. He knew the carpet sellers would search the German for any items of value and then would share with their brother. He would, and had in the past, done the same with them. The alley was more about family and relationships than mere sellers of products or providers of services.

The man's glare pierced the gloom of the alley both ways. His tongue clicked almost closed mouth. The boy slid from behind the curtain and nodded at the pointed finger.

Turning, the pigment seller secreted the small valise under his arm and moved between the curtains. Past the small bed was another curtain. He disappeared into the long hall, his slippers scuffing in the dark. He began to hum a small tune he had heard during his college days at Cambridge.

Another small boy materialized from the shadows of the alley. He knew there would be no more buyers for the night, but it was his duty to watch. His brother adroitly rebuilt the shape of the cones and swept the threadbare carpet. His fingers touched the red cone and then rubbed the carpet to replace color which hadn't existed there since his grandfather was a child.

The butcher bid his last patron a healthy life. He reached up and untied the canvas curtain. The meat disappeared. The alley dimmed as each merchant closed for the night.

03 SETTLE IN

Thorny looked up at the pink veil on Mt. Tom and the lower crescent of pink on the ridge creating Mt. Humphries. She even smiled at this site as a little girl. She never tired of walking into town in the dark. As the road straightened, the stars would begin to disappear from the night sky. At a quarter mile from the junction of Highway 6 and 395, she was walking down the middle of the smaller highway. The main highway, 395, became the main streets through all the towns in the Owens Valley. She watched the black separate into grays and not quite black. By the time she reached the stop-sign, the pink was just a blush.

She would always stop and lean against the signpost. Watching the hazy blush become a light pink on the rocks showing between the snow patches. Some mornings, the two mountains looked like they were bursting with a flame within. When the mountains were shown with a fresh-covering blanket of snow, Thorny never even gave them a glance. The fresh snow and pink never reached the same visceral fire.

Thorny could hear the truck coming. Without turning, she knew it was old man Jessup. The truck had sounded the same for most of twenty years. She also knew if the man touched the brakes while approaching the sign, the heavens would open and take him without delay.

The truck rattled through the stop. If Thorny tried, she knew she could walk faster than the man drove. The single anemic *aaugaha* of the horn had started a few weeks before.

"Mornin', Chief."

Her eyelids gently fell shut. The greetings about town had started a few days later. She figured before she reached the police station, she would be greeted at least twelve times each as police chief, mayor, sheriff, councilman, and judge. Not once would anyone just say hello or call her by her name. She groaned. The town was having their fun, but also, it was their way of showing their appreciation, if not respect.

Even Monte had taken up whistling cheery senseless tunes. His take was it was the town's way of welcoming her home. There were days she thought about climbing the ladder and waiting out the days in the civil defense tower with Bill. The man was at least creative as to what he saw. A crow could be a SPAD airplane from the first World War, or a small dark gray cloud could become a zeppelin. The saving grace of spending time with Bill was he would never see her as the mayor, chief of police, or a judge. To at least one man, she was just Miss Wallace.

The pink had become a yellow-red stone on the mountains. The sun had risen and was warming the valley. Thorny pushed off against the post and walked across the highway. It would be the wrong side of the street eventually, but in less than a block, there were roses, and then gerbera daisies. The planter box sat under a cracked pipe. The leaking water was enough for the volunteer plants to grow. Thorny had asked around, and there seemed to be nobody who would miss the occasional handful of flowers.

She pulled a few dozen weeds from the planter. She laid them on the concrete to dry. In a few days, she would crumble them and spread them back in the box—returning them from whence they came. She pinched off the six roses and a dozen daisies. The small vases on the six tables at the Bib would look cheery.

The sound of two large motorcycles roared in from north of town. The two bikes swept around the large turn. The two riders could have been riding in a Model A for as close as they were. Thorny couldn't see but would almost bet their knees occasionally touched. The men had met during the Great War. Some would say they were real brothers, who had finally met in the trenches of France. The only thing for sure was they must get a lot of bugs in their teeth because they were always smiling.

The motorcycles slowed and eased into the small parking lot in front of the garage. The sign originally had a painted picture of the two on motorcycles racing with hats turned backward, goggles above the smiles only inches from the handlebars, and the two men bent over and racing with the wind. Now the sign simply read, 'The Right Brothers Mechanical Repair.' There weren't enough motorcycles in the valley; so, cars, trucks, and even tractors would be seen in the shop.

Thorny noted the large banner over the door, advertising 'The Race of the Century.' The all-out race was to be four hundred miles. It would start at the train crossing in Mojave. They would start in the coldest hours of the morning—to beat the heat of the desert. The end would be at the last streetlight in Carson City, Nevada. The winner would get a thousand dollars and his motorcycle. But the race's true purpose was to raise money for the new wing of the Northern Inyo County Hospital. The big contributors were the manufacturers of the two large motorcycles. Roy favored his heavier red American Indian Chief. Mace would ride his pride and joy Harley Davidson. Both motorcycles were powered by engines known as Flatheads. Both had displacements of eighty-inches. The two manufacturers were putting up twenty-five grand each for the hospital.

Thorny waved back at the chorused calls of 'Morning, Chief.'

Thorny could have walked the length of Main Street and only

once or twice have had to dodge a car. The street was empty in the crisp early morning air. The sidewalk was no colder on her bare feet than the asphalt of the street. Bishop was slow to wake, but it was also the time of the day Thorny liked the most. The fresh daylight was holding its breath with an expectation of anything. The sun rising in the cloudless sky boded simple and gentle movement below.

The two women who cleaned and then helped the owner at the Men's Fine Clothing nodded as they passed. "Very nice flowers, Mayor."

Thorny returned their nod. She smirked at the retreating twitter of gossip.

"Who do you think the flowers are for?"

"I don't know for sure… but, Gladys said… and you know how much of a gossip she is…"

Thorny almost turned at the short gasp.

"Why, he's old enough to be her grandfather…"

Thorny crossed the street and stepped onto the soft dirt that paved Line Street. The long tent that, for a few months every early spring, adorned the front of Victor's Leather, had been put away until next spring. The mule teams were in the high valleys, delivering food, people, and fingerling trout to the lakes and streams.

A quart jar sat tucked under the front steps of the Bib. Thorny could see the light in the kitchen. May would be busy baking biscuits. Thorny stuck the bouquet in the jar and put the whole under the small hose-bib. She filled the jar halfway and set it on the second step, out-of-the-way of the door. She knew they would be on the tables when she returned with Monte.

<hr>

THORNY GRUMPED with a smirk at the growl behind the door. Either Monte had slept in, or he was in the middle of buttoning his shirt. She listened for the sound of feet.

The sound was of shoes on the hardwood floor—shirt.

The door swung open a couple of inches. Thorny pushed and saw the backside of the retreating man.

"You're getting better at waking up with the rooster."

The man buzzed his lips and grumped. "Don't talk to me. I'm old, and I haven't had any coffee yet. Was there a paper on the stoop?"

Thorny leaned back and looked around. Monte's 'stoop' was a six-foot square of concrete in front of the door. She had yet to ever see the paper thrown to land on the pad. "No."

The voice drifted back from the bedroom or bathroom. "Check the Pyracantha bush. The young Smith boy has a habit of throwing the paper like a tomahawk." Monte came out of the backroom cinching his belt. "After the war is over, I might pay to get his eyes checked and buy him some glasses. He's got a good arm, but he pulls to the left." He looked up in expectation.

Thorny laughed. "You have a mirror. Or did you become a vampire overnight?" She stopped and thought. "It is vampires who can't see themselves in the mirror isn't it?"

The man harrumphed. "Who cares. The beast doesn't exist. Grab the paper and let's go—I'm starved."

Thorny poked at his slight acknowledgment to older age. "Yes, you look so starved."

"Behave."

Thorny raked her claw at the errant set of curls on the side of his head as he passed her for the door. He shied as his own fingers came up to complete the unseen work. "I told you to behave."

Thorny grumped back at him. "Act your age."

"The flowers look lovely, May." Monte leaned and smelled the single rose set with two daisies.

May stood next to Thorny and snuck her arm around the younger waist. "Yes, I have a very high placed gremlin who magically brings them to my doorstep on Sunday mornings. Heaven only knows where they find such treasures in this mule-bitten town." She leaned over and gave Thorny a kiss on the cheek, the hug and kiss returned.

"Daniel went about the neighborhood yesterday, pulling me a huge basket of dandelions, and last night, he was down fishing and found some ferns, still with the fiddle-heads. So I made us a cheese and greens quiche. The biscuits are about to come out, and as soon as the girls get here, we can have brunch. Make yourself comfortable—Monte, if you would be please a gentleman. You know where the coffeepot is." She turned back toward the kitchen.

Thorny sat before someone pointed at the seat at the head of the table and demanded she sit there, instead. "Where is Daniel this morning?"

May's head poked out the kitchen door. "My son? Are you asking a serious question? You know how religious he is... He's in church." She disappeared as they all heard the dinging of the timer clock.

Monte and Thorny looked at each other with smirking smiles. "The church of the river." Fishing. Since the stock market crash in twenty-nine, it had been the fastest growing church and religion in the valley. Anyone living in Bishop knew the banks of the Owens River, wandering down the middle of the Owens Valley. On any given Sunday, the banks would be spotted with religious anglers. The Great Depression had taught many men how to catch fish, which led to simply fishing. Years of a diet consisting of field-gathered greens and trout, led in better times to settling for any cut of meat other than fish. But, if a man was fishing, he was excused from any other chores around the house. Daniel was one of the few who still went to the river to collect fish, instead of lying in the grass and passing the day in quiet, relaxing solitude.

They both turned at the hollow sound of shoes on the wooden porch. The door opened, and the two women stood, removing their shoes before entering the house.

Monte snapped his fingers as he finished pouring Thorny's coffee. He quickly poured the other four cups full, then retreated to the door. Hugging the two women in passing, he removed his shoes.

Thorny stood with a smile. "Inez, Bertha, we are just getting started. May made us biscuits and quiche, so please be seated." She hugged both women as May brought a large glass pie pan. May nodded back toward the kitchen for Monte to fetch the biscuits.

As May stood at the corner of the table, she slipped off her shoes. They all sat. The blue and white checked gingham tablecloth shone in their eyes as they took hands around the table. Their smiles reflected in the warmth of their grips.

May looked about the table. "I call this meeting of the Sunday barefoot posse to come to order. Dig in."

The first few minutes were taken by serving food and the first bites. Inez turned to May as she chewed on a small bite of biscuit. "I see Danny was successful in getting you some more Cardamom."

May reached out with a laugh. "Shh, we don't want Thorny to know my secrets about cooking. Next thing you know, she'll get my job too."

Bertha sniggled. "She better not come looking for my job."

The four looked back at the young woman hanging her head, focused on her food. There was a soft growl, making the older four laugh.

Feeling safe enough to poke the snarling beast, Monte continued the teasing. "Which is the problem, Thorny? The cooking or the other jobs?" He leaned away from Bertha who was quietly trying to push his wayward curls back into place.

Thorny looked up through her eyelashes. Her chewing was slow. Finished, she swallowed as she sat back, wiping her mouth. "All of it. I can burn a rat or lizard on a hot rock, but beyond that..." She sipped at her coffee. "The town... well, the women of the town want to give me all the jobs abandoned by the men who decamped. The problem is I don't want the jobs. There are plenty of smart, honest people who can do an excellent job at these positions. I think we should find the right people for the jobs and let them do the work. There are some who could use the pay, something I don't need now." Her voice trailed off. Her focus slewed down along the table in thought.

Bertha—only a few years older, but as the town whore, so much wiser than her age—cleared her throat. "Are you asking your barefoot posse to find the right people for the jobs?"

Thorny blinked and looked up. Her face was like a person waking from a dream. "I guess I am." Her smile was conspiratorial. "What a great idea. You four know the people in the town, and I'm only new back."

Inez snorted. "What Birdie and I know about the people in the town..."

Bertha squealed in laughter.

Monte grumped. "You girls are just nasty." His hand and napkin were quick to hide his smile.

May smiled sadly at the mischievous three. "Intimate knowledge, from being the town's prostitutes, is much better knowledge than no knowledge at all. But seriously..." She gave the two women and Monte a hard eye. "We each have unique views into people lives. There are subjects men will talk about to their barber, which they would never share with a woman they are having sex with. The same goes for a small café. I hear more information about how people conduct their businesses and lives than others would ever think."

The three women looked at the only male. His toes curled as he wished he could cross his toes. "A good barber never talks and tells."

The retired prostitute laughed. "Good thing Bishop doesn't have one of those barbers."

Thorny detected a warm glow creeping around her uncle's neckline.

As the laughing died down, Thorny eyed the young prostitute whose apartment and business was the entire second floor over the court and police station. The young woman took a second glance down the table.

"What?"

"What about John for chief?"

The young woman's lips came together in a mew as she thought. May raised a finger. "If I may. I'm almost positive he never climbed those stairs, and if he did, I'm certain I don't want to know. However, as honest as he is, I would hazard a bet he would turn down the offer."

"Why?"

"His comfort is in going home at night. He will man the desk from sunup until dinnertime, but don't ask him to work and miss dinner. He also likes to read his books in the evening."

Thorny nudged her head sideways and squinted. "What sort of books?"

"For himself, I think he likes to read about world history. But for Nancy... He reads her poetry by Chaucer, and sonnets by the bard among others."

"So, he would work hard as my second in command, but not the chief?"

Monte closed one eye. "I think you might want to retain the position and the opportunity of power it provides. If you are going to investigate old cases, it would be good to have the power of police chief in your front pocket... so to speak."

Inez winked. "And then you could move the hog leg to your hip instead of down your behind."

Thorny reached inside the back of her pants and withdrew the automatic pistol. She laid it on the table pointed to her side. "It might be more comfortable, but I think it would scare the church ladies."

Bertha stared at the size of the large semi-automatic weapon. She mussed softly to herself. "Not such a small hog leg."

Thorny ignored the other young woman's fascination with the weapon. "What about a judge?"

May coughed softly. "The reason the last judge was probably on the Water & Power's bribery payroll was that the judge position doesn't pay enough. If you could convince the county to increase the pay, you might convince one of your law school friends to move to the backwoods. I'm sure they would get reelected until they died of old age."

Thorny looked down at her right hand. "Damn. I didn't expect much from this meeting, so I didn't bring a notepad and pen."

May excused herself to get more coffee and said note-taking materials.

Monte leaned his head as his eyes drilled holes in Bertha. She blushed and pulled her hand away from his head. "What?"

"Well, did John ever climb those stairs?"

Bertha softly snorted a tiny puff of air and looked to the older Inez. The retired former town whore shied her eyelids and swung her head. "Not with me. I tried, but I think the man was pure when he married his woman. Without a doubt, he worships the ground she walks on."

Bertha turned. "I'll vouch for the same."

"It's not much of a notepad…" May stopped in the doorway. She eyed the four who looked ever so much like children with their hands in the cookie jar. She lowered her eyelids as she rolled her eyes. "As I was saying… It's not a large pad, but it's what I have." She put the coffeepot on the trivet and sat. Her eyes drifted from one to the next. Nobody was making eye contact or making a sound.

She turned and leaned in and growled at Monte. "Give it up, Geronimo." The man was not the same warrior his great-uncle was… but then, he didn't count out his grandmother, either.

A poke of Bertha's finger in his ribs was his end. "The consensus is John never did climb those stairs."

May sat back with a satisfied smirk and looked at Thorny. Thorny softly chuckled as the other woman wiggled her eyebrows as if to say, this is the way things get done.

"Moving on to mayor."

The front door swung open, and May's son Daniel backed in. Three fishing creels hung from his neck and shoulders. He turned and froze. "Oh." He took in who was at the table. The only attorney sitting at the table leaned back with her arm over the back of the chair.

"Looks like a weighty haul there, Daniel. Remind me what the limit is again."

"Ah, jeez, Thorny, the Fish and Game officer is right behind me."

"Are all of those creels yours?"

He moved the small curtain on the door's window. All of them could hear a truck or rattle-can car pull up to the curb in front. He looked back at Thorny in panic.

She rose and pointed at the kitchen. Grabbing her pistol, she shoved it back into the holster in her pants and strode to the door. She glanced at May in question.

The woman shrugged. "I think it's Mike Hollister. June and Addison Hollister's boy."

Monte nodded. "He was about three or four years ahead of you. He is kind of a pretty boy."

Thorny nodded as she opened the door and stepped out. "Good gracious, as I live and breathe, it's Mike Hollister. How long has it been, Mike? Six, eight years? How are you?"

The four listened to a muffled conversation through the windows and wall. The young Daniel peeked around the corner.

Without looking at him, Monte quietly asked, "How many, son?"

The boy coughed in his fist with a mumble. May interpreted. "I requested twenty-two, and my son went to church shopping. I expected nothing less from him."

The door opened as Thorny stepped back in as she waved. "I'll see what I can do, Mike. Good seeing you. I'll let Daniel know if I see him." She quietly closed the door and returned to her seat. The pistol returned to the table, pointing away from the others, but in front of her.

She cleared her throat. The young man's head appeared from

out of the kitchen. "Mike said the large eddies, off the north end of the new runway, were showing signs of too many large brown trout. He just thought you might need to know in case your mother wanted to put up some trout on the menu."

"So I'm not in trouble?"

Thorny gave him a hard look. His head disappeared into the kitchen.

Monte watched the grown woman. He had watched Thorny grow up since she was barely knee-high. She ignored him as she made a fuss over sipping on her coffee cup.

He cleared his throat. "You might have got away with that, except I already knew your cup was bone empty."

The three women took a hesitation before laughing. Even the leader was not beyond being called out for cheating.

Thorny eyed the man with one eye over the top of her cup. She put it down and patted her mouth with her napkin. "It would appear the county doesn't pay their officers enough, either."

The thin folder landed on the desk with a cloud of dust. Thorny pulled back from her work, waving her hands in the air to clear the cloud.

"What in Hades are you doing, John?"

The policeman stood with his hand grasping his belt buckle. Thorny didn't know if the man had ridden in the Wild West Show, but she did know the Buffalo Bill buckle was genuine. She also had been informed of there being fewer than forty of the buckles cast. The bronze didn't tarnish because of the gold content in the metal. The gold had come from the mountain, not twenty miles from where she sat. It was almost as if she could feel the pull of the metal from the mountain.

Her right hand fell to her lap and softly felt for the lump in her right pocket. She usually knew when John was close. The skeleton hand in her pocket, cast from pure gold, would become extra warm. She didn't understand what it meant, but its affinity to the buckle was the least of its unsettling traits.

She still couldn't figure out where the hand went when she removed her pants. She even tried holding the gold sculpture in her hand as she slid off the clothes. She never felt it leave or disappear

—it was just gone. In the morning, she would chance to put her hand in her pocket, and the gold hand was there. These days, she relaxed and let the item come and go as it needed. It was a Paiute artifact with Paiute lore. Thorny's bond with it had been sealed one fateful night with the guidance of the tribe's last great medicine man—her best friend's grandfather.

She rolled her head to the side and gave the officer a hard look. "Well?"

The man's mouth wrestled with the lips and tongue. "It's your next case."

She leaned over and looked at the desiccated folder. "Fresh this morning, I see." She lifted the cover and looked at the paper inside. There were no forms, just writing cribbed on a few torn pieces of paper. Intrigued, her eyes searched for a date. Seeing the date, she fell back in the chair.

The man waited calmly as he knew the woman was studying him for any humor. There was none. The man seemed to lack any humor in his body—even down to the large bone in his arms.

"I'm guessing 1869 isn't a joke. Care to explain?"

The man shrugged his eyes and brows. "I figured if you're going to dig up the old cases of unsolved crimes in the valley, may as well start with Robert Bishop. He was the first murder."

"Bishop. As in this Bishop?"

"It was named after Robert's father—Samuel A. Bishop. He's the one who first brought a bunch of cattle up this way. Eventually built a ranchero named Saint Francis Ranch. The rancho was up near clear water coming out of the large canyon we now call Bishop Creek. In those days, the water was free flowing so I would suppose it was a lot more than just a creek. In the summer, they probably ranged the cattle up there in Upper Buttermilk—good lush grass and cooler evenings. The Saint Francis was the start of the dude ranch."

Thorny smiled. She remembered John loved to read history books. The older, the better. "When did he bring the cattle?"

"Early, about 1860. But, by 1862, he had started the ranchero, and a small town was being built in his name. He also had started a family, but he never married."

Thorny pursed her lips. "Robert."

The man nodded. "There was also a Mexican squatter family down near the waste-gate, this side of Big Pine. They were growing hard root vegetables for the miners. He took a liking to the daughter. She was only fourteen, but when he left, she was about to pair... um... give birth."

Thorny frowned. "And Robert...?"

"Half Paiute. She gave Robert his father's name but eventually married in the tribe. I saw a reference once as to his half-sister, but there never was a recording of the name."

Thorny fingered the cover open a few inches and stared into the folder as if looking for an answer. "So, we have a half-breed bastard child born in 1862, but murdered seven years later. There was plenty there for someone to hate... but enough to kill?" She looked up. "Why?"

John smiled and stood taller. "That is what you get to figure out."

Her eyes danced over the paperwork on her desk. Much had been ignored for years. "In all my spare time..."

John smiled and turned, walking back toward the front desk. "That's right, Chief." Pulling out his pocket watch, he looked at the time. "Or, should I say, Mayor." He glanced back. "You have a city council meeting in about ten minutes. Don't be late. The cookie ladies don't cotton to no tardy city officials."

The swearing was almost silent. She stood, stuffing her pistol back in her pants and holster. "Where is the meeting?"

"Methodist Church. You now have seven minutes."

She closed her eyes and bounced them open wide in exasperation. "Well, it could have been the Catholic Church, I guess." Nine blocks further.

"WE COULD HOLD SOCIALS. They raise money." The woman's face was as evocative as a stone brick. Her eyes seemed frozen halfway between intent and frightened but matched her frizzy penny-copper hair somehow.

Thorny had a quick thought about the pistol down the back of her pants. This was exactly the sort of church lady who would be frightened by the large weapon. The side holster was sounding more and more appealing. "Are you proposing to hold a social every month?"

The woman blinked. "Socials raise a lot of money. I don't think there will be a need for more than a few a year. Why, just last year, we had an ice cream social and raised almost a hundred dollars."

Thorny nibbled at the inside of her lower lip. Her eyes slid to the right. Beatrice Wainwright was known for her level-headed thinking. She taught second form mathematics as well as home economics at the high school. The look on her face was of a parent listening to her children when she knew the answers but wanted them to work their way to the solution on their own. Not for the first time, Thorny wondered why she was the mayor and not Beatrice.

"Bea?"

The woman's face rose as she leaned back and away from the question. "I'm still listening to the ideas for solutions."

Thorny stretched her head back and twisted her neck until she was rewarded with a few soft cracks. "How many more solutions would you like to hear before you jump in?"

The woman's eyes leveled. She knew they were well matched. The rest around the table were merely window dressing. "Three."

Thorny's response was soft. "Three." The woman hesitated and then dipped her head.

Thorny turned her gaze on the bulky woman in robin's-egg blue at the other end of the large table. Even on a warm summer day, her hat, jacket, and white gloves were still in place. Just the edge of white lace hinted at a handkerchief tucked in hiding at the end of either sleeve. An image floated in Thorny's mind of the woman sitting in her undergarments while her husband went over every inch of her face and neck, tweezing any hair which would dare to grow and show any color. The woman was the quintessential maven of propriety. "Marvella, is three the magical number for you too? Or are you willing to float an idea yourself?"

The woman almost flinched at being called on. The sum of her duties was to sit, be seen, and be a presence of the status quo. Being forced to put herself forth bordered on ridicule.

She softly cleared her throat. "Three sounds like a reasonable number."

Thorny looked around the table of soft nods and eyes frightened she might call on them next. Not for the first time, Thorny halfheartedly wished she could have been dealing with their husbands instead. But most were dead or serving somewhere else in the world.

"Okay, here is the problem. The changes I will be proposing will require a tripling or more of the current annual budget. We also will need to float three bonds. One to pave Line Street from Main to the hospital." She pointed at Marvella. "Yes?"

"Are you proposing the economy of macadam or the expense of asphalt?"

"Which returns the longest value for the money spent?"

The consensus mumble sounded more like somebody's burden instead of Eve's husband.

Thorny's eyes rolled low in acknowledgment. "Next, the primary school is falling apart."

One of the younger women raised her hand. "Is the roof leaking? Because the roof on my house has three leaks, and if my husband doesn't come home soon, I'm going to run out of pots when it rains."

Thorny closed her eyes to think. "The roof leaks, there are a dozen cracked or broken windows, many of the floors are spongy from rot, room seventeen is closed because one of the janitors fell through the floor, and then there are the insignificant things that haven't been fixed since 1930."

Marvella cleared her thought. "How do you propose we raise all this money?"

Thorny's face turned to stone. Her eyes never left the challenging lock with the woman who saw herself as the Queen Bee.

Thorny rocked forward in her chair. Reaching, she drew out her pistol and quietly placed it on the table. "You wanted three more suggestions. Well, here they are. First, I take my pistol and go pay Elisha Jacobson a visit. I'm sure the money in the back would cover at least the roof on the primary school. It might even pay for the new judge, a city controller, and a raise for the new police lieutenant."

Nine of the eleven women had a hand to their mouths. Thorny was talking, and Marvella hadn't batted an eyebrow. Thorny liked the grit in this woman more by the minute.

"The second suggestion is to hold up every car or truck which passes through town. I think a two-bit toll for passing through our fine town seems fair enough."

The woman in robin's-egg blue stirred. "You could go rob the mobsters at the dude ranch."

Thorny winced. "I tried it. It netted the town just enough to cover John's usual monthly income for the next two months. No, the mobsters are even out of money. Danny Rambino was the one who suggested the toll on those passing through. If they can afford to drive around, they can afford to help this town."

The curly haired blonde, Thorny seemed to remember as a little firebrand in high school, raised her hand. "Will there be a toll placed on someone walking everywhere?"

Thorny almost smiled. "She already pays. The day you want the job at the pay I've been taking for all seven jobs, you are welcome to get sworn in."

"What are the qualifications needed for the job?"

Thorny's voice turned to ice. "Kill the person you are willing to replace. Bring your own gun."

Marvella's hand slapped the table a little louder than she had meant. Her voice was lower—almost embarrassed. "Okay, Thorny, you've had your fun. What is your serious suggestion?"

Thorny nodded slightly and almost smiled. Lying her hand on her pistol, she stood. "There is only one choice. We will be voting to raise property taxes come the first of November."

"How much do you propose?"

"About twelve dollars each household. I will also task the county tax collector down in Independence to start lien sales on properties more than five-years in arrears. They will mail out letters of sixty-day notice. After, I will have the sheriff start marking notices in the Inyo Register. All sales will be cash and final."

The young redhead whimpered. "But twelve dollars is a lot of money…"

Thorny turned on her heel. "I'm sorry you feel that way. There are city and county employees who must live on less each month. Nobody has had a raise since 1928. If you think you can't scrape together the dollar a month, then hold a social. Maybe you ought to hold a bunch of socials to help people pay their back taxes and save their homes. Many of you have husbands in the war. They are getting paid less than they made here at home. Everyone has some Victory Garden. We are all struggling to hold our homes, our lives, our families, and our town together until the war is over. I'm the lucky one here. I have a farm supporting the two people who run it for me. I don't take any pay for the jobs you wanted me to take… I'm not complaining—it's how I can help this town and county keep running. The tungsten mine is running at twenty percent. The mill at only slightly more—but there are no more men to hire. We can all huddle and hide our heads and wait for your husbands to come home, but what will they come home to? A cowering wife, a bank-rupt and falling apart town, and a county run with criminals in charge—isn't a very attractive inducement to return home." She sighed and looked each woman in the eye. The last was Marvella—whose head dipped a fraction of an inch.

MONTE CROSSED his legs the other way. Shaking out his newspaper, he looked over the top at the statue of Amelia Earhart standing in his doorway. He studied the sag in the shoulders, and the soft distant stare.

"How was holding court today?"

Thorny budged and finally rolled off the doorjamb. "I think the ladies auxiliary and flower club has finally met the Thorny in Miss Wallace."

"With understanding or just horror?"

She climbed into the second barber chair and sunk into the cushion. "Hopefully with more of the former. But I fear some of them were overwhelmed with the latter."

They both looked up at the sound of a soft knock on the door-jamb. A storm of robin's-egg blue filled the wide door.

Monte lost his voice. Thorny's eyes slide with disgust at the man lack of decorum or courage in the face of a potential storm. She turned to the woman. "Marvella?"

"I've been thinking."

Monte recovered and stood. Offering out his hand toward the long bench along the window. "Would you like to come in?"

Her spare nod was his only acknowledgment. The mass of robin's-egg blue settled into Monte's seat and turned it to face Thorny. "Twelve dollars will not be enough. Even if you collect every back tax, they still won't be enough."

"Why?"

"My guess is you haven't really gone over the books. Book-keeping is my expertise. I was a bookkeeper before I married Mister Oskar and for the first twenty years of our marriage. Find me the books, and I'll have you a better number, but I'm guessing it will be closer to twenty-dollars."

Monte guessed at the gist of the conversation. "Why so high?"

Only her eyes moved to his place on the long bench. "If this war is anything like the last big war, it will take the men about two years to come home. About two years after, they will understand they are home, and it's time to make a family. Once you release that genie from the bottle, there will be many children needing space in a primary school which is already falling apart."

Monte almost smiled as he sat up straighter with a noisy intake of air. Her plump left index finger shot out in a point and then turned up. Effectively shushing the man in his kingdom.

"The people living on Elm Street will want their street paved. The people on Short Street will point a finger at Elm and ask why they got more than the Short. We can only do so much, but it will go around and round this way until the entire city is paved. But, by then, we will have a larger problem as the primary school explodes, but the children are too young for high school. Meanwhile, the mine will be running two-shifts to mine enough tungsten to keep the lights on in America with men coming home and turning off those lights and making more babies. It happened in 1920, and it's going to happen again. Mark my words, this town will grow, and we will need more taxes to buy the services everyone is going to want or need."

Thorny leaned back. "Whew. And you figured this all out on your way over here?"

The woman flailed a hand. "Oh, heavens no. My Oliver and I have been hashing this all out for close to two years."

Thorny raised her eyebrows, and her head rolled over to look at Monte. His chin nudged back at the large woman in his chair.

Thorny looked about the floor a moment and then looked Marvella in the eye. "How would you like to be mayor?"

The woman's face cracked, and Thorny worried about the cackle coming from her convulsing throat. The woman gathered her control. "Um… no. But I am willing to be city controller for half the current pay until the war is over, and an extra ration of butter."

"So, who do you think should be the mayor?"

"This fall run Bea up the flagpole and see how many support her. My guess is there aren't enough men to vote against her come November. Any mother who has had a daughter in her home economics class is thankful for the woman who taught her daughter how to cook and sew. She understands economics and what this city will need for the next twenty years. She's the one I want to work with."

"Why her instead of me?"

The woman moved her mass and stood. "Because, unlike you, she doesn't have a big pistol jammed down the back of her dainties." She winked and nodded at Monte. "Mr. Geronimo, as usual, it's very nice to see you in the peak of health."

Monte watched through the window as the woman crossed the street and progressed down the shaded side of the street. "I'll be all go to hell." He turned around with his hand scratching at his head.

"What's wrong?"

"Her husband."

"Because they talk about the economic condition of the town?"

He looked up at her. "No. Because I was one of his pallbearers sixteen years ago."

05 JAKARTA, INDONESIA

4 MONTHS BEFORE

The rust on the scow was peeling in hand-sized flakes. The rotting metal leant a biting singe to the port and the fetid wet air. The jungle was a quarter mile from the port, but the stench of the composting vegetation compounded the sensory soup of broken-down ships, tied in strangleholds to collapsing docks. The small shipping port should have been left to wash out to sea in the last century, but there were still certain creatures whose needs for such a remote transfer point outweighed the desire for safer accommodations.

The man in the sweat-stained white linen suit stepped hesitantly onto the dock. Looking up the dock toward more buildings, he glanced at his small gold wristwatch in irritation. His pencil line of a mustache twitched in irritation as he listened to the tiny finches sweeping in and out of the bones of former warehouses lining the length of the pier. His gaze returned from down the pier to what was left of the warehouse in front of him.

The grayed green square columns rose to the small third floor of the building. In colonial days, the top floor would have been the office of the customs officer—placed there to make sure the king received his due. The windows shot out long ago were nothing more than a few teeth of glass glinting in the sunshine. The man could see the heat-faded sky through the broken windows where there once was a roof. His eyes slid shut as he thought. *In a hell like this, everything dies before its time.*

The sound of a small car rattling to a stop at the foot of the pier woke the man from his stupor. He turned to watch a massive man grow from the one door like a genie from a small bottle. The top of the car was well below the dark man's armpit. As the man walked out on to the pier, the man in the white suit could see the gold glinting in the other's left earlobe. The kaftan shirt was as dark as the man's bald head. His slacks appeared as if they might have been white or cream at one time.

The man in white removed his dark glasses as the other came within a few paces.

"Salaam, Alaikum."

The dark man stopped and squinted. The light was strong but not glaring. "Wa Alaikum, salaam." He turned and, motioning with his hand, retraced his steps. The other man followed.

On the roof of one of the dilapidated buildings, a sniper withdrew his rifle. Turning, he rose and walked away from the parapet and toward the stairs.

Unbeknownst to the sniper or the dark man, another person lowered his binoculars. Leaning to his right, he turned the crank on a field radio. The charge to the battery would only last a few minutes. Gently mounting his hand to the telegraph key, he tapped out a code. Holding the small speaker to his ear, he waited for a confirmation. Four measured pings. Message received.

The front passenger seat was missing. Suffering with a sigh, the man sat in the back of the small car. In his mind, the obvious filth on the windows was repeated many folds, and anywhere his clean white clothes or skin touched. He tried not to touch anything, and if he could levitate, now would be the time to do so.

The small car sagged as the driver gathered his mass behind the wheel. The passenger studied the seat for signs of imminent collapse. The engine rattled to an approximation of life. The tires crunched or squished on rotting fruit as it carved a slow turn and retreated into the jungle.

The ride was not anywhere as smooth as the Phaeton had ridden about the countryside south of London. He wished he was there now. His small indiscretion with a young son of a diplomat had sealed his fate to be banished to the outback of the world as a courier of only God knew what.

The man drew himself up as he closed his eyes. It was bad enough the driver had no regard for avoiding large potholes in the road. Now he was driving through a large crowd of filthy untouchables and their predilection toward marketing meat hanging naked to the sun and flies of the world.

"Most unsettling," the man murmured through a delicate linen handkerchief held to his nose against the sickening stench.

"What you say, sahib?"

"Nothing. Nothing at all. Just get us there. Please."

The driver smiled. There were other ways to get where they were going. But he knew this way would be the most repulsive to an Englishman in a white linen suit. He jerked the car left to miss an ox cart. He watched in the mirror as the man almost fell over. He would try harder next time if he were driving him again.

The car lurched right off the street, the driveway pocked with disrepair and destitution. The driver tapped at the breaks to bring the whole lurching to a standstill before the once-extravagant set of steps. The colonial hotel had seen its best years several wars before. The façade of the small run-down hotel was scaled with faded paint and crumbling plaster. Faded colors from previous generations showed through as lines rimming where plaster and paint had chipped out or fallen off. Garbage heaped near an open window. Rats played on the rotting mound and dragged at bits of what the man imagined to be fresh flesh.

"Oh my." The man held the scented handkerchief to his nose and mouth as he stepped out of the car. The dark man opened the wide metal-laced door to the hotel. He waved in the shattered Englishman. His smile glowed large—as if showing off Buckingham Palace. The Englishman's eyes drifted shut as he quietly groaned and entered.

A mange-bitten gray dog lifted its head at the man's entrance. At the site of the second man, the head lowered, and the beast resumed sleeping. The driver walked past the Englishman and down a hallway. As they passed the small man behind the check-in desk, the Englishman took a second glance. The shabbily uniformed man looked like a bored Malaysian. But the demeanor and shadowed attentiveness were much closer to the Gurkhas he had met in India. The fearless killers had been in the British Army for close to two hundred years. The man knew the Nepalese fighter would have at least one deadly blade near at hand.

"This way, sahib." The dark driver showed his hand at a doorway. The Englishman took one last furtive look back at the Gurkha. Things were not what they appeared to be.

A small woman in the traditional dress of Malaysia and Java rose from the desk. The small office was clean and simply appointed. She bowed in greeting. Her decorative green and gold dress crinkled in the hush of silk. She turned toward the door to an inner office. The twin Webley revolvers were in crossed holsters spanning the small of her back. From the wear and dark of the leather, the Englishman was sure the woman was not shy about using them. The sound of his commander's voice rung in his memories—faint from years before, during his first tour of India. *Just remember, Colt may have won the west, but Webley won the rest.*

Her voice was soft. "The commander has been expecting you." She knocked twice and then opened the door. The glue-chipped glass of the door sparkled with the sun streaming through the large office windows.

The officer continued to read something on typed paper. His

right hand seemed to be a snake of its own accord. It fetched a cup from a matching saucer. The Englishman could see the light glowing through the thin bone china. It reminded him of the full set of china, dating to Charles the second, lining the sideboard of his family's estate in Leeds. He wanted to groan with the loss.

The officer placed the papers on the desk and taking up a pen, signed them. He put them aside and looked up.

"I take it you are…?"

"Jones. Robert Jones. Well, for this trip at least."

"Right." The man stood and walked to a chest. Opening the wooden door revealed a large safe. The man spun the dial and then opened the heavy door. The hinges were silent.

Removing a small valise, he turned. He held out the leather case so the Englishman could see the official swastika burned into the top.

"Am I expected to go flouncing around with a case marked by the Nazis?"

The colonel's mouth twitched at one side. He smothered his urge for a sarcastic retort. He knew more about the man in front of him than most anyone else in the world. The diplomat's pubescent son was his wife's step-nephew. He pointed toward a Gladstone satchel sitting on the low table in front of the divan.

"The grip has a false bottom."

Placing the valise next to the squat luggage, he motioned toward the divan. Demonstrating, he manipulated the fixtures on the case.

"Push in these two feet and slide them sideways. This locks the release in the open position." Opening the case, he reached in and drew out the bottom. He opened the valise and drew out eight velvet drawstring bags. He massaged the one with his thumb. The sound of small rocks chittered softly. He placed the bags in the bottom of the grip. Replacing the false bottom, he drew back the two feet, a soft click all the two men could hear.

The colonel looked up. "I'm afraid you cannot trust anyone else to lift this bag. The eleven-kilograms of uncut diamonds will give it away. You must make carrying this look effortless. Your success, and most probably your life, depends on it. Do you have any questions?"

"Eleven-kilograms of...?"

"Raw diamonds from the mines of central Africa. Roughly fifty-two-thousand carats. Once cut, they should respectably be worth fifteen million to twenty million pounds sterling—or a small down payment on what we owe the yanks so far."

The courier tapped the top of the empty valise. "Compliments of Hitler himself."

"Hmm, quite so."

The man stood and pulled at the bottom of his uniform jacket. "David will have brought the Bentley around and will take you to your ship. I'm not sure if I envy you or not. I understand your berth is a stateroom behind the bridge. I would imagine this to mean you will be dining with the captain most nights."

The Englishman leveled his gaze at the older man. He felt the prick of the stab at his expense. "I'm also sure you are familiar with the tramp steamer and the route I'll be subjected to."

"Vividly." The officer's face steamed with hatred.

The courier knew when he had been dismissed.

The battered car and Arab driver stood at the curb. One last insult before the long abuse across the coldest part of the most southern Pacific Ocean. The man shuddered at the thought of stop after squalid stop through South and Latin America before arriving in Los Angeles. Three months lounging aboard a passenger liner like the glorious Queen Mary was one thing, but a tramp freighter with its filthy smelling crew was another. He hoped someone had thought to stock at least some good novels aboard. Hopefully, this time, in English instead of the vexatious Pashto or Arabic.

As a courier, his life, clothes, and reading were at the whim of others. His only control was the suit he wore ashore and protecting the satchel. Everything else must be disposable, and therefore, never carried aboard and always left behind.

As they stopped, the man surveyed the ship through the dirty window. Stepping out of the car did not improve the sight. In fact, the smell made it even more damning. The stevedores and crew were just finishing loading part of the dry hauler's cargo bays. The deep bay closest to the bridge, and the man's quarters was nothing less than bat guano from the giant caves of Java. The constant humidity of the sea air guaranteed to keep the manure moist and at the crowning of its stench.

Thorny had eaten more tea cakes, homemade cookies, and 'we're-so-glad-you're-the-new *fill in the blank*' cakes than she had during the first twenty-six years of her life—before there were rations on butter, sugar, and flower. When she sat at the dinner table the night before, after walking seven miles home, and had only wanted a glass of water, it caused Mrs. Ferguson to raise an eyebrow. After the explanation, she had patted Thorny's hand and told her she would take care of the women in town.

The fact was, Thorny liked it. She wouldn't admit it, but she did. All her years growing up, she walked barefoot except in the winter cold, but her uniform of the day was bib overalls over a home-sewn flour-sack shirt. Her hair was always cut by the barber who many referred to as the *niggra*. The word was a mispronunciation of the Mexican word *negros*—meaning black. The amusing part was Monte didn't really care. He was Mexican Sonoran Apache Indian. His uncle was the famous Geronimo. Monte was Monte, unless he was Mr. Geronimo. Apart from Monte, few people paid the young Thorny any attention. She was the barefoot girl—if they noticed her at all.

So the attention was something she was reveling in as she turned in to the barbershop.

The man smoothed out his pencil line of a white mustache. His mouth hid his quick smile. "Sacramento called. The governor just resigned, and they want you to fill in."

Thorny slouched into the second barber chair. Her hand reached up and performed a time-honored one-finger salute.

Monte chuckled as he folded the newspaper. "Was it cookies or cake…" He stopped himself, and with exaggerated eyes, stuck out his hand. "Wait… Mrs. Timkin… Oh, you had that flakey confection with nuts and dripping with honey…" He snapped his finger with one eye closed.

"Baklava."

One last snap of the fingers and he pointed. "That's it. Did you bring poor Monte some?"

"I had one piece. If you want some, you figure out how you're going to sit in her parlor and listen to her prattle on about her tiny dog, Snookums."

He grumped back into his chair. "I'm on a diet." He looked over at her with a glowering flutter of the eyes. "I'd rather chew my own leg off."

"Hmm, I was considering doing just so. Why does a mayor have to attend a meeting of the Daughters of the Revolution?"

The man laughed. "Because, my dear, you are one of them."

She looked down at her modest breasts and slender, youthful body. "I don't think so."

THE OLD APPLES jostled dully in the canvas knapsack. Thorny reached back to the seat to grab the canteen. Looking through the window of the old Model A, she noticed the top of a large black tank just cresting above the dense brush. The truck belonged to her best and oldest friend. She grabbed the second canteen. She knew Charlie would never drink from the Owens River. As a Paiute Indian and the current chief of the local tribe, there were certain mystic quirks to his nature. One was his having never touched anything of the water of the river, and yet, it was his favorite water to canoe on.

She retreated out of the car as she nestled the second canteen of water in the knapsack. An image flittered through her mind. The tall giant of a man canoed, standing up as if the longboat was a pole skiff. She wondered if he had ever fallen in, but she knew it was not her place to ask.

Thorny walked through the tall brush drawing life from the nearby river. Her footsteps were light on the early summer grasses.

"Did the lizard fart a few minutes ago? Or was it Heather's growling stomach?" The deep growl of a voice led Thorny to the proper clearing.

Thorny laughed at the man spread along the large log, with the mule bent over his head. The equine nose was resting on the man's chest as his hands massaged both shaggy cheeks. If mules could purr, Thorny knew Heather's purr would be long and loud by now.

"I think it was more like a tiny tree frog snorting." Thorny draped the knapsack to the ground by the log. "About two more minutes and Heather is going to be asleep in your lap."

At the sound of her name, the mule lifted her head lazily. She took a step toward Thorny and nuzzled her chest and then slid her nose down until her forehead was pushed against her friend. The apples would come later.

Charlie sat up and looked out at the river. His double braids dragged sluggishly across his broad back. Thorny noted the small feather at the end of one. She thought about the date or at least the season. The small white feather would be in remembrance of his younger sister. Thorny thought about the day Charlie trusted her enough to introduce her to his sister. The small form of a child lain twisted by polio. She was silent but seemed to enjoy her brother's attention. The next early summer, she was gone.

Thorny also knew the double braids would be back for the Fourth of July. Each braid would have a single feather in each side. The crow feather for his mother, the eagle feather for his father. Fourth of July was the day Charlie became the single lineage from his grandfather—to be the next chief of the Bishop reservation of the Paiute Nation. Even after Charlie and Thorny sliced open their thumbs and pressed them together to become blood siblings, he had never talked about the explosion. Thorny never asked.

The man turned his head and looked back over his shoulder at Thorny and Heather. Even through her dark green glasses, she could see the mischief in his eyes. "Why, you look downright mayoral standing there with an ass in the sunshine."

Thorny grabbed Heather's ears. "Don't listen to him, Heather. He's just angry it's hot, and he can't go swimming. And don't worry, we don't have to share the apples either."

The man barked a laugh and rolled forward. Straightening, he held up a large grain sack. "I would be surprised if she'll take an apple. She got most of my spring harvest of carrots and several pounds of large wild asparagus."

Thorny kicked at the log with her bare heel. "Why you warty old toad, you picked asparagus and didn't have me to dinner?"

"Figured it would steam nice with a goat leg over a small fire. If we root around, we might even find some baby potatoes to go with it." He looked back at Thorny. "You think we can find a cast-iron skillet up at the mine, to take and leave at the hot pool?"

Thorny blew out her lips as she thought about the mining camp a couple of miles away. She had been bored and had searched the old camp for every cooking utensil. The stack of skillets ranged from a two-handed deep skillet with a lid, to a small one perfect for stirring up a couple of eggs. The final count so far was ten. "We might find one or two."

She looked again at the white feather. "Is there a reason we're going up to the pool?"

He chuckled. The rumble sounded more like an avalanche of

large boulders in a distant valley. "Because the water feeling good isn't enough of a reason?"

She lowered her head and looked through hooded eyes. The rest of the mountain rolled into the tumbling rumble. They had teased, cajoled, and poked each other since they were waist high to the grandfathers who raised them.

Finally, he looked down at the grass before looking out at the river slowly boiling then smoothing out in a brown mirror of the sky above. His sigh was quiet but long and deep. "I just don't want to be in the house for a few days."

Thorny thought about his dog, which she called his *wife,* and the other animals of his small barnyard. "What about your wife?"

His back heaved a fast chuff. "The dog snores. Besides, Brenda from down the road wants to see if her son can take care of the animals. We can let her know we're heading up the mountain, and if the dog wants to come, it's her choice."

Thorny laughed. "She is one spoiled wife. She knows better than to go camping with us. We'd make her sleep outside."

"Huskies are spoiled by nature."

"She lies too." Thorny liked the large dog but was also amused by the dog farting and then scowling at whoever was close as if blaming them for the offense.

Hours later, Thorny hung her feet in the pool of hot water. Technically, the land belonged to her, but she never felt the ownership. It had always felt like she was privileged to come on the land and soak in the restorative water. The pool had been formed by their grandfathers and three others. The only one left of the original builders was Monte, the barber. The original land claim was taken out by one of her other pseudo-uncles, Ulysses.

She turned back to face Charlie, fussing with the small campfire. The large cast-iron skillet spanned the gap between the three rocks. He fed the fire small sticks, each slightly larger than the last.

Thorny looked back at the pool. "Do you think if I submerged a couple of lambskins in the pool like Ulysses did, they would trap the gold?"

The man snorted. "You're asking the wrong mountain. The mountain holds the gold, and it is your spirit guide. Ask it to guide you on what to do for the gold you need." He looked up. "Is this a need, not just a want or a whim?"

"There are a few things that need to be done, and I don't want to cut into the money being paid for the water in Round Valley."

"Is this gold for you to use for you… or for someone else?"

"There are a few people who are breaking laws to make ends meet because the county can't pay them more. I thought if I could help…"

Charlie looked up toward the darkening sky through the tops of the trees. "I'm not telling you not to do it, but it is a very wet grassy edge of the river."

Thorny leaned over and washed her hands. She could smell the dinner, and her stomach was growling. "I think it's called a slippery slope."

Charlie raised the wooden spoon to his lips and blew gently. "I only know the water. You inherited the golden skeleton hand—the mountain is you. You ask the rocks if they will give you the gold you want." He dished out the food onto the two enameled tin plates. "If the rocks of the mountain will give you the gold, the water will bring it to you."

Later, as they shucked their clothes and eased into the bone-warming water, Thorny looked up at the dark trees she knew marched up the side of the mountain. This place had always felt as much her home as the ranch or the deserted mining camp across the river. Now, it felt even more restorative, and it wasn't just the water. She could feel the minerals in the water. She couldn't explain it, but she knew Charlie had grown up with the same understanding of a sense that betrayed understanding. The mystical world of his grandfather and the broader setting of the relationship the Paiute's had with the world around them.

She fingered the small leather pouch hanging from her neck. By their humming, her thumb could feel the difference between the quartz crystal and the gold nugget. She knew other people couldn't feel it, but for her, it was there.

Her eyes closed as she sunk into the water to her chin. "You told me the petroglyphs of the hand read differently with the palm up or down. Can you read the glyphs?"

The deep hum from his chest next to her radiated through the water and confirmed her question, and his being awake. As children, she had once teased him about being so talkative. By high school, he had become almost monosyllabic.

"You said it read about my being the mountain or about my receiving from the mountain. Which is which?"

He sat up. Thorny could see the moon reflecting in the pool was now reflecting its light in the muddy whites of his eyes. His eyes searched back and forth across the water. "If I give you something like pinion nuts, how do you hold your hands?"

"Palms up."

"That is how you receive. When your palms are down, and you place them on the ground, you give of yourself to the mountains."

"But what am I giving?"

The large man shrugged the shoulder closest to her. Without seeing his lips, she knew the lower was pushed out until the wet inner pink was exposed. "When you plant a seed or a flower, you push the ground down around it. Do you say a small prayer?"

Thorny snorted. "Prayer? Me?"

His face turned. There was no smile. "Do you think something like, "grow, little one"? Or is there a thought about what the plant will look like full-grown? When you seed the rows, are you thinking about schoolwork or the plants you are planting?"

She leaned back against the side of the pool. "Sure, but it's not like a prayer."

He leaned back in a mirror of her, his bulky arms crossed. "But it is. It is a prayer at the most basic level. You are speaking to the seed directly and asking the dirt and earth to help the seed to grow into what you will receive."

She thought about the springs and summers, following her grandfather as he guided the plow, cutting the single line of the turned ground. The seeds would fall gently from her hand as her bare feet would replace the dirt. The seeds felt sweet in her hand or claw, but it was touching the soil with her feet. She could feel the sense of the dirt, the earth, all the way to her gut and chest. A feeling she had never stopped to think about.

"I guess I have been connected all my life."

The hum vibrated through the water. Thorny could feel the difference—there was now a smile in the small waves.

The morning light was creeping down the mountain. Thorny huddled under her blanket, breaking small twigs and feeding the fire. The huge lump under the other blanket moaned. "It's too early."

Thorny knew Charlie hated waking up early. Most of his life had been spent living with his grandfather. The old chief and tribal shaman rose early to make a fire and then stand with his arms raised in greeting to the pinking of the sky before the sun would crest along the White Mountains. As children, the two rose and stood with their grandfathers in supplication to the dawn.

For Thorny, it was a take it or leave it habit. For Charlie, it was now his choice as an adult and the tribe's chief to forgo the ritual. He would create his own dawn ritual by calling a song of snoring.

"The deer have already passed. They were headed for the higher Coyote Flats. The buck was a nice looking six-pointer."

The lump curled tighter. "White woman lies."

"I have coffee."

"White woman lies even bigger. The fire isn't big enough for coffee. You're still snapping tiny twigs."

Thorny chuckled and snapped a stick as thick as her thumb.

The loud throaty snap caused the lump to roll over with a toss of the blankets. The single glaring eye took in the tiny fire and the coffeepot sitting to one side. The growl was more of a distant rumble of a rock slide. "White woman lies like husky at home."

Thorny carefully fed the bigger stick into the fire. "Don't bad-mouth my sister. She told me you fart in fresh sheets."

The two poked each other casually. The teasing and their easy friendship were a large part of what Thorny had missed in the big city. For eight long years, she had felt a hole in her soul and days. When she figured out what it was, she slipped out of the shoes and the city that were pinching her feet and soul—and returned home.

"How long have you known about the golden hand?"

"I heard stories when I was growing up. There is much lore surrounding the hand." The giant rose and dipped his cup in the warm water of the pool. Walking over to a small tree, he carefully watered around the tree. He patted the top of the tree, as if like a dog or small child. Returning for coffee, he sat back down. He ignored Thorny's look at the tiny tree and him. "I think I was maybe nine or ten when Ulysses pulled it out of his pocket. Several men were standing there at the Sticks Game, but only my grandfather and I could see it. For years, it was a mystery to me."

"Are you saying only a few can see it?" She poured herself the last of the coffee and set the pot aside.

The man looked up at the cliff rising through the trees. His lips to the mug, he paused. "Maybe." He sipped and thought about the question. He looked out the side of his eye at her. "Who couldn't see it?"

She pinched at her upper lip. She could feel the firm ground begin to turn to something shaky. This was one of the discussions where her education and knowledge of the world started to become something worthless, or at least confusing.

"I showed it to Monte, and he saw it, but when we went back to the bank, I laid it on some of the paperwork. The people at the bank made no comment. It was as if they couldn't see it. So I chalked it up to the distraction of the piles of folders on the table, or just being discrete. Then the other day, I had changed my pants. My coins and the hand were on the tack table. There was nothing else there. Mr. Ferguson came in and put a bill down next to where the coins were, but the hand wasn't there. After we spoke, I was putting the coins in my pocket, and the hand was already in there. It not only doesn't get seen, but it moves to stay close to me."

"Are you uncomfortable about it?"

She rolled her lips and stared at the reflections in the pool. Her eyebrows rose as she toyed with her coffee mug between her right hand and her claw. She looked over. "I just wish your grandfather was here to explain it."

"So you're okay with it moving to be with you?"

She flicked the last of the coffee and grounds at the brush behind her. "I seem to be more than just okay with it. I think I'm more comfortable with it being close."

Charlie watched as she rinsed out the grounds from the pot. "It used to be with Ulysses, but where did you find it?"

She straightened in thought. "It was right on top of all the folders and stuff in the bank box. There was a letter under it, but nothing anywhere even mentioned it. It wasn't until I talked with your grandfather, I had any hint someone knew anything about it."

Charlie cleared his throat as he stood. "It chose you. It knew Ulysses was gone, and you were next."

"But you can see it." She drew it out of her pocket and held it out. The skeleton hand cast in gold gleamed in the sunshine.

Charlie didn't move to touch it. He nodded. "Keep holding it out."

"Why?" She frowned and shied her head sideways.

He smiled. "Let's see who can and can't see it."

Thorny heard what Charlie had been listening to for a few minutes. She huffed through a small breathy smile.

The voice was low as it filtered through the trees. "This better be the right place. There weren't any street signs or sidewalk to follow."

Thorny smiled at Charlie. "Come on in, Peter, but you're too late for coffee."

The sheriff deputy pushed aside the last limb and strolled across the clearing. Seeing the pool, he let out a low whistle. He stuck his hand out and shook Charlie's hand. "Is it as warm as the steam says it is?" He turned and shook Thorny's outreached hand. The golden hand was gone.

Charlie's one eyebrow rose. "Go stick your hand in, Pete. Feel what you missed last night."

As the deputy knelt at the pool, Charlie asked quietly, "Is it in your pocket?" Thorny shook her head and shrugged. She knew as they walked down the hill, the weight would return.

"Wow, this is really warm."

Running her hand through her short loose curls, Thorny smiled at the boy in the deputy. "If you forgot your bathing suit, you can always borrow one of ours."

The man dried his hand through his long blond hair. Looking from the large tall Paiute to the slender smaller woman, he laughed. "I don't think either of your suits would fit me."

Charlie smiled. "Birthday suits fit all sizes."

Pete rolled and sat on the raised rim of concrete and stones. "Sure, tease the city boy."

"You're getting better, Pete." Thorny winked. "You found your way up here."

The man blushed. "Yeah, it was so easy. I've been thrashing around in those bushes for the last hour and a half or so. How come you never cut a trail?"

Charlie winked at Thorny, confirming he had been listening to the deputy, raised in Salt Lake City, beat his way about the mountainside since sunup. "What are you doing up here?"

"I got a call last night. The deputy and both prisoners down in Independence were found dead around two this morning."

"Shot or food poisoning?"

"Neither. The prisoners were in separate cells, and the deputy was at the inside desk."

Thorny pointed at the trees the man had just fought with. "We were just leaving. What can we do to help?" She grabbed the smaller of the two rucksacks with her claw. Slinging it onto her shoulders, she reached through the strap with her right. Charlie pulled the larger through and onto his one shoulder. The pack wasn't large enough to fit him properly.

The lanky deputy looked at the forest with a resolved forlorn look. Thorny patted his shoulder. "We'll show you the trail, but you aren't going to like it."

As she turned the man toward the trees, her hand dipped into her pant's pocket. She showed the skeleton hand to Charlie. The twitch in his eyebrow was all the conversation they needed.

Thorny gently grabbed the deputy's left arm and pulled him toward a large rock outcropping. The path was head-size rocks and shale flake. Thorny thought about how the seemingly unstable edge of the field of rocks had never slid around, but she could see where small slides had possibly prevented others from coming this way. Not once did they have to battle a branch or dodge a bush. It was as smooth as any trail in a park.

"So how can we help the Inyo County sheriff this morning?"

"The sheriff wanted to know if you could also add 'deputy' to your list of jobs?"

She pulled the wireframes around her ears and glanced back through her green glasses. "You do know it's Sunday, don't you?"

His Adam's apple bounced once as he swallowed. "They left the bodies where they were. Someone figured you would want to see them in place. From what I understand, it's not pretty. You could probably say no, and nobody would fault you."

She looked back along the trail toward Charlie. He nodded. She knew his cousin's Chevy would be faster than the Model A.

She looked at her newer friend. "How 'not pretty' is it?"

"All three were voiding from everywhere. The older deputy said it appeared they were even bleeding from their eyes, nose, and ears."

"All three."

The deputy nodded.

She turned back and continued walking. "I guess we better stop and see if Doc Denton is up for going down with us."

Charlie added. "His son, Bob, is here from medical school. Maybe a little trial by fire?"

She glanced back. "They give the interns time off?"

"I think he finished and was doing some surgery work back there in Illinois. Maybe we get lucky, and he's been doing some work with the coroner."

As Thorny continued down the trail, she thought about the young doctor she had met years before. Two things had stood out about him. One was the hair-lip scar bisecting his wispy moustache, and the other was the continuous smile matched only by his happy about life attitude. She also remembered the truly awful but funny hair-lip jokes he told. He had directed her to make sure to tell him of any new ones she had heard so he could be a fountain of jokes. His self-deprecation had put her at ease, and she allowed him to examine the burn scars of her left hand and arm. He had tested her strength and was genuinely surprised and happy to find she had kept a powerful grip. Both had recognized the power of other's assumptions of them being less than they could be. Thorny remembered it as a moment of *I see you for who you really are*. They were separately in common.

The stucco lace pattern of bad paint over poorly chipped and rusting paint slid smoothly under the man's knuckles. The cotton slipper-shoes of his native country were silent on the scarred linoleum floor of the passageway. The folded straight razor lay secreted flat on his left palm as his fingers spread wide, balancing the tray with a copper heat-cover over the plate. The naked lightbulbs overhead flickered from the inconsistent electrical supply while the ship was alongside the quay. The man turned at the end of the passageway. The time-marked wooden door was on his right.

He knew the Englishman would be in the cabin. The man never came out of his cabin, except at night when they were at sea.

The best time to perform certain acts was when the rest of the crew members were busy exchanging cargoes. The man stopped at the door and listened. His breathing was slowed. Controlled.

His one index knuckle fell lightly against the cabin door.

The soft rustle of a newspaper came from behind the door. He listened for the sound of the drawer sliding closed. It always slid closed with a dull thud.

"Come."

The Malaysian's hand fell to the unpolished brass of the door-knob. As the door swung, he slid sideways through the opening. "Good morning sahib."

The man sat in the sunlight streaming through the porthole. He waved his hand distractedly in the air as he mumbled a greeting. "Good morning, Mohinder."

The Malaysian responded softly as he set the tray down on the small desk. "Guaspari, sahib. My name is Guaspari." Forty-two days, the Englishman had never repeated the same name. Forty-two days, Guaspari corrected him. It was a dance before he placed the straight razor to the man's neck.

Removing the heat dome from the plate, he took up the twin tongs. With only the tips, he pried apart the two ends of the towel. He could hear the Englishman sliding down in his chair with his head back against the top-rail. The man moaned softly in expectation.

Guaspari drew up the towel. Turning, he drew it apart at the critical moment and wrapped the man's face. Even in the heat of the subtropic day, the steam rose from the towel.

The walnut-hued fingers deftly stirred the brush in the bowl. The soap and water mixed from froth into a cream. Too fast and you got bubbles, too slow and you only had soap flakes swirling in hot water. Guaspari watched the steam on the towel as his hands felt the right speed and consistency of the soap.

Setting aside the bowl, he reached over to the towel. One deft move and the wrap became a warm pile in his hand. He placed it on the plate and replaced the cover. The razor reflected dully in the old copper.

"What port are we in today?"

"Peru, sahib. I believe the city is named Lima." His accent pronounced it as the green citrus fruit. The bored Englishman didn't correct him.

There was no rough stubble to create sound. The thick lather slid onto the man's face like paint. Both men understood a weekly shave would have been more fitting, but the days in the cabin wore on the one man. The ritual of being serviced, even as minor as a daily shave, provided a needed break.

"What are they loading here?"

The thin small finger cleaned a bubble of white foam from the man's lip. "I believe it is fertilizer, sahib. It comes from the giant vampire bats who live in the caves at high altitude, sahib."

"I thought we loaded the bat guano in Chile?"

The silver blade flashed at the man's neck. "Maybe so, sahib. These are not part of my job, sahib. I only know you will have steak for your dinner tonight, sahib." He wiped the blade on his apron next to the bloodstains from dealing with the meat.

"What will you eat?"

The man's mouth stretched his upper lip as he drew the razor's edge down the other's lip. "Curried sea bass with fresh potatoes, sahib. As you know, my religion forbids me from eating meat."

The man waited for his lip to be clean. "But fish is allowed?"

The copper dome flashed, and the warm damp towel moved about the man's face. "Yes, sahib. The fish is not an animal. It is more like a potato of the sea." The towel plopped on the copper cover. The man shook a small bottle, the astringent mixed with lime zest, providing a sweet smell for the rest of the morning. Rubbing some between his hands, he then wiped the Englishman's face.

The man was already half dozing. The narcotic in the soap lather had worked its magic. The man would drift in a mental haze until dinner.

Quietly, the Malaysian cook picked up his tray and left.

The four of them looked more like they were holding up a bank than examining a crime scene with their wet bandanas hung around their necks. The sheriff and another deputy stood helplessly facing them. The stench seared their eyes, and they took frequent breaks to stand outside breathing fresh air.

The older doctor had been in surgery, but the son offered to take his place. The younger doctor's turn at an operation had started late the evening before. The younger Denton had worked with another until just before dawn. Bob snored the entire ninety-minute drive. He woke bright-eyed and energized as if he had slept all night.

"We'll have to get them on the table to be sure, but I'm thinking somehow they ingested arsenic. But I also don't like the sulfur smell in there, either."

The voice was flat and nasally, but the words were clear. Thorny squeezed the wet towel to her eyes. "Once you remove the outhouse smell, the rest is a bad mine. But how could they get enough arsenic to kill them?"

Bob rinsed his mouth and spat. "There are many ways. Arsenic is in the ground, and it leaches up into certain plants. The bitter in apples is a combination of cyanide and arsenic. Farmers have been breeding apples and apricots for generations to drive the poison out of the fruit. There is still a lot in the seeds of apples and the pit of apricots. An old war trick was to grind up the pits and steep them in a tea to make a final gooey mess. You dip the tip of an arrow in the goo, and you get poison to at least make a mess out of your victim's nervous system." He waved his thumb toward the wall of the jail. "You saw what happened. Their guts probably let go first from both ends. The bleeding was probably the last to happen. The vital organs, once failure begins, fall apart pretty darn fast."

Thorny looked at Charlie as he retched into a coughing fit. He finally drew himself up and gave her a hard look. "Paiute's never used medicine to kill. Apple seed paste with clay could reduce a fevered skin like a boil."

Bob twisted his smile at a thought. "Hmm, I might have to try it sometime. You can show me how to mix it."

The rumble was soft. "Grandfather tried two winters ago." He didn't have to explain. The former chief had also been one of the greatest respected shamans of the Paiute Nation.

Pete wrung out his bandana. "But how would you get them all to eat whole apples?"

Thorny opened her mouth and then stopped as she put her hand out to the doctor's arm. Bob looked at her as she explained. "Go easy on him. He grew up city. He's from Salt Lake."

The three chuckled at the one's expense. Bob cocked his smile. "That's the bugger of it. They would have to each eat a small truck-load of apples to get enough poison to kill them." He turned and squinted at Thorny. "If I remember right, you used to pal around with the old miner named Flapjack."

Thorny nodded. "Ulysses."

Bob smiled. "He was a pretty smart fella. He probably taught you about the miners having canaries in the coal mines." She nodded. "The gases are close to the same. In these mountains, there is more arsenic than there is cyanide, but the miners used sparrows around here. Cheaper to buy and easier to catch."

Thorny dipped her head as she ran her claw through her short curly hair. "The gas leaks through fissures in the rock. In closed spaces like mines, it lays low because it's heavier than air. By the time the miners know there's a problem, they stumble and fall into even more of the stuff."

Bob looked up at the sheriff. "I'm guessing, but maybe it's been chilly these last few nights?"

The man shrugged. "Probably enough for the deputy to have closed the back door. Usually, it's open to allow fresh air into the concrete building. The prisoners aren't always religious about their bathing habits."

Thorny frowned. "But surely deputies have closed the door before? The winters must be cold in there."

"Not really. The wood stove heats the place nice and toasty, even with the back door cracked a bit so there's fresh air for the stove."

Bob stooped to rinse his bandana. "So the back door is supposed to always be open for fresh air?"

"Well, there's no hard rule... but even when I was a young buck, slick-sleeved deputy, you close the door, and real soon, it smelt like a bad night in the outhouse."

Thorny spit out the water and hitched at the back of her pants. "I didn't look at the floor... but I'm guessing there are some cracks in the concrete?"

"Always have been. When they built the jail, the sheriff had to tie his prisoner to a bed in his house. One prisoner was a strapping young cowpoke with a silver tongue. The sheriff's daughter took a liking to him and cut him loose in the middle of the night. The next morning, the posse tracked the two kids up over the White's into Death Valley. The posse turned around. They didn't have the stomach for the valley. The sheriff didn't care about the cowhand, but he wanted his daughter back. Nobody ever heard from him again. So, in the heat of summer, they poured the concrete and started building walls."

Charlie snorted wetly. "So it cracked from drying too fast."

The sheriff rolled his eyes in a shrug. "All to hell. We have always called it the spider floor."

Bob chuckled. "That must play hell with the minds of drunks."

Pete nodded. "The occasional scorpion and tarantula reinforce the stories. But yes, the smell and bad construction are some of the reasons why they have plans to build a new sheriff's office and jail over nearer to the courthouse."

Thorny bent over and poured the bucket of water on her head. Looking sideways at the sheriff, she summed up the situation. "I'm guessing those plans were drawn up about 1929?"

The man rocked with his frustration; his lips tight. "The county signed off on the construction October twenty-first at the end of business. Construction was to start the next spring. We've been waiting for spring ever since."

She slowly rocked her head and body agreeing.

"Whenever we think we're a little ahead and can start, something else happens. A while back, we were toasting with a few beers —we could start with the money we had. It would get the basic building built. We figured as things moved along we could get the wiring done and the plumbing—pay as we go."

She roughed up her wet hair as she stood. She could see the darkening around his neck and ears. She was expecting the major vein in his forehead to burst at any minute. "This party was on…?"

"A Friday night. December fifth. By Monday afternoon, the contractor had called. Three-quarters of his men were on the bus to the induction depot, down in the city. Even if we could afford to do the work, there weren't enough men."

Charlie cleared his throat. "What did you use the money for?"

The man could feel he was not being called on the carpet but was among those who might help him figure out what to do. "We had a mandate since thirty-six to pave the Main Street. The state would pay for a third, federal picked up a third, and we almost had enough. The guy we hired has a son with polio…"

Bob smiled. "So the home out west is still taking in polio victims?"

The sheriff nodded. "The man took what we had, paved two miles of Main Street, then oil and hard rolled six more miles of our streets. We got the better of the deal."

"The boy?"

"Died the next spring. His heart just stopped fighting. I'm not sure if it would have done any good to get him up here any sooner. I met the boy. He had a smile as big as his heart, but at fourteen, he looked like a ten-year-old but weighed less than the six-year-old daughter of one of our deputies."

Dr. Denton stepped to the door and leaned his head in. Turning, he screwed up his face. "We might let it air out some more. Where do you want me to do the autopsy?"

The man took a deep breath, his hands jammed down deep in his pants pockets, and he looked north toward Big Pine and Bishop. "There's a table still at Doc Miller's old place, but everything else you'd have to bring here. The only funeral home is Decker's in Bishop. If you want, we can load them in a truck after the sun goes down and haul 'em up there."

"I know his embalming equipment. It's almost city complete. I think it would be better there than upsetting people at the hospital. Room is tight at the hospital, and they don't have a cold room."

Thorny kicked at the dirt. "Which… is what the big race is for."

"Dad said something about a race, but it didn't make sense."

The sheriff chuckled. "It's the one time I won't be able to write a ticket for those two men and their damn motorcycles. They're holding a four-hundred-mile race from Mojave to Carson City. The race is raising money to add a wing onto the Northern Inyo Hospital. It will triple the beds and give them room for several other services this valley has needed for a long time."

"Why Mojave to Carson?"

Pete held up his hands. "I've got this one." He smiled broadly—he could finally contribute. "There is an electric stoplight at the railroad crossing in Mojave. Three hundred ninety-eight and a half miles later, or there abouts four-hundred miles, there is the next electric stoplight in front of the Silver Nugget. The two racers are Mace and Roy from Bishop. They work on anything mechanical these days, but their love is motorcycles. Mace rides only Harley Davidsons, and Roy only rides Indians. Roy always paints his red, and Mace likes black. So, they talked the two companies into sponsoring the race and kicking in twenty-five thousand dollars each to the construction fund. I've heard talk about the three casinos in Carson and another in Gardnerville will make up the rest for the hospital. They have all agreed to kick in ten percent of all the bets to match the contribution by the California betting."

"Betting? In California?"

The sheriff winked. "Nobody wins anything with the California betting. Your bet is placed on who you think will win. but the money all goes toward buying beds and equipment."

Thorny smiled crookedly at Charlie. They both knew there was more betting going on elsewhere. She turned. "Last I heard, the Harley was ahead."

She looked at the sheriff. "So one of your guys can bring them up tonight?"

The man held out his hand. "Sure thing, and thanks for all you coming down. I know this wasn't how you'd like to spend a Sunday."

She winked. "It goes with the job, Sheriff."

His sigh was as sad as it was tired. "It do that." His shirt hung with the top four buttons unbuttoned. Thorny noted the pajamas underneath and the red burn in his eyes. She knew she would never want his job.

Thinking, the sheriff looked at the doctor. "You want us to wash them down first before we bring 'em up to ya?"

Bob held out his hand. "That would be most appreciated. And… um… I won't need their clothes. If you could…"

The man's face snarled at the thought of the smell. "We'll shuck 'em out here on the gravel before we turn the hose on them. Don't worry none about the clothes. If the dump don't get 'em…" he pointed at the rusted fifty-five-gallon drum, "…the burn barrel will."

Guaspari slowly ground the powder to an even finer powder. Before it would turn to dust, he spat in the mortise to grind it as a safer paste. The Englishman was becoming more and more used to the dose with each shave. The white porcelain mortise and pestle were tan in color from the years of grinding many different narcotic drugs to mix with the soap during shaving, or into soups for dinner. The man was hired more for his pharmaceutical knowledge than his cooking skills, even though the recipients of his culinary skills never complained. As for those receiving the drugs, they never talked back.

The portal hatch opened from the outside. Guaspari listened to the footsteps on the metal deck. The hesitant slide of the outside of the left foot would mean the boilerman, Miko. Guaspari wrinkled his nose at the thought of the man. His hand continued to slowly grind as the hatch banged closed—rusted metal on rusted metal. The ship was diseased and dying. Rust blistered any paint, and the energy of muscles to grind the paint and rust to clean metal had long been viewed as a waste of time.

The smell of garlic, diesel fuel, grease, and a body unused to taking a bath, wafted in ahead of the man stepping through the doorway. The formerly white jumpsuit was painted and stained with grease, sweat, and fuel. The lightest areas were those bleached by the fuel. The man's slippers were threadbare and all but silent, only the light hush as the one edge dragged forward.

The cloud of the man's offensiveness swirled around the cook as he carefully ground the poison with the pestle in the mortise bowl. The light blue flower was now a fine azure paste of poison and saliva. The man considered using his urine the next time. The passing thought almost brought a small smile to his face.

The prickly face of the porcine man leaned close as he looked at the mixture. Guaspari shied his eyes from the open front of the man's clothing. Too often he had seen where the opening ended, and the buttons were missing.

"Did you want a shave today?"

"With that?" He nodded his head at the mix. "Not likely. It would probably kill me." He stuck his almost black finger in the simmering soup. Pulling it out, he stuck it in his mouth. "Hmm, the last of the goat?"

"Lamb."

The man farted with a sinister snarl. He scratched somewhere in the lower area of the jumpsuit—where, Guaspari didn't want to know. "Same thing. Always with the halal. I can't wait to get to Los Angeles and have a steak from the forbidden animals."

The cook shrugged as he poured the mix into the shaving bowl. "The swine will someday turn on you, and it will not feel as good as you think." He grated the end of the soft soap into the bowl. Using the back of a spoon, he mashed the soap and opium into a paste.

"When will you use the other?" The boilerman nodded his head toward a cabinet on the bulkhead.

The cook's hand stopped. He drew erect as his eyes slid closed. He counted three heartbeats and then looked at the other man. "His mind will not leave San Diego. Only his body will arrive in Los Angeles. You are too impatient. One day it will get you in trouble."

The man rolled his finger through the soup one last time. He sucked it dry. Turning for the door, he retorted as he scratched at something between his butt cheeks. "Not before the pig does."

The cook opened the oven. Holding the two towels, he drew out the plate with a damp cloth folded on it. He placed it on the tray and covered it with the copper dome. Arranging the rest, he turned to the strop. He dipped his fingers in a kettle of warm water and sprinkled the long leather belt. The razor flashed open, and he stared through the one grimy porthole as his hand passed back and forth. He let his mind retreat to the small village on the hillside. He had learned to cook from his father, to shave men from his grandfather, and how to drug or kill from his mother.

He wiped the blade down along his apron and then back. Placing the edge on the tip of his fingernail, he slid the nail the length. It was smooth as oil on water.

Closing the blade, he placed it in his open hand. Pulling the tray out from the table, the edge clicked softly against the middle of the tray. He kept the tray to one side of his head as he walked down the hall.

At the door, he knocked softly.

"Come."

11 COLD TABLE FACTS

The hot wind blowing off the desert tugged at Thorny's memory. The rotten smell was not the usual pungency of rabbitbrush. It had heavy notes of skunk, rabbit, and last night's elk steak.

Thorny stood with her hand on the haunches of the last cow in the barn. The light of day was wiped like paint on a canvas—it was a fog of reds and oranges in the smoke of fire. The desert was ablaze, and she couldn't move. She wanted to turn around and tell her grandfather she wasn't strong enough.

"You must stand when others cannot. You are the angel with the burning sword, Thorny. Vengeance is needed—for the valley to survive. You are the mountain who oversees the valley."

"But I'm a woman." She wanted to turn and fall into his arms.

"You are the chosen one, little Thorny Lizard." She could hear the Great Chief, grandfather to Charlie. Why was he here? "You have always had your feet buried in the dust of the valley, but your heart is the mountains. The White Mountains are the old and are the side of your heart which takes back the tired blood. The Sierra Nevada Mountains are the new and give the refreshed. You are the center which creates balance."

She tried to turn but didn't know where to look. The desert storm became redder and hotter.

"Listen to them, Elizabeth." The voice was Ulysses, her mentor. She had so much to ask of him. "They know the truth. I left the golden skeleton hand for you. It was always for you. I knew it was yours the moment I first touched it. I was only to hold it for safety until you were born. Let it guide you. Your heart will lead you to the truth."

She could feel him fade. She wanted to cry out. Tell him not to leave her—again. She had so many questions. She wanted clarity.

The hot wind ruffled her curls and filled her nose.

She could feel her grandfather was still standing behind her. She opened her mouth. The hot wind blew and filled her, so she couldn't speak.

"Ask the mountain, Thorny. You will know the truth. I always taught you to know the truth."

Thorny stirred and finished his words. "Everything else is just a story."

The hot wind ended with a sneeze. The wet snot on Thorny's face woke her. The dog startled, and Thorny was looking at the wolf face of Charlie's dog.

Thorny laughed lightly and reached out. The dog moaned and rubbed her face in Thorny's armpit. "Did I startle you? I think we were both dreaming." She tried to reach back into the dream. There was... someone... and they were telling her something. It was important... or it was... only a dream.

She rolled over on the bed and waved her feet over onto the floor. She sat up, rubbing her face with her palm and claw.

Something in the dream...?

She stood and aimed for the back door.

"It's indoors now." Charlie's reminder from his bed on the couch was more of a volcanic rumble.

She adjusted course. He had added a bathroom onto the house a few months before. She chided herself. She knew about the addition. She had used it many times before. Why was she so disoriented?

As she walked through the door to the room, she heard Charlie roll over and mutter. "Heathen."

Using the outhouse had never bothered her. Growing up, the outhouse faced the sunrise, barely to the right of White Mountain. Sometimes she would go in the middle of the night and stay —sleeping sitting up, with the door open, just to watch the sunrise.

Thorny returned to the main room of the small house. The bed was made, the couch back to being a couch, and Charlie was making coffee. The black and white husky who he varied between calling her dog, fluff face, hair-ball, or wife, was eating her breakfast.

Thorny leaned her shoulder into the large man's back and hip. He didn't move. He always seemed to be a stone wall or rock. Thorny knew it had to do with his size eighteen boots—custom-made by the town's saddle maker, Victor. Her focus was out the crystal clean window. The pinto horse, too small for Charlie to ride, cropped at the fresh hay in the trough. She had initially wondered why he would take in a worthless horse until she watched it walk. The better word would be limp. The small pony understood the day Charlie brought it home with a large wrap still on its leg. The two would cuddle sunshine or snow.

"I had a dream this morning."

The man grunted as he mixed the eggs.

"I think the chief was there trying to tell me something."

Charlie never moved his body. His long arms moved the bowl and poured out the scrambled eggs into the warm cast-iron pan. He paused and then set the bowl and fork aside. "What about Ulysses?"

The horse moved to the watering trough. Thorny scratched lightly at the side of her face. "I think so. I think even Pop was there."

She could feel the muscles roll in his back. It felt like a large sack with snakes in it. "I don't remember what it was they were trying to say. But I think it was important."

Charlie stirred the eggs. "Do you want toast?"

"Have any jam?"

"There's a jar in the cold box. I think it's Huckleberry and rose hips."

"Sure. Thank you."

His head snapped up. "Thank you?"

His body bounced lightly, and before Thorny could respond, he had spun around. "Who are you and what have you done with my friend who never says thank you?"

She growled as she chuckled at the honesty of the teasing. "You want to lose your left manhood?"

He turned around as Thorny stepped over to the breadbox and drew out the loaf of bread. Slicing off two thick slabs, she placed them in the toasting rack and set it on the gas ring.

Both were softly laughing.

As they ate standing at the sink, Charlie remembered where the conversation had left off. "Who had the last words?"

Thorny studied her friends face. "They come to you too." The statement was in no means a question. It was about settling their equal standing.

She started to take a bite of toast with homemade jelly. The smell was of the fruit and bitter rose hips. The lack of sugar convinced her she never wanted to have jelly any other way. She watched the man nod.

She pulled the toast out of her mouth, his mug freezing at his lips as he saw her face was a question mark. He lowered the enameled mug, and she worried her tongue at the center of her lip. "Why would the last...? No. Why not ask who spoke first?"

His chest expanded as his head rose. She had never paid attention to how much air the man's chest moved.

"When spirits come to you in dreams, you are the one who spoke first. You have always asked a question of your guardians.

The first to talk is the dog in the yard, yapping in the night. They are there to wake you and make you pay attention. They have nothing to really say. They are just making noise—barking at the shadows from the moon."

"But why the last person. What makes them the important one?"

Charlie smiled around his mug as he drained his coffee. He held up his index finger. She knew from their twenty-plus years he was about to make his point and win the discussion in one move. She almost groaned. Her piece of toast was at her mouth.

His one finger turned and became two pointing at his eyes. Look or watch.

He picked up his plate and placed it in the tin pan of soapy water. "Because they had the last word. Argument or message, they won or finished." He looked down at her last two bites of toast dripping with jelly. He grabbed her hand and turned the toast. In a flash, he had bitten off half as he turned and walked away.

She sagged against the cool enamel of the sink front apron. *Damn, I hate when he does that.* She looked at the last bite of toast.

"You know I'm right." He closed the door to the bathroom.

Thorny looked at the piece of toast and mumbled. "Yeah, that too." The movement near her leg caught her eye. The dog was looking at her and the last piece of toast.

She sighed as she leaned over. "You might as well." Thorny ruffled the dog's ears as it chewed in delight.

THE TALL WINDOWS, facing north, provided almost enough light to work. The medical work light made the interior of the cadaver glow. The young Dr. Denton bent over examining the cavity of the chest. The air from a large fan placed near the open doorway pulled at his curly hair. His moustache hung heavy—smeared with Vicks to battle the smell.

Bob looked up at the sound of the metallic ding. The alarm he had set had gone off. Controlling his urge to work for just a minute more, the doctor stepped away from the table and walked outside through the open door. He looked down the side of the building where the tall window was leaning against the wall. He had removed it and tied a fan in the hole. With luck, this autopsy wouldn't end with his death, as well.

The truck and deputy had arrived shortly after midnight. Even with the wind in the back of the truck for forty-five miles, the bodies still gave off the scent of death with an undertone of cyanide and almonds. Bob had thought about doing the autopsy on the back of the truck, but the deputy pointed at the small church next door and mentioned there was a prayer breakfast every morning until the war was over.

The two had looked to the windows as the last choice. The embalming room had two doors, but the second led into the sanctuary and other public places where the poisonous fumes would linger. Bob woke the mortuary owner up and got permission to take the window out. The air had remained static in the summer night air until he rigged the fan and propped the door open. The deputy had suggested setting an alarm. The autopsy advanced in fifteen-minute intervals with fifteen-minute breaks in the night air.

Thorny and Charlie found the young Dr. Denton passed out over the mortuary's typewriter. The short but concise autopsy report lay at the end of the desk. Charlie went to find coffee as Thorny sank into the lounge chair under the window—reading.

Charlie returned with three mugs of coffee. Thorny looked up and wondered if every medical or adjunct medical establishment was supplied with the thick white coffee mugs from the navy.

Handing the mug to Thorny, Charlie took the autopsy and eased into the other chair under the window. Sipping as he read, his tiny hums and tongue clicks interjected into the metronome tick of his right foot against his left.

Thorny listened and smiled loosely at her memories of them studying in the library. If they would sit across from each other, her feet would find their way between his. The right would pass over hers to tap Charlie's left. She teased him in the seventh-grade about his 'chirps and burps.' When they were in high school, he had passed six feet, and his voice rumbled like a team of mules on Line Street. His chirps and burps had become deep rumbles and hums, and he had added a wet sucking click in his closed mouth. The sounds, or lack of, told her if he found anything of interest. When Charlie's foot didn't move, and he made no sounds, she knew he was only reading what he had to read or to be polite.

The half-dead body draped over the typewriter stirred. A wavering hand mopped at the drool smeared along the side of the doctor's face.

Thorny wondered if she ever looked as bad studying in college for her law degree. She hoped she hadn't, but figured it came with the territory. "There is coffee to the left of you Bob."

A red eye rose over the carriage of the machine. It blinked twice then the head ground its way to look at the desk. The body moved sparingly. The mug slowly rose to the lips as the zombie carefully leaned back into the desk chair.

Charlie raised the report and held it out. Thorny watched the young doctor breathing in the vapors of caffeine. She placed her hand on Charlie's arm and lowered it back to the armrest. There was plenty of time, but now was the time to watch the restoration.

Charlie and Thorny exchanged glances. This was an old routine from their teenage years. Charlie's grandfather was the tribal chief and shaman. Occasionally, he would sit in the yard—unmoving. The longest vision quest was shortly before they graduated. He had laid out a couple of blankets in one corner of the corral. Charlie came home to find he was making his own Thursday dinner. In the morning, he had been late to school, having done both men's chores with the house and the animals.

After school, Thorny had come home with Charlie so they could study together. The house was empty, and the chickens were roaming the yard. Charlie pointed to the far corner of the corral as he pitched feed for the chickens inside their pen. Thorny checked the nests for fresh eggs and held the nine in her shirt.

Slowly washing the eggs before combining them with the other eggs collected the last two days, she watched the elderly man. He never moved. Charlie laid the circle of oilcloth in the earthenware crock. They placed the eggs point down while the pot of isinglass cooled in the sink. When the layer was completed, he carefully poured the warm liquid over the eggs until they were covered. The gel would keep the bounty of eggs until Christmas.

"It's amazing he never moves. Not even to go pee."

Charlie pushed the heavy wooden lid into the mouth of the crock like a plug. Standing, he looked out the open back door. "He hikes many miles in his quests. When he is done, he will sleep many hours."

"How do you know when he is on a quest and when he is sleeping after?"

Charlie walked closer to the back door. The boards of the floor creaked softly with the man's weight. "When he is on a quest, he seems to be dead. When he is resting after, he is sleeping the sleep of the dead." He turned and smiled at his friend. The face grinding back and forth in her hands meant she understood the Paiute mystic joke.

As the two longtime friends sat in the mortuary office, they watched the zombie at the desk. All three were working on morning coffee.

Thorny leaned closer to Charlie. "Dead or just sleep of the dead?"

The man chuckled the sound of large glass marbles in a leather bag. He was amused.

The lids covering bloodshot eyes rose. The one hand raked at the tossed-about curls. "Give me another five minutes, and I'll be ready for surgery." Draining the last of his mug, he rose. At the door, he paused distracted. "I'll be back."

Charlie's face pulled back on the side as he ground his head on his shoulder to face her. "White man have small bladder. It only holds enough until morning."

Thorny buried her nose in her mug. "Yes, I heard the tiny Paiute bladder this morning. Sounded like scared lamb on flat rock."

The teasing never stopped.

"Saving buffalo herd for afternoon garden watering."

The two were still shaking at the ever-growing bragging when the doctor returned. His hair was combed—almost. The mug was full, and his face was as promised—alert. He sat his slender leg and haunch on the end of the desk as he sipped on the mug.

"The two prisoners?" Thorny started.

"From what the deputy, who brought them up, said—one had been there a month, but the other was arrested..." He looked around. "What day is this?"

"Monday." Thorny frowned at Charlie who nodded. She turned back. "Monday."

"So the poor guy was incarcerated last Monday night. Something to do with drunk and disorderly with a shotgun. I guess the man he disordered is down in the Southern Inyo Hospital recovering from a backside of buckshot. The prisoner was charged with drunk and disorderly, but his real sentence was this here." He pointed at the small stack of autopsies. "I called down to the university in Pasadena last night. Dad had the telephone number for the seismology laboratory. There is someone there around the clock to change the shaker papers or something." He rubbed the heels of his hands on his eyes. "Anyway, there seemed to be what they think was a shift or slip, last Thursday. I'm just conjecturing here, but my guess is there was a pocket or something, and it got released. The prison just happened to be in the path."

Thorny sorted the three reports. "The deputy..."

The man's lips pulled back as his face winced. "He was walking dead a year ago. Half of his lungs were just hard charcoal. His liver was fat and rock—it's why they call it rot-gut. Even his pancreas reeked of arsenic. You can call down there, but I think they will tell you he was slowing down and sick a lot. So they let him babysit the jail for the night shift."

Thorny shrugged her eyebrows. "No foul play."

"Plenty."

She looked up at the doctor.

"That jail should have been torn down the day it was built. If you looked at the window bars, the reason the window didn't open was from the concrete rot. If a couple of prisoners wanted out really bad, they could pull the whole window structure apart. The jail's success was they arrested honest criminals. The real crooks were the ones who built the place."

"Do you think they can use the jail?"

"For what? As extermination chamber?"

She nodded as she furled her lips. The truth was obvious, and it took the lives of three men to turn the light on it.

"Sometime in the next few days, could you work up a report so they can condemn the building?"

"What will they do for a jail? I can't see them holding prisoners up here in Bishop and then driving them an hour or so to appear in court."

Thorny cocked her eyebrow and rolled her head to look at Charlie. "Guess, I'll have to go to work."

Charlie laughed and pointed. They'd fill the doctor in when he woke up—again.

12 PORT OF LOS ANGELES

The police officers stood at the door, considering the small cabin. The one body sat in the chair with its feet crossed on the end of the bed. One arm hung. The hand's fingers curled slightly at the floor. The white starched shirt looked as if it had been worn for days but was otherwise pristine white. The cadaver's hair was oiled, well-trimmed, and combed. Other than the tattered slipper on the one foot, the man would be what the two detectives would have called a fop or a dandy.

The detective dressed in the gray suit pushed his fedora back on his head and leaned over, slowly examining the body from the pedicured toenails to the sculpted wave of the hair. There was absolutely no sign of struggle. The body was lacking any signs of having been shot or stabbed. The one arm was draped casually across his waist. "I think this fella was so relaxed he didn't even enter rigor mortis."

The detective in the brown suit removed his hat and looked about the room. The room was as neat as the body's shirt—starched but lived-in. "So the stiff is shaving. He mops up his face and decides to cool his heels. He sits down, relaxes, and passes away. Something doesn't add up here."

Gray bent again and looked closely at the soap on the body's face. Standing, he steps to the small sink and opens the efficiency medicine cabinet and mirror. He waves his hand to show there is nothing there then stoops to look in the empty set of shelves under the sink. He glances over at the open-faced Gladstone bag.

"I'll bet you lunch there's no shaving kit in the bag."

Brown pinch-shuffled the fedora's brim through his fingers. "Why?"

"I don't think he ever had to shave himself." He took one of the small hand towels and wetted it. Stepping to the body, he wiped the side of the jaw. The skin wiped clean and smooth. "He didn't need a shave, but he liked the ritual of having someone shave him."

Brown considered the idea. The cabin was small but clean. There were no luxury appointments, and yet everything about the body screamed upper-crust. "What was he doing on this rusted tub?"

Gray rocked his head and body as his lower lip eased forward. He twitched his head toward the dark corner of the cabin—behind the open door. "That will be for him to tell us."

The pool of blood flow framed out almost a foot away from the small crumpled body. The body had been kneeling at the small cabinet. The dark line of dried blood on the throat just below its ear suggested the throat had been sliced with a sharp knife.

Gray caught the eye of the larger of the two uniformed policemen. "Roll him over, would you."

The two uniformed officers shared a look. They had been in the same situation many times.

Crossing the legs, the officer twisted the small body. It rolled in place. The head moved, but rigor had dulled the looseness. Most of the clothing that had touched the floor was soaked with the man's blood. The neck bisected with a thin line of congealing blood. The slice was from ear to ear—severing the carotid artery.

Gray squatted. His fingernail picked at the white flake on the body's apron. He raised the test sample to his nose. Almonds.

He carefully lifted the one corner of the apron. The dry blood splatters didn't penetrate the heavy cloth. The blood was never fresh or in volume. He thought a moment and stood. Brown was used to letting the older detective work out a scene.

Gray leaned over the passive body, his nose almost touching the body's mouth, and then he stood and smelled. The tiny amount of scent in his nose smelt of almonds.

He looked at Brown. Pointing to the prim Englishman, he concluded, "First victim. My guess is this was not the first drug he had gotten in his morning shave, but this one meant to kill. My guess is there is some mix of opium or similar plant that put him to sleep and allowed the cyanide to bring him the rest of the way to here."

Brown nudged his chin at the blood-covered body. "And him?"

"Ah, yes, our mysterious killer, barber, and cook. Why was he also a victim?"

They turned at the light knock on the doorjamb. A man in a gray flannel suit stood in the door. His coat was open to expose the badge on his belt. The butt of a .45 peeked out from his armpit. Gray guessed there might be a twin on the other side.

"Slumming, Carlson?"

"Just in the neighborhood, Vern. I thought I'd stop by and see if I could lead you to the next clue."

Gray flushed at the collar. "What does the FBI have to do with a murder in the L.A. Harbor?"

The FBI agent stepped into the cabin. "I might ask a similar question, Tom. Since when does the Los Angeles Police Department step off dry land and take over investigations from the Harbor Patrol or Coast Guard?" His glare was pure cold iron. The two had history, and they weren't beyond taking it up in public.

Brown cleared his throat. "Before anyone draws a weapon, is there a point to this pissing match?"

The two held their stare and then turned on the younger detective. The only one without any gray hair.

The FBI looked toward the cabinet near the head and hand of the bloody body. "Did you happen to find a small valise with a swastika on it?"

Brown lowered one eyelid. No cop liked getting punked on a crime scene. "No, did you lose one?"

The federal agent turned toward Gray. "He's been sitting too close to you for his own good."

"How do the Nazi's figure into this?"

"They didn't… until maybe this. Four months ago, off the coast of Africa, a shipment of uncut diamonds was stolen from a Nazi go-between. The man turned up floating in the tidal basin of Dar es Salam, Tanganyika, with a knife lodged in his heart. The diamonds found their way into the hands of our English allies." He pointed at the reclined body. "This was their man assigned to safeguard them from Asia to here. He was to disembark last night when the ship docked and come directly to the west coast British Embassy in Brentwood. When he didn't show up by this morning, they called us."

Gray flexed his eyebrows and looked back at the Englishman's body. "How many diamonds are we talking about?"

The FBI agent thought about not sharing the information but then acquiesced. "About eighteen pounds. Four bags about the size of a cricket ball." He smiled slightly at the reference meaning nothing to the two detectives. "Four hardballs." He held his two fists out. "Or about a quart and a half."

The twin whistles were low and appreciative.

"And they were in this Nazi valise you're looking for?"

"He could have changed them out to something that wasn't so obvious. I know I would have."

Brown stepped around the blood pool. The door on the small cabinet was slightly ajar, and he used his one fingernail to swing the door open. There was nothing in the cabinet.

Gray and the agent looked around the sparsely furnished cabin. To one side of the service lavatory was a half-opened Gladstone.

Eschewing procedures, he picked it up and looked in. His face slumped. Turning, he held it out to the agent.

The agent looked in. His right hand slid in and pulled on the edge of the bottom. Withdrawing the false bottom, he reached in and felt around. In the one corner, he found what he had heard—a soft rattle of something loose and tumbling. He drew out the small rough stone. Even uncut, the light from the porthole shone through dully. The stone was the size of the end of his index finger.

Brown pointed down at the bloodied body on the floor. "So where does this guy fit in?"

The special agent shrugged. "From what we have determined, he was the cook and might know about certain drugs. He was also the barber, and so he put the drugs in the soap, which would make him the killer, but who killed him? Well, that could be anybody's..." The agent's voice trailed off as he studied the body. He squatted as he moved slightly to one side. "What's that sticking out of the cut on his throat?"

Brown stepped back nearer to the wall and bent down. "Where?"

The agent stepped around Gray and grabbed the threadbare hand towel hanging from the ring next to the lavatory sink. He stepped to the body on the side with the least blood on the floor. Squatting down, he wrapped the towel around his index finger and thumb.

He probed with his index finger, and the small lump, sticking up through the cut, moved. He pulled the towel tight over his finger and thumb, taking hold of the small object. Pulling slowly, the straight razor withdrew from the man's windpipe.

Gray hummed low. One of the first things you learn in homicide is the telltale signs of who did the killing and what kind of murder it was. Numerous stabs to the heart area would call for a visit to the estranged ex-lover. The murder was one of emotional rage concerning the heart, but they don't touch the face they fell in love with. Spur of the moment shootings of a husband catching his wife with a friend usually bare out a previous knowledge of the affair spurring the man to go buy a gun. Strangulation is personal and often a man. Poison is predominately a woman killer. But one stands out above all others. The insertion of the weapon in intimate areas of the body.

"Insertion…"

The agent held the razor up by the tip of the tang. He turned it around, carefully looking at the handle. "I would have expected this inserted down the mouth, or in his ass… but I guess with the throat open like that…"

Brown frowned at the agent and slowly shied his face toward his partner. He had risen through the ranks from fingerprinting to financial crime to detective. He had never dealt with the street or homicide.

Gray caught the move and silence. He was getting used to explaining the grittier facts of life to the sheltered man. "Our victim here and his killer were homosexual lovers. As it would appear, the killer didn't exactly like the stiff but was engaged with him to be on the inside of what was going on. So, when he killed him, he presented one last display of homosexual hatred—he shoved the weapon down into the place they had until now been having sexual relations."

Brown's frown turned harder as one eye squeezed half closed. The burning grease from his gears grinding in his mind was too much for the agent.

"Oh, come on… did Bill find you in a seminary? The stiff was sucking his cock. He didn't want to, but it was part of the job. So, when he killed him, the killer hid the razor in the man's throat." He held the razor forward slightly. The younger man recoiled against the wall. Neither older man laughed. They could see life had just mule-kicked the younger man in the delicate parts of his body and his mind.

The agent turned to Gray. "Tell me you remembered to seal the ship and keep everyone off and on."

Gray rolled his eyes up into his lids closing them in a facial shrug. "We locked the ship down as soon as we got the call and got here. Unfortunately, one of the crew from the engine room had taken a tumble down some stairs as they were docking, and he was taken away by the port authority to get medical treatment."

"Where did they take him?"

"Check with the securing officer at the bottom of the gangway, but I think they said San Pedro Mercy. The guy had taken a tumble. His face had gotten as bad as his ankle and ribs."

The agent stared at the detective. The seconds were their own conversation. The detective could feel his edge of control slipping away.

Gray's shoulders slumped as he caved into himself. "Shit on a hot sidewalk." He turned and looked for another towel, finding the only one was draped on the other stiff. He swore under his breath as he grabbed the soap filled towel. Rinsing it in the sink, he moved to the body on the floor and started washing the right hand. The man had put up a fight.

"Rickets," he called for the uniformed policeman outside the door.

"Yes, sir?" The officer leaned into the opening.

"Find out where they took the engine guy and call over there to make sure he's still there. I want a team on that little..."

"Yes, sir."

The agent chuffed a single breathy laugh. "You honestly think the guy ever made it there?"

The detective held his look. Finally, he crumpled. "Not just no, but hell no. But at least I've got it covered."

"The question you might also ask is who took him there." The two detectives stared blankly at the agent. They all knew the truth to what the man alluded to—more than one person.

Gray looked at Brown and nodded. "I'll go."

The agent and senior detective continued to search the small cabin. Apart from the shilling and a two-pence coin stuck down under the seat cushion and bed mattress, they found nothing for their efforts.

Brown looked at the agent with a hang-dogged face. He then looked at the body draped languidly over the chair and end of the bed.

The agent chuffed softly. "I know. The one person who can no longer appreciate the only decent chair…"

The two sat as one on the bed. A mutual dislike for the other's position, but they waited quietly. It was the nature of their jobs.

Gray stopped at the door and softly talked to the uniformed officer. The officer glanced in and nodded his head. The detective thanked him.

"Did you two find anything?"

The agent held up the two coins. Gray's face fell and turned dark. "Turn them in at the lost and found."

Brown smirked at the comment. He enjoyed his partner's snappy commentaries. He could judge the mood by the level of the cutting edge. "What about the engine guy?"

"Never showed at the hospital."

The agent ground the back of his neck into his collar. "Who took him?"

"One of the dockhands said there was a black Chevrolet waiting at the end of the dock since they tied up the ship. When the engine guy came down the gangplank, the car drove up, and they were gone." He held his hand up. "And, before you ask—he said the driver was a man wearing a fedora down over his eyes. In the early light, he couldn't see anything more."

"What year? I mean new or an old beat-up dying car?"

"He thought it was a Deluxe or a Supreme. Either way, it was a standup and from the late thirties. He did think one thing was odd. There was only the taillight, but he said by the white letters over black, it was Nevada or New Jersey license plate."

The agent thought about where he had trained and where his

parents lived. "White over black. It could also be Washington state or Mississippi."

"Washington maybe, but not Mississippi."

"Why?"

"It had a seaport entry decal on the bumper. It would need to be near a coastal port. He said they have to be renewed every year."

The agent rubbed his chin with his open palm. "San Pedro is a long way from Mississippi, Washington, and especially New Jersey..."

"He also said it was a three-by-three."

The agent smiled with a smirk. "Washington and Mississippi are still on the one-letter and five-number system. Nevada followed California several years ago and converted to the three-by-three."

Gray swallowed a chuff. "Now all you feds have to do is find a standup Chevy in Los Angeles that's from Nevada."

The agent's smile was more predatory than humored. "Haven't you heard? We have a whole team just for doing those kinds of shit work. We call them the Los Angeles Police Department.

"Ass."

2:30AM

"Good morning, race fans. This is Tom Holloway, reporting from a chilly night in the Mojave Desert of California. We are standing outside a large concrete building that's usually only used by the Southern Pacific Railway repair crews. But tonight, there have only been two people allowed inside the building. Those two men are the competitors in the Race of the Century, being held here today.

"The two men are Mace Gilbert, who will be racing for Harley Davidson Motorcycle Company, and Roy Tollofson, who will be racing on his traditional red Indian Motorcycle. These two men are the tightest of friends and are also business partners in a motorcycle repair shop in Bishop, California—the town they expect to pass through about six o'clock later this morning.

"The racecourse today is four hundred miles of some of the most grueling highway conditions. I have here with us today the fastest man on earth, Barney Oldfield. Barney, you drove this same length of highway just one month ago. Welcome, and tell us about what these two men are facing today."

"Thank you, Tom. I'm honored to be here today. As you said, this race will cover some of the hardest conditions for a motorcycle, much less a racing motorcycle. They will go from here at an elevation of seven hundred feet, up and over three mountain passes reaching as high as eight thousand feet. Most of the highway is dirt. Some of the course is oiled-bitumen macadam, but also some of the more treacherous areas are pure volcanic silt, which can be as slippery as ice."

"Barney, the silt sounds dangerous, but what's the harm in skidding out into the desert. After all, isn't it just sand?"

"Tom, the silt isn't in the desert, it's in two of the mountain passes. The most dangerous being Dead Man's Curve about ten miles this side of Lee Vining—one of their pit stops. But let me walk you and the listeners through the four hundred miles."

"Sounds good, Barney. Let's start with the railroad crossing. Why start here?"

"Tom, even with a long race, you want a fair start. Now we know that for most of the race, Mace and Roy will be riding knee-to-knee."

"Why is that, Barney?"

"Safety, Tom. Anybody who is standing on the course will probably only be near the fueling stops. That will leave about three hundred and ninety miles where they are alone. If something is to happen to one of them, the other man is there. Remember, these are best friends who work together, and probably was the best man at the other's wedding. They're going to be out there to not only beat their friend but also look out for his safety."

"So back to the railroad crossing."

"Right. Three months ago, the railroad installed an automated crossing arm here at the town of Mojave. There are red electric lights that will be flashing while the arm is down. At exactly three this morning, the representative from the Southern Pacific Railroad will raise the guard. When the lights stop flashing, the race has begun."

"Why three o'clock, Barney?"

"The first hundred miles are as pure desert as it will get. Even right now, at the coolest time of night, the temperature is only fifty-eight degrees. They need to be out of this hot desert by five o'clock. The heat is their enemy. It makes the fuel thinner, and their motors will burn through their fuel before they get to the next fuel stop."

"What are the highway conditions for these first hundred miles?"

"Actually, barring them hitting a mule, a rabbit, or a tortoise in the dark, this is as good as it will get. While the temperatures are cooler, they will be running flat-out on asphalt—thanks to the WPA. They expect to hit speeds well over one hundred across the flats."

"I understand to conserve fuel; they will be running without lights. Is that wise?"

"Look up, Tom. What do you see?"

"The full moon. So it's going to be a big headlight."

"Right, but after the flats, there is a stretch of highway they will have to turn on their lights. That stretch, we call the roller coaster. In there, they will have to watch for animals and areas where sand may have blown across the oiled macadam. This can make a curve become a slip. When I ran this course last month, it was almost over before it started. The fourth roller into the canyon almost called me home. But I had four tires on the road, and they will only have two."

"The roller coaster brings them up to the mouth of the Owens Valley. So are they back up to top speed or are there still dangers?"

"At the top of the rollers is a long narrow lake. If the temperatures have kept the valley dry, there won't be any fog. But if there is, they will be hitting the fog until just before Owens Lake where they will hit the real desert of the Owens Valley. Once they fuel, they have a long run to Lone Pine. The highway is well maintained and clear. I would expect them to be back up to their top ends. This whole first half before sunrise is where they have to log the fastest times. They will lose a lot of speed later in the passes."

"But don't the high speeds burn more fuel, Barney? They only have so much in the tanks, and there are only eight pit stops along the route."

"You're right, Tom. They will be burning through their three-and-a-half gallons of fuel much faster than someone driving the forty-five-mile-an-hour speed limit. But that's what makes this an interesting race instead of a leisurely drive. They have only nine hours to cover the entire course. This means they have to average almost fifty miles each hour."

"But they have to stop for fuel."

"Right, and those pit stops take time. They will need every ounce of fuel, and they don't dare spill a drop. So it is a race against time but also one demanding they conserve their fuel."

"And the real fuel burning will happen in the mountains. Let's talk about what comes after Bishop."

"That's right, Tom, but the town of Bishop is another important mark. This is the point where they will be leaving 395 and heading out a smaller highway toward Nevada. Highway 6 is almost straight as an arrow with only a low rise. Because this stretch of the race is in their backyard so to speak, they know and have practiced racing on every mile of this stretch. This is also where their pit stops are less than fifty miles apart."

"Why is that important, Barney?"

"Speed, Tom, speed. They will probably make up a lot of time between Independence and across the Aberdeen flats. The highway between Independence and Bishop gets a lot of use, and, by racing standards, almost dead straight and flat. We should see them hitting speeds of eighty or eighty-five along those stretches."

"But aren't the motorcycles able to top over a hundred?"

"Very capable, Tom, but the pit stop to pit stop run from Independence to Bishop is forty-seven miles. So they will be holding back while they are trying to gain time. Where we expect to see the two hitting over one hundred is the straights between the railroad station of Laws and the old stagecoach station of Benton—their next fuel stop, which is only thirty-six miles. They have been riding the highway and figuring out the speed to fuel ratio under all sorts of conditions. I think we will see the real test of these two and their machines on this and the next section."

"This is where the dirt and mountains come into play.

"Right, Tom. The mountains are where the real race gets to the nut of the fruit. Straight out of Benton Station, they turn left and right into the winding grade of volcanic glass ash from the Mono Craters and the sand from Granite Mountain. It's the hardest pass on the motorcycles, going from an elevation of four thousand feet to almost six thousand. It is the combination of these two elements that make this potentially the most deadly section of the race. Combine this with the fact the stretch of road is rarely used, and you have danger. They need to make good time, but if anything happens, they are pretty much on their own. The Mono County sheriff will follow them from Benton, but still—anything could happen."

"Just one officer?"

"When they leave Benton, their next fuel stop is at a small place at the bottom of Mono Lake, named Dog Town. It is only forty-one miles but could take between thirty-five and fifty-minutes to get there—depending on the conditions. The arrangement is that if they haven't shown up by the end of an hour, a search team will be sent back down the race course."

"Couldn't that be dangerous? I mean, if they aren't expecting any traffic, and they come around a tight mountain curve right into a car or truck…?"

"Tom, the last ten miles are pretty open, so they would see anyone coming. So they are pretty confident it would just be a safety measure. These two are used to racing on these conditions, so I'm betting they even beat the thirty-five-minute time."

"Whew, but they are still in the slippery volcanic ash?"

"Correct, and that's at Dead Man's Curve. But there is another problem also, and that's the altitude. The thinner air makes the engines run less than efficient. So they will have rolled in some retard on the spark. That also burns more fuel. But, the big worry will be getting around the curve and into Lee Vining and more fuel."

"That's a pretty short run, Barney."

"Yes, but the topping off is critical as they will be facing a big hurdle next. The curves out of Mono Lake Valley are stacked for a fast ascent to well over eight thousand feet on the Conway Summit."

"Does Mono Lake and the alkaline cause them any danger or problems?"

"If there is any morning fog, I would suspect it will have burned off by the time they get there. If they are on time at Lee Vining, I would think they won't have any more trouble until they start climbing up out of the Bridgeport Valley. Those switchbacks are sharp and not graded well. Most of them are flat, so I would expect them to drift through those. But if there is much new loose sand, they could be losing time there."

"After Bridgeport is the Walker River Canyon."

"Right, and because of the river, they don't oil the macadam. So the best they can hope for is the highway department has rolled the heavy steamroller through the canyon to give them a solid road. But the curves are nasty with a solid wall on the left, and the rushing river on the right. There is no room for a mistake here. But, at the other end, is Topaz Lake on the Nevada border. They get fuel and a smooth climb up and over the Topaz Pass. The lake on their right is a beautiful sight, but they probably won't be stopping for a picnic."

"Right you are, Barney. Now they are on a straight shot across the high desert of Nevada. Take us through the area and bring us on home to Carson City."

"That's correct, Tom. The climbing and nasty winding roads are done. Here is their last chance to make up for lost time. They know to make the finish line at noon they have to race full out."

"But watch the fuel at the same time."

"Right, they have only one last pit stop. But the pit stop is restricted to only three gallons of fuel. They need to have close to the other half-gallon in their tanks to give them a full tank for the last forty-eight miles, and a race to the finish. Too fast and they will be pushing their motors home. To slow and they may lose. So the real race, for my two-dollar bet, is going to be on the streets of Carson City just before noon."

"How many people do you think will be in the three casinos when they race past?"

"Tom, my guess is about the same number as will be in the capital building hard at work."

"Barney, I see the large doors to the warehouse are being opened, and the two men will be pushing their motorcycle to the start. What do you think has been going through their minds tonight?"

"My guess is we will see very shiny motorcycles this morning. If they are like me, I would have taken advantage and stripped every-thing I could off the racer and polished everything else."

"The polish helps it slip through the wind better."

"Right. Also, look for them to have replaced the large seats with small metal pans with split-hide or pigskin suede glued to the metal."

"Less weight?"

"Yes, and the rougher leather keeps them from slipping around in the curves."

"Fenders?"

"Gone. Those things are heavy, and I don't think we will be seeing any rain today."

"How about the footboards or sidewalks as they call them?"

"I'm not sure. I watched them practicing a bit last month. Both of them ride flat-footed and light on the seat. They might have replaced them with pegs. We'll see in a few minutes. I see them starting to roll out now."

"Barney, they will have nine hours to run this entire four hundred miles—you drove it this last month, how hard is this going to be?"

"Tom, I wouldn't want to be in their seats today. I ran the course in a stripped-down Oldsmobile runabout. We took over five hundred pounds off the coupe and put a hundred-gallon gas tank in it. I didn't really have to stop for anything that wasn't important. Even with all that, I ran the course in only nine hours and seventeen minutes."

"There you have it, folks. The fastest man in the world, and this race must beat his time. The racers are crossing the track, and in minutes, folks, the arm will be brought down. We can see the polish gleaming on both motorcycles, just like Barney said they would. Barney, I want to thank you while we have a minute. You drove this long racecourse to bring us this special insight into the unusualness of this race."

"Thank you, Tom. It has been a pleasure being here today. But let's not forget what this race is all about."

"That's right, Barney. This isn't just about Harley Davidson versus American Indian, but about the hospital in Bishop, California. Both motorcycle companies, as well as many others involved in today's race, have made pledges to help build a new, much needed, wing on the hospital. This race has raised almost all the needed hundred and twenty-five thousand dollars for a new surgical and recovery wing."

"No better cause for such a great race. Win, lose, or draw, the donations will be building something that will last for many decades to come."

"But let's not forget the winner's purse, Barney."

"That's right, Tom. The winner today will walk away with his motorcycle and one thousand dollars."

"And, the loser, if there is one, only gets his motorcycle and five hundred dollars. Folks, I can see the man at the switch. We are on countdown… and in four, three, two, one… there goes the arm raise, and… the lights have stopped, and as you can hear the roar of the motorcycles, we have a race. This has been Tom Holloway bringing you the beginning of the Race of the Century starting from Mojave, California. Stay tuned to this station as we bring you updates from our reporters as they call in along the racecourse."

The road from Fallon, Nevada, was hot, long, and dusty. Even with the canteens of water and thermoses of tepid coffee, by midafternoon, Thorny and Pete were both exhausted.

Pete had pulled over to use a tall sagebrush. Thorny found a low wash behind a fuller bush. Relieved, they sat on the running board of the car in the shade. Pete stared at Thorny's boots.

Her voice was low and almost a desert breeze. "What?"

He pulled his eyes with his face and jaw. "Nothing really." He sipped on the canteen. The water was bitter from the metal. "I was just thinking about your boots."

She blinked hard and looked south down the highway. Looking back, she squinted behind her green glasses. "What about them?"

"We left Bishop at four this morning."

"So...?"

"You still have them on. Even after we dropped off those two corporals at the brig. You could have taken them off... but you haven't."

Thorny looked at the battered aluminum cap of the thermos which doubled as a cup. She swallowed the last sweat-temperature swig of the morning's coffee then screwed it on the empty thermos. "Do me a favor. Spit out there on the road."

She watched through the crack between her cheek and the glasses as the man massaged his mouth around trying to work up some spit. She waited.

"Can't."

"Why not?"

"Too hot, and I don't have enough water to make spit."

Thorny nodded. "Then just step out there and put your hands down in the dust of the road."

The deputy looked at her and then started to chuff. "Is this something like when you beat your hand to show me how you don't feel pain? Because I already know the road is hot as hell."

Thorny stood. Placing her hands in the small of her back, she bent backward—stretching. "So you're not going to do it?"

"No, ma'am. I may be a deputy in a beautiful valley what gets hot as the third ring of hell, but I'm not stupid enough to go burn my hands on the highway."

"How do you know it will damage your hands?"

He pointed. "The air is still dancing seven feet above the ground. I wouldn't even want to walk far on this road."

He stopped and looked back at her. She had been watching him figure it out. Her slim smile curled a fraction more. "Keep figuring things out, Pete, and one day, you'll be the sheriff himself."

His left shoulder slumped as his right hand pushed on his thigh. "But you'd already figured it out…"

Thorny laughed softly. "No. But thanks for the compliment." She looked north up the road. Her face frowned into a squint as her voice trailed off to a distracted tenor. "Remember, I grew up walking barefoot on these roads. I already know when to keep my boots…" She turned to the back of the car and opened the trunk.

"What's wrong?"

Her voice echoed from deep in the trunk. "Is there a pair of binoculars in all of this crap?"

"I keep them under the front seat." He turned, opened the door, and drew them out of their case.

She took them and looked north up the highway. "Why the…?"

"What are you looking at?" He tried to see what could have gotten her attention.

She handed the binoculars to him. "Top of the run. Second rise, not the third."

He dialed in the focus. He frowned down around the eyepieces. "What… their moving… but…?"

"I saw them crest the top rise. I expected them to clear the second rise a minute later. But they're stopped up there. Not on the rise but behind it so it hides them."

"What are they?"

"Not what, but who." She took the binoculars from him and slipped them back in the case. "You know about the race coming up next month." He nodded. She opened the door as she twitched her head back toward the north. "It's Mace and Roy."

Pete started to turn. Thorny stopped him. "Just sit back down. Is there another canteen?"

"No."

"Well, we just have to act like we have water and coffee."

They relaxed with their backs to the car doors. Their feet were crossed out in front of them as they sipped on their air-filled canteen and thermos, relaxing and enjoying the late afternoon as it washed across the expanse of high desert.

The large motorcycle engines were muted as the desert sucked the pounding sound out of the air. Lazily, Thorny turned her head, and Pete followed suit. They watched the approaching pair.

The black Harley Davidson and bright red Indian glided to a stop. The rumble became a soft pounding as they idled. The beats were half noise and half a vibration felt in the chest.

Thorny hefted her soft silver cup as if making a toast. "Afternoon, gentlemen."

Mace raised his goggles. "Well, mayor, what are you doing out here?"

Roy added. "You two need help?"

Thorny noisily sucked the last of the coffee from her cup and snap-waved any left at the dusty road. No darkened spots appeared in the dust. "Nah, we're fine. We just stopped to take a break and watch a small herd of Tule elk over along the base of the alluvial fan. You two out practicing racing in the slippery deep dust or something?"

The two men exchanged glances. "Yeah, something like that."

Pete frowned at the shade of evasiveness. "I thought the race was all on 395?"

The two looked more like schoolboys caught peeking into the girls' locker room than fifty-year-old men. Something was up, and it wasn't the sun.

"Most of it is. But, as Thorny figured out, there is a lot we can practice out here to prepare for the worst the 395 can throw at us." Mace looked to Roy for confirmation. Thorny thought the nod was a little too energetic.

"Which do you expect to be the worst? Around Owens Lake or up near the Mono Craters?"

They both smiled. "Deadman Curve."

Pete put the cap on his canteen and stood. "How fast do you think you can take it?"

Mace cleared his throat. "Roy's better at slipping around tight curves, but I would guess if it's loose, neither one of us will take it faster than fifteen or twenty. The volcanic dust is made of glass, and you can go sideways and flat over the cliff in a heartbeat."

Thorny made a show of standing. "How sensible is the eight-hour deadline?"

"Nine hours. We start in Mojave at three in the morning to beat the lower desert heat. We've got eight fuel stops along the way, spaced out about every fifty miles. Those will be the time killers. Through much of the run, we can hit eighty. On the oiled macadam, we could hit a hundred or more, but then we burn too much fuel and don't make the next stop."

Thorny cut him off. "So it's a balance of going fast enough to make the stroke of noon, but not so fast you burn your fuel and wind up pushing the bikes. Why can't you carry more fuel?"

Roy skidded his jaw sideways. "Them's the rules. Harley against Indian, eighty-inch flathead against eighty-inch flathead, three-and-a-half gallon tanks. Mace and I weigh almost the same, and we've both been riding motors since we stole two motorcycles just outside Toul, France, after we took it from the Germans."

Pete took the thermos from Thorny and stowed it and the canteen in the trunk. "Well, gentlemen, our workday isn't done, so we'll leave you two to your racing, and we'll go take care of county work. Good luck to both of you on the Fourth of July. What time do you think you'll be through Bishop?" His hand rested on the door handle.

Mace lowered his goggles. "Bishop is the midpoint, but we need to be fueled and shunt and climbing this grade before six-thirty."

Pete showed surprise. "Holy Toledo, three hours from Mojave. That's a blistering speed for even a car with plenty of fuel. I don't know if you two are racers or daredevils. But still, the best of luck."

As they drove away, Pete and Thorny exchanged knowing looks. Something was not right.

THORNY STOOD in the empty lot and looked up at the tower. She could just make out the top of a white helmet moving back and forth behind the low wall. "What's the report, Bill?"

The man came to the wall and looked down. "Hello, Mayor. All quiet this morning."

She smiled. It was about to not be. "Permission to come up."

"Come ahead. Company is always welcome." The man waved her up.

Thorny shifted the rucksack to both of her shoulders and began to climb the first of the three ladders. As she climbed, she thought about the ladders and those in the mine on her property. They could have been made by the same person.

The man with thinning gray hair and even fewer teeth gave a large smile with a hand up and into the ten-by-ten watchtower. The small table, stool, and tin bucket with a neatly furled and hung rope were the only items besides the man. She noted a small book on the table accompanied by a canteen. There was no log book, nothing to write a report with, nothing to track sightings of enemy airplanes.

The man stood with a bent back and a defiant twinkle in his powder blue eyes and toothless but warm smile. "This question you have on your face must be a doozy for you to climb the forty-one feet just to ask it."

"Who said I had a question?"

"Well, there… I'm a-tryin" to figure out who done climbed up here. It's either the mayor to give me grief about the lack of reports, the chief of police to arrest me for dereliction of duty, or the little barefooted girl in bib overalls who would climb it just for fun and because she was curious."

She cocked her head slightly as she studied the man. There was a lot more going on here than she had thought a year ago. Anyone in town could tell you Bill Worth was three jokers and a face card or two light of a full deck. But it had slowly worked on Thorny since Monte told her about someone noticing Bill standing on top of the empty Civil Defense building, watching for enemy airplanes. So they had built him a watchtower from timbers the Los Angeles Department of Water and Power had stored nearby. Supplies were always disappearing from the storage yard.

Her lips furled as she thought how to start. Her shoulders shrugged out of the arm-straps of the rucksack, and she caught it with her left claw. Swinging it up to the small table, she noted the title on the book. It was a small collection of poems by Robert

Service. She moved the book to the upper corner. "Which do you like best? The Bandicoot, the Yukon, or Malamute?" She turned to find the man smiling with the loose lips pulled up on the one side.

"Eustis always said he had the smartest granddaughter this side of the Marian. The Chilkoot Trail was what Mr. Service wrote about. The pass up over to Bennett Lake was daunting, and his description could make your blood freeze. That seven-mile trail alone killed more ambitions and dreams than all the women who've lived since Helen of Troy." He smiled as he watched Thorny's passive face turn to a restrained surprise. "The Bandicoot is a tiny marsupial from down there in that Australia place." He held up his thumb and fingers to show a size about the likes of a mouse.

She turned and drew out a thermos. "I brought coffee to ease the throat while we talk." She noticed him eyeing the rucksack. She said nothing as she brought out a clear half-pint bottle with no label. She stacked a couple of sandwiches next to it. "May said you prefer your ham and cheese chopped and the darker bread. So the top one is yours."

His head ticked up at the thermos. She pulled out two enameled tin cups. Taking up the thermos, she handed the half-pint of moonshine for him to govern for himself. If the man poured a shot, it was shy by at least a tablespoon. Taste over intoxication.

THEIR SANDWICHES WERE HALF GONE, and the coffee had demanded the second thermos, but no more of the seasoning. They both sat on the floor—leaning back into the wall. The roar of two motorcycles on Main Street a couple blocks away gave Thorny pause in her chewing.

Bill didn't even miss a bite. "The boys." It was a statement of note. He swallowed and started to take another bite. He noticed Thorny was looking at him. He rested his sandwich hand down in his lap. "What?"

Thorny rinsed her mouth as she thought. "Nothing gets past you, does it?"

"What are you asking? And is this the chief of police, the detective, or the Thorny Lizard asking?"

She smiled at the full nickname her grandfather and pseudo-uncle, Ulysses, had called her. "I'm not the little girl anymore, but I also don't feel like the others, either. But I also don't think you are lost in your head and can't tell a crow from a SPAD airplane from the Great War in France."

The man shrugged his eyes and took a small bite of his sandwich. "People didn't pay much attention to the little girl in the bib overalls, but I could see her watching everything around her. You might have lacked for a mother, but between your grandfather, Ulysses, Monte, and the couple who sharecrops your ranch now… you had the best this town could offer." He leaned his head back to rest on the wall as he looked past the roughly built ceiling.

Thorny finished his thought. "But you were watching…"

His head fell forward and bobbed gently. His face only turned halfway as he shyly looked at her. "Try me."

"What's your report for last week's Tuesday?"

"The official report I yell down to the idiots who ask me for the spotted airplane report… or the report on your town?"

Thorny chuffed. She liked this man more and more with every surprise out of his mouth. "Both." She took a bite and chewed slowly as she listened.

"The SPAD was a red-tailed hawk. We have a nesting pair in the tall trees on Hubbard's hundred acres. From Line Street, it would be the fifth or sixth tall tree, but there is one taller. The two Fokkers were the pair of eagles nesting just east of Bishop Creek. They like to fish in the pond behind the lower power dam." He looked at her.

She rolled her finger in the air for him to continue. "And the town?" She stuffed the last bite in her mouth.

"It looks like the new couple on Elm Street are preparing to be parents. The cracked sidewalk in front of the Miller's on Mason Street is because of the lack of deep water across the street. The cottonwood is looking for water, and the new owner is trying to keep his lawn green. But this time next year, he'll have a sidewalk to trip someone, then he will be looking for you to do something."

She gave him a side look. Her one eyebrow as raised.

"I wake up before dawn most days. I walk three or four miles to keep my arthritis from settling in my back and legs."

The motorcycles roared back down Main Street, headed the other way. Thorny notice the man glancing at his wristwatch.

"Too short or too long?"

"What?" He frowned at her in confusion. She noted how few wrinkles he had.

"The boys...?"

His face smoothed as he looked in the direction of Main Street. "No, about right. They ate at Roy's place. His wife must be working the late shift."

"How do you know they ate at Roy's. I seem to remember they both live out that way."

The man's tongue curled around in his lips as he considered what it was prudent to tell. He drew out his blink as the side of his face stretched. "If they ate at Mace's it would have been just long enough for a glass of water, a rotting apple, and a stop in the outhouse."

"Hard times aren't universal, but only an apple?"

He bobbed his head slightly. "They gleaned every field this last fall. Business is terrible, or they would have to practice racing in the evening when it's cooler. Mace's wife also works at the market, when she doesn't get enough hours throwing booze for Clarence. I've watched her poke about the trash cans to save thrown-out food. I don't know what's going on, but they are sorely hurtin'. I'd be rooting for him to win the race, but I know Roy and his girl are hurtin' right alongside them. I don't know if a $500 purse can solve their problems, but I hope for their sake it can. They're nice boys, and I've known them since France, but I wish this race could do as much for them as it is for the hospital."

"Where are they getting the money for all the fuel?"

"The motorcycle companies. I also think the county has somehow allowed them off the rationing. Heck, most people right now could give you half of their ration cards and still never use what they have left. There's three cars on the west side with flat tires. One went flat two years ago. People are just walking. Now they smile and tell each other if our mayor can walk, so can they." He looked at her with a tighten smile as he silently laughed at teasing her.

"Are you trying to get fired from this job?" She tried to keep a straight face, but she barely got the words out.

He squeaked before they both burst out laughing. "I've been meaning to ask for a raise. But now I think you're thinkin' of taking my job too. Do you even know what a SPAD looks like?"

"Sure. It looks just like a crow."

As they sat later in the warmth of the tower, Thorny's mind churned. "So why do you do this?"

"Because the town built this tower for me."

"Weren't you on the roof of the defense building watching for planes?"

"No, I was up on the roof looking at the condition. Tar-shingle roofs don't last long in this heat. That roof is only a gentle slope because we don't get heavy snow. So it gets strong sunshine from sunup to sundown. It just bakes the tar right out of the papers. There were two small leaking patches then. There are five now."

"Then where did the spotting airplanes come from?"

"He closed one eye and rolled the other. "Have you ever drawn water from a well with a rope and a bucket?"

"Sure, who hasn't?"

"Does it look like you're doing anything else?"

She thought. "Um... no."

"Now imagine you're seventy-two, been through two wars, and

don't suffer kindly a fool who ask what you're doing on top of a building poking at the roof with a stick."

Thorny pictured the man on the roof and started to laugh. "Spotting enemy aircraft. Who would be so dumb...?" She held out her hand. "No, don't tell me. I most certainly don't want to know."

The man stood and stretched. "It doesn't matter anymore." He looked at her. His face was stone serious. "You done killed him already."

"Chief Reseda?"

The man nodded solemnly, but she could see the twinkle returning to his eyes. "Can I tell you about some other dumbasses in this town?"

She stood and rested her hand on his shoulder. "No. I'd rather find them on my own. But I still don't understand why you keep coming up here. It has to be boring, and the ladders can't be easy."

"Hah. The ladders are easy. I spent most of my time in and out of mines. If Ulysses gave you the mine stake up Silver Canyon, you should know there are two mines. The lower was a rip-roarer in its day, but it petered out. I helped dig the upper. We followed the veins, and the most ladder we put in was four 4-10s. The last one was a mistake. Only after they got the shaft down 3-10, they lost the vein below but found trace up top. By then, the bunch had gone to hell, and we went our separate ways. I heard the French were hiring pilots, so I went to France to fight the Germans."

"You flew SPADs?"

"The death traps? Oh hell no. I was a mechanic. I kept them flying until they didn't. France is where I met the boys. They were mechanics and could fix anything. They stole some motorcycles and brought them back to the base. We heard the red pants were looking for their motors, so the painters repainted the motors in the blue colors of the Service Aéronautique. The red pants suspected, but they couldn't prove the battered, dirty motors were theirs, so they left. We washed them and tuned 'em back up. The boys became quite good at... um... rescuing, shall we say, needed supplies. They also were daring and when we needed to get a message through by ground? Off they would go. And, usually, they would bring back a shopping list of needed supplies. One Christmas, they came back with a small pig riding on the gas tank between Mace's legs and arms." He stopped and looked at her. "Oh. But it's not what you wanted to know."

Thorny thought about the lack of stories she had gotten from her grandfather Ulysses and Monte. The three had been in Cuba with Teddy's Roughriders. Her grandfather had also served an abbreviated time in the trenches along the River Somme. Shortly after Thorny was born, he was brought home and suffered the rest of his life from the Mustard and Chlorine gas attacks.

"No, it wasn't what I asked, but I liked your answer more. I've only been back a couple of years, so there is a lot of catching up I need to do." She looked around. "And this view is like nothing else in town."

Bill chuckled. "Unless you nailed the roofing on the steeples in town. Up there, it's just you and the birds." He nodded off to the west where a shadow in the blue sky hung in a slow dance on the thermals.

"Hunting?"

The man shook his head. "He's just out playing in the thermals. Birds of prey are the biggest children when it comes to thermals. I've watched them lift and drift on a thermal by the hour. The rotting garbage of the dump creates methane gas. Combine the gas with the heat of the day, and you get a powerful lift for the wings of an eagle."

Thorny stowed the thermos and wrappings. "I'll leave you the canteen."

"Thank you for lunch and the visit. You're the first I've ever had. I don't need the water, I brought my own, but I appreciate the gesture."

Thorny rested her hand on the metal, but then pushed it an inch toward the man. "It will give me an excuse to come by again."

The man's tongue curled gently at his lips as he nodded once. "Thank you. I'd like more visits."

As Thorny reached the bottom of the second ladder, she looked up at the hatch. "Hey, Bill?"

The man's face appeared above the opening. "Yeah, kid?"

"I really did enjoy our time."

"So did I. Stop by anytime."

She looked out across the top of the buildings. The air wavered and danced with the heat. She thought about the cold of the last winter and looked up. "What do you do when it gets cold?"

The man laughed. "You're the first to ask. I stay home. It gets bloody cold in the winter and after all, who's going to check on my being here. We all know there are no enemy airplanes."

"Good morning, race fans. This is Jimmy Johnson in the studio. For those of you just tuning in or waking up, the Greatest Race of the Century started at exactly three o'clock this morning in the California desert town of Mojave. The two racers are Mace Gilbert on his eighty-inch black Harley Davidson and Roy Tollofson on his eighty-inch red Indian Chief. The two men have had only one month to get used to their racing motorcycles. From what I have heard, they hardly slept for all the practicing they have been doing. To go over what makes this race so special, I have John Roberts of the American Motorsports Association here in the studio with me. Welcome, John."

"Thank you, Jimmy. It's an honor to be here this morning."

"The honor is ours, John. First, what exactly makes this the race of the century? And why is it important?"

"Jimmy, for forty-two years, the fans of the Massachusetts motorcycle have argued with the Wisconsin motorcycle company. Both are fine motorcycles, and both played their parts in the Great War to help with winning the war. The races over the years, from road to hill climbs, have fallen both ways. It has always been about the rider."

"But today, John, the machines are the perfect match. What about the riders?"

"Jimmy, the two men are as perfect a match as their motorcycles. During the Great War in France, the two ended with motorcycles in their possession. There are stories of the two of them riding knee-to-knee with artillery shells or bombs falling all about them. They became tested best friends. After the war, they returned to Bishop, California, where they will ride through in just a couple of hours. They opened a motorcycle shop which has grown into a full automotive repair. They live almost next door to each other and were best man in each other's weddings. Just like the Harley being two-and-a-half cubic centimeters larger than the Indian, it is rumored Mace is a quarter-inch taller and five-pounds heavier than Roy. Jimmy, this couldn't be more textbook of a match up. For nearly thirty years, the two have been by each other's sides."

"Thanks, John. Ladies and gentlemen, we have Dutch Gertzen on the phone, calling in his report from the middle of the desert at mile marker forty-eight. Dutch, are you there?"

"I'm here, Jimmy. The racers were burning up the desert tonight. They wheeled in to the pit stop at exactly three-twenty-seven. Roy, on the Indian, was pulling his friend with a rope. When they got within twenty-yards, the big red Indian ran out of gas as well. I spoke to them while they had a sip of water and their tanks topped off. By their estimates, they are running about four minutes fast. In these first miles, the highway is mostly oiled hard-pack. Roy almost hit a rabbit, but Mace narrowly missed a tortoise. They have some moonlight left, but they still must run under the laws for lights. The hooded covers only allow them so much visible road ahead, and it has nothing to do with driving at night at ninety-three miles an hour. They felt upbeat and think they can make up more time between here and Little Lake—their next pit stop. Jimmy, back to you at the station. This has been Dutch Gertzen in the middle of the Mojave Desert."

"Wow. Ninety-three miles an hour in the dead of night. Would you do that, John?"

"Jimmy, I've ridden well over a hundred miles an hour, but it was in the middle of the day on an asphalt oval track. I can guarantee you, I would not be out there doing what these two men are doing tonight. But when I spoke to them a week ago, they were laughing about riding across enemy lines with no lights."

"So this ride tonight is old hat for them?"

"Jimmy, they live in the desert of the Owens Valley. So riding in the middle of the night for them is about a skill of sensing what is out in front of them. Like I said, it is not a skill I've developed. So my hat is off to them."

"Well, there you have it, folks. The racers are crossing the hot start of the desert and pushing their machines hard. This is Jimmy Johnson with the Race of the Century. We'll be back with the next update shortly."

"I thought I'd run up and see if you were here."

She looked around the mine cabin and the large lump on the one bed.

"I went by your house, and even your wife wasn't there." Thorny blew on the small fire in the shavings and tiny kindling. She noticed the work Charlie had done on the mining cabin. "The tar paper on the outside will make a huge difference this winter when the wind comes roaring down the canyon."

She ruffled the ears of the dog they referred to as Charlie's wife. "I bet he's been starving you. You have to come to me for any love and affection."

The dog leaned her head into Thorny's thigh and crotch. She rubbed and squirmed as the sharp fingers of her claw probed the fur on the dog's forehead and played with the ears. Thorny pulled more kindling off the top of the woodstove and pushed them into the growing fire.

"Are you going to wake up, or just lie there pretending to sleep? I haven't even gotten a morning groan." She kept feeding the fire as she glanced at the large pile of blankets on the one cot.

The low rumble sounded almost like an earthquake in the

mountain. "The coffee isn't made yet."

Thorny ruffled both sides of the dog's head as she kissed the nose. "Silly frog. He didn't think I might bring coffee in a thermos." She smiled as she talked to the dog.

The blankets shook as the man rose and stumbled out the front door. There were effects, which once woken, could not be ignored.

Thorny piled in more of the larger kindling and a couple small splits of old timbers. The old dried timbers from the mining camp burned hot and fast. Thorny had noticed the small stack of arm-thick logs of black locust. The iron-hard wood was stubborn to start burning, but once lit, it would burn all night, leaving hot coals for the morning.

She stepped to the new dry board Charlie had been building for her. She pulled some fresh meat wrapped in waxed paper from her knapsack. Picking a couple of pieces, she tossed them in the air for the dog—they never hit the ground.

Drawing the can of coffee to her, she spooned some grounds into the enameled pot she had found one day in the half fallen-down barracks. It wasn't as fast as frying coffee in the iron skillet, but it made more. She poured water from the bucket standing on the counter. Charlie must have brought it in the night before.

She dipped one of the cups into the water bucket and sipped on the well water. The crisp metallic flavor of the chilly water drew her back to her time spent at the mine with Ulysses. As she stared out of the recently cleaned window, she could hear her surrogate uncle explain the difference of the well water from the well in the valley. The arsenic gave the bite, but it was the iron in the mountain that provided the metal taste.

"I thought you brought the coffee." The deep voice was a warm mock threat on the back of her neck.

She caught the movement of the large hand out of the corner of her eye. The hand flipped another piece of cubed meat behind them. The gift was rewarded with the sound of scrambling claws and a jump in the air. The landing was soft and quiet for an eighty-pound dog. But the wife was a Paiute dog and knew the ways of sneaking and quiet—for rewards.

Thorny slid her hand into the rucksack and drew out the thermos. "Don't whine, little frog. More is on the way." The two could smell the cast-iron of the woodstove heating. Soon, the large Indian would forgo the two blankets he stood wrapped in.

He portioned out the coffee in the two blue-speckled enameled cups. "Did you bring eggs from the house?"

She drew out a much-reused egg carton. There were seven brown speckled eggs. He gave her a hard look. She glared defensively back. "The white hen was having a bad morning. I think I startled her and she pecked me, and I grabbed the egg too hard. You should feed them more eggshell to strengthen their eggs."

"Didn't you stay out at the ranch last night? You've got plenty of eggs out there."

She turned from the window and leaned her lower back against the dry board counter. "I was going to have dinner with you last night. You weren't there so I just stayed. Little Tito came by to feed the animals. I helped him with the hay; he's too small to do the horses."

The man shrugged. "He's only seven, he'll grow. I feed him much elk jerky."

Thorny stuck her face in her cup. "I'll watch for the antlers to start growing."

The large man eyed the number of eggs. "Were you staying for breakfast...?"

She laughed and rubbed his tummy. "No, my starving tiny tree toad. It's Sunday and I have a meeting."

He ignored her stab at his size and appetite. His head bobbed up as he remembered. "Ah, the Hidden Skull and Death Society. How could I forget?"

She sensed a shadow of resentment of his not being included. "There's much girl talk, and anything about a mystery I share liberally with you—who else would have my back?"

He stared out of the window silently as his left hand probed along below her beltline. The .45 wasn't obvious to the casual observer, but his hand knew enough. He had also helped her kill hundreds of bottles and tin cans, at the dump, as she practiced her quick draw and shooting. The OK Corral wouldn't have stood a chance against her. She practiced with the same focus she had applied to her schoolwork. It was as if the use of her pistol was a tool for her life.

He thought about the bullet breaking her arm in the spring. He glanced down at the arm and her using it. Anyone else would have been in a cast much longer and still overprotecting the arm. Thorny hadn't spent three weeks in the cast before she soaked the plaster off.

"So what are the Skull Diggers up to?"

She rinsed out the enameled cup and set it on the drainboard. "They're still working through the large box of old cases Harold and Ulysses left. There is a lot there to go through."

He smiled as he looked sideways at her. "And then there is the Bishop case…"

She snorted at the first murder case in the Owens Valley her officer had suggested. She turned and leaned back against the counter. Her eyes bounced around the single room of the cabin. The two cots and table didn't fill the cabin that was probably built to bunk four or six miners. Now it was a comfortable size for the two of them to come visit for the peace and quiet.

Charlie's chest rumbled as he prepared to clear his throat. "You had another reason for coming up here this morning. I have coffee, jerky, and can make my own fire. You haven't chewed on your left lip once, but you're still working on something."

Thorny chuffed. "Red man saying white woman obvious?"

"When buck on top of doe during rutting season not shopping for new drapes."

She thought about all the observations Bill had talked about. Things that were plain to see—once you were told where to look.

Thorny walked everywhere, but she never walked to see, only to think. Now she would need to do both just to keep up with her new friend and his set of eyes.

"How much do you know about Mace Gilbert and Roy Tollofson?"

Charlie knew this was neither a snowball question to melt with the afternoon sun, but also not the real question. The real question, he knew, would come later.

"Good mechanics, good motorcycle riders, both married, live out toward the hot spring hill..." His voice trailed off. "Not much. Why?"

"I'm working on it..." She shoved the fingers of both hands in her pants pockets, holding her arms close to her body. "If you had work to do, would you go practice hunting during the day?"

His body struck a deep tone. "Hmm, I hear their motorcycles many places in the valley as I deliver fuel. I haven't thought about it in those terms, but I'm guessing you have a thought on it?"

"Someone mentioned they had gleaned much of the orchards and truck farms this last fall."

Charlie rolled around against the dry board. His face was looking out the window, but she knew it wasn't what he was seeing.

"Times are tough for many people. It's not just the war and the rationing. People who took on two hundred gallons of heating fuel in winter's past only took maybe a hundred this last year. People wear an extra sweater, and if they have it, they put extra blankets on for the winter. I think one time or more almost everyone who could gleaned these last few years. Not everyone has trees in their yards."

Thorny thought about the fruit and nut trees in his and her yards. Between the growing elk herd coming at dusk to eat her alfalfa, plenty of produce from the truck farm, and the eggs from her hundred or so chickens, she was close to the most well-off person in the valley. The strange relationship she had with the mountains disclosing veins of silver to her, or the younger mountains producing nuggets of gold, was a bonus that allowed her not to have to work for a paycheck. When the nation needed untapped water, the mountain gave it to her, but sensing the flow of water was Charlie's warrior spirit.

She reached out with her claw and gently gripped his arm in friendship. "Do you need bullets for your rifle?"

"Got plenty. What are we hunting?"

"Perhaps it's time to thin the herd of elk. The real heat is coming on and the barn is cleaned. We can make a ton of jerky for the winter and some fresh meat for those in need."

He smirked evilly. "Are you going to let Mr. Fish and Game come and play?"

She bumped off the dry board and snorted. "I heard he's the fastest field dresser in the north valley."

The man chuffed. "Is that a challenge?"

She paused at the door. "Take it any way you want, but the work needs more than just one man." She looked at the full sun on the mine site. "I need to get down the hill. If you're done up here, I'd like to go up the mountain for some hot water tonight." She saw his nod and stepped out of the door.

THE FRONT DOOR of the Bib restaurant opened as Thorny stepped up on the porch. She expected the red hair of the town's current whore, but instead, was greeted by the dark, slicked-back hair of the FBI.

"Hello, Stan. Fancy meeting the FBI here." She glanced down at his mirror-polished shoes. "Hmm, must be here on business."

A delicate hand wrapped around his arm from behind. It didn't shove him out of the way as much as he sidestepped to reveal his wife, Ruth. "Ignore the cretin, Thorny. We just arrived about five minutes ago. Monte and May were filling us in." She looked down and spread her hands out presenting her stockinged feet. "At least one of us was paying attention."

Thorny stepped into her hug. With her claw, she gently punched at the Special Agent and friend. Ruth stood on her toes as she hugged the taller woman. "We're here on business, but I think Stan wants to talk about it in private."

Thorny snickered. "I never thought I'd get to say this, but you can tell these people everything. They're my posse."

Ruth pushed her back as her face opened in surprise and delight. "You have a posse? I'm so jealous." She turned to her husband. "She has a posse. Who could have imagined such a thing?"

Stan strained one eyelid closed against his stretching face and smiled. "Oh, I could imagine it. After all, she's holding down every job except governor." He looked at the other two. Monte and May shrugged with smiles and nodded.

Ruth and Thorny jerked apart at the sound of the door opening behind them. Thorny laughed. "Here are my other two. Right on time."

THE SUNDAY BRUNCH was down to cups of coffee and the last crumbs of a coffee cake. The seven had run through the six old mysteries they had settled on two weeks before. The only one with any side-note was the murder of a man while his wife was away tending to her ill mother several states away. The man was found with a cooking knife in his chest. Only the handle was showing above the chest where his heart was. Days after, another miner had pulled up stakes and moved with his wife back to Colorado. A few neighbors remembered she had a pair of dark black eyes and what appeared to be a broken nose. She had said she fell down the stairs, but all the houses in the mining town of Rovana had a single step for a stoop, as they were all single-story homes. Nobody was buying her story. Not then, and with the knowledge of the other miner's death, not now. But there didn't seem to be any evidence connecting the two miners, or the one miner and the other's wife. So the investigation was filed in the bin with the rest of the head scratchers. Even if it did have a wink and a nod to go with it.

The younger of the prostitutes raked her fingers up into her red curls as she leaned on her elbow. She slowly blinked. "Tell me again what these diamonds are worth?"

Understanding the woman's view, Ruth smiled as she taunted the young woman. "They think they are just shy of twenty million dollars."

Bertha lowered one eyelid in warning. "No. I meant after they're cut, polished, and on a deserving girl's finger."

Thorny knew the young working girl and where her mind wanted to go. "Unset, they are only worth north of twenty-five or thirty million?" She got the small smile she expected and continued. "Once they're ready for a girl's finger, they can push those numbers closer to two or two-fifty—with the right jeweler."

Stan and Monte's foreheads both furrowed. Monte hadn't said the larger number. Thorny leaned back as she knew she had jumped far ahead of the FBI agent—or, with his wife working ostensibly for the same company, *agents*.

Stan cocked his head sideways as his wife interceded. "How did you get the larger number?"

Thorny's smugness was cut short as May calmly reached over and put her hand on the back of Thorny's shoulder. The chair eased back to the four legs securely planted on the carpet. May nodded her acknowledgment and for the young woman to answer the question.

Thorny gave her a side look and then focused her attention on the two federal agents. "I've been… um, how do I say this without it sounding wrong? I've had reason to become involved with the jewelry industry as of late."

Monte chuffed as he leaned forward with his elbows on the table. His oiled black wavy curls shined in the light from the high window. "She can tell you this week's spot price on all the precious metals."

"Only gold and silver."

Ruth cocked her head as she rubbed her neck. Thorny guessed it had been a long drive up in the night. They would have left the south Los Angeles bay at or near midnight. "Why not platinum?"

"It doesn't come from the Americas. I think it's mostly in Russia and maybe one of the minerals in Africa. My jeweler could tell you. He deals in metals used in jewelry. It's why I know about silver and gold—I sell the ore to him. He smelts it down to pure and then can certify it."

Inez sat up straighter, and her head moved back as her eyes opened wider. She dabbed her napkin at her mouth. "May I ask how much?"

Thorny's smile wasn't patronizing but close enough. She watched as the previous town prostitute smiled back knowingly. "Enough... just enough."

The older woman's smile breached by the tiniest of tongue wetting her lips. The eyelids shuttered halfway in understanding. "Ulysses taught you well."

Thorny's head dipped as she turned to the FBI agent. "Why do you think the diamonds will come through here? There must be plenty of stonecutters in Los Angeles. There is a street... a whole area. I can't remember the street, but there are many of the strict Jews who work in the business... the ones with the long curls by their ears and they wear those black hats."

Ruth bobbed her head. "Fairfax. They are Hassidic Jews—orthodox. Mostly they work in the designing and casting the metal. The Fairfax neighborhood makes probably most of the jewelry for the western half of the United States—but they don't cut diamonds there." She waved her hand as she sat back. "Oh, I'm sure there are a few cutters near the jewelry market who can cut them, but mostly they grind or lap the colored stones. It is a whole different process and training."

Thorny fidgeted with her finger, tracing the squares of the blue and white gingham tablecloth. "But it still doesn't answer why you think the diamonds will be brought through Bishop. And even if they were, how would we know? How big is fifteen pounds of uncut diamonds?"

"It's closer to around twenty-four pounds, which is about a quart and a half... give or take."

Everyone turned toward Bertha. The redhead's neck flushed, and she looked like a shy schoolgirl caught peeking into the boy's bathroom. She wore the white blouse; the only piece missing was the tartan academy skirt. "I know math. I mean... I can do math problems in my head. Sometimes it's a comfortable place for my mind and attention when my body is doing what it has to..." Her voice faded off.

Ruth reached out her hand across the table. More a gesture than a touch. "It's all right, sweetie. I'm sure only one other person at this table understands, but we can... um..." She turned toward Thorny.

"Commiserate?"

"Yes. Commiserate."

Stan nodded his head at his wife agreeing but turned to the young redhead. "But how did you conclude a quart and a half is what I want to know?"

"Well, you told us the carat weight of the rough stones. I have some unset stones. The five together is about the size of a grape. I took the total, added twenty percent to allow for airspace between the stones, divided by the grape size and adjusted for the container, and it looked like a quart canning jar and a pint jar or six cups." She looked at the blank looks. "What?"

Monte drew in a breath through his nose. "You have an amazing talent there."

Inez smiled and patted the younger woman on the thigh. "Yes, yes she does."

"Can you tell me how much fuel I used driving from Los Angeles?"

"Sure, Stan. Which car, what was the temperature on the desert while you were driving, how fast did you drive… and a few other things."

Ruth coughed a laugh. "Not fast enough. I do the driving across the desert. He's hell on wheels on the city streets, especially in the middle of the night when there is nobody else, but when he hits the dark country, my eyes are better."

The man's stoic face confirmed the statement as fact.

Thorny persisted. "One last time. So why here?"

Stan smirked with mutual understanding. "The car and driver who picked up the boilerman from the ship had, we think, Nevada plates. They were white over black. So, either Washington, Nevada, or Mississippi. There are no stonecutters in Washington or Mississippi. If you were going back east, you might as well go to New York. For that, you would get a flight with American or Pan Am."

Thorny thought about what Wilber had said, in confidence, about shipping the gold and silver ingots. Post office and no insurance. "Why not just ship them?"

"Give up control to the chance they might get lost?"

Monte lolled his head toward Thorny. "He does have a point there."

"Where would they be taking the stones in Nevada?"

Ruth put her finger up. "There is a stonecutting school in a small town called Minden. They are the only school outside New York or Antwerp, Belgium. We think they will either take them there or to someone who has trained there. We have some leads, but just nothing to really point you at—right yet."

Stan finished. "We just wanted you to be aware of the situation, so if we call with an emergency—you will have all the background." He smirked and tipped his head at his wife. "And we don't have to be back in Los Angeles until midafternoon on Tuesday."

"I'll call Danny and tell him to throw some mook out into the desert and make room for two federal agents."

"Good morning, race fans. This is Tom Holloway, reporting from a chilly night in the California Desert. Two men are the competitors in the Race of the Century, being held here today.

"The two men are Mace Gilbert, who is racing for Harley Davidson Motorcycle Company, and Roy Tollofson, riding on his traditional red Indian Motorcycle. These two men are the closest of friends and business partners in a motorcycle repair shop in Bishop, California. They expect to pass their shop shortly after five o'clock, later this morning. But, right now, we are going to Red Tyler at the old Olancha stage station—the second pit stop. Red, are you there?"

"I'm here, Tom, and so are Mace and Roy. As the officials top off their tanks, let's see if I can get a word with Mace. Mace, this is less than an hour into the race, but how are you two doing? I notice you both coasted in—dead empty on fuel."

"That we did. We pushed a little bit hard, but the roadway was oiled this spring, so we were looking to gain some time we expect to lose in other places."

"How are you two doing?"

"I can't speak for Mace, but it's downright cold this morning."

"Folks, that was Roy on his Indian Motorcycle. The temperature is in the low sixties, but with a windchill of close to a hundred miles an hour, you can bet it is very cold. Dawn isn't until 5:47 this morning. Is this going to be a problem, Roy?"

"Strong coffee with lots of honey."

The sounds of the two motorcycles starting and roaring away drowned out anything being said.

"There you have it, folks. The two racers are cold, but just got gasoline and refueled with some strong coffee loaded with honey from their backyards. The motorcycles are running strong, and they are out of here at Olancha Station with seven minutes in their favor. The sky is clear, and we're an hour and a half away from sunrise. We should have a great day for this race. Tom, back to you in Mojave."

"Thanks, Red Tyler, and we'll be looking forward to you narrating the race later this summer at Pike's Peak in Colorado.

"Folks, the race officials there at Olancha Station made a note of Mace adjusting his choke a bit. It may have been for the cold, or it may have affected their fuel consumption, too. They both filled up, and the temperature is standing at fifty-three degrees there at Olancha Station.

"They have gained some altitude but will have close to a flat run to the old stage stop and Pony Express station at Aberdeen and their next fuel stop. Those who are just joining us, we are getting reports from the pit stops for the two motorcycles who are racing four hundred miles across some of the harshest highways and conditions California has to offer. This race is between a Harley Davidson and an Indian motorcycle, but this is all about raising the money to build an important addition onto the Northern Inyo Hospital in Bishop, California.

"Tom Holloway here, coming to you from Mojave, California. And we'll be right back after we hear a word from our sponsors."

The steam provided some sense of privacy, but adulthood provided more. The men took the uphill side of the pool—Charlie's preferred seating. The hot water swirled in, and it was the last section to mix with the cold spring-water fed by the snowpack from years gone by. The women clung to the warmer section, originally built to accommodate Charlie's grandfather, and Thorny's desert-rat adoptive Uncle Ulysses. The older men had always enjoyed the warmer water on their aging bones and joints.

The genders held their own low volume conversations. But, by the hand gestures of her lifelong friend, Thorny could tell the men were talking about hunting. Specifically, bow versus rifle. She was sure it would eventually get around to an invite for a weeklong camping trip into the Sierra Nevada Mountains. At worst, she could see the FBI agent being invited to take part in some pouching of the large Tule elk on Thorny's ranch.

"What are they talking about?" Thorny jumped mentally. She realized she had been watching the dialogue of Charlie's hands and had stopped talking minutes before.

Thorny snorted softly. "Charlie is almost up to inviting Stan to go hunting this fall. He used to take a couple of weeks at the end of

September with his grandfather. They would fish and make fish jerky as well as take a deer or two. I'm not sure it was as much about the food as it was about the bond the two shared."

"What about his parents?"

Thorny's two fingers rose out of the water, and she flicked a small stream at the men. The water only made it halfway, but it was met with a similar splash from the other side. Charlie had never even looked. The two had been connected since they were waist high to their older men. Most of the time, they rarely had to say or ask; they were already comfortable knowing what the other was thinking.

"His mother died shortly after he was born. I always assumed it had to do with the birth. I saw a picture once, and she wasn't even my size. His father was what they call an itinerate cowpuncher. He used to work the stockyards in Yerington, Nevada. When we were around eight or nine, he just didn't come home. There was talk of him drinking and an accident with the cows or something, but I don't think even Charlie ever found out the truth. But his grandfather was always there until last year." She glanced over at Ruth. "Now that I think about it, it might be why he has never made any effort at finding a wife. He never saw much need or advantage in those kinds of relationships." The story was a fabrication, but it was easier than trying to explain a mysterious explosion on the reservation which took both lives and three others.

"He has you."

Thorny lowered her chin to her chest and thought without thinking. She looked up at the large shoulders and head in the steam. Turning her head, she engaged Ruth. "Our relationship… Well, there isn't any romance there. We've been friends since we were just a little frog and a thorny lizard. At times, it's as if we know what the other is thinking. We care deeply about each other, but it doesn't go beyond. In a lot of ways, we are about all we have left. When Monte is gone, we are the only family left."

"But you love him…"

Thorny shrugged her eyebrow and mouth. "To do so, I would need to be able to feel emotions. The same as I can't feel pain goes for what everyone else experiences as emotions."

The woman wiped at her hair on her forehead. "But you care about him…"

"Deeply. But those butterflies in the stomach, the ache at a loss, the crying at hurt… I don't have the… um… capacity. I know he can feel pain, but he doesn't display his emotions anymore emotive than I do. So, in a way, we make a good pair—just not a match. Besides, he already has a wife." Thorny smiled as she turned her head to look at the large mound of fur. The two sparkles of moonlight in the dark fur told her the dog was still awake and watching.

Ruth turned and looked at the dog. "It would be nice to have enough room for a dog like that. I know Stan would like a larger dog."

Thorny rose out of the water to sit on the concrete berm, leaving her feet and lower legs in the water. Ruth joined her and looked at the scaring in the moonlight. "Is there feeling in the scaring?"

Thorny smoothed her right hand up the scaring on her left arm. "More than most people give credit for." She looked up as her right hand slid down. "Do the scars on normal people lack feeling?"

Ruth motioned toward her husband. "The scar where the bullet came out of Stan last winter is still numb. There is some numbness in his back where the bullet went in, but not like the chest. But you said you can't feel pain. So, where you got shot…?"

Thorny thought about how to explain how it felt. "Have you ever had a stuffy head cold—one that aches from the throbbing and being inflamed?"

"Sure, I have terrible sinuses. When a cold gets in my nose, I feel miserable."

"But it doesn't hurt as much as ache."

The brunette swayed her head back and forth.

"The arm felt the same way. Like I had a bad nose cold in my bicep and shoulder."

"But no sharp pain?"

Thorny snorted. "You met the deputy, Pete. I explained to him about it, but to drive the point home, I took a large piece of firewood and started pounding my hand into the table. It scared the heck out of him." They both started laughing. "He thought I had gone crazy, and he was next."

"Lizard…" The caution rumbled across the pool. It made the girls laugh even harder.

Stan rose out of the water and sat on the side. "What are you two cooking up now?"

Thorny giggled as she looked at the fuzzy form across the pool. She turned into Ruth's shoulder. "I'm not saying your husband is a stuffed shirt… but I never thought he would take us up on coming up here tonight."

The two muttered so the men couldn't hear. "Why, because we would be wearing only our smiles?" The woman looked across the pool and started laughing. "Honey, what was the name of the place we stayed at for our honeymoon?"

"Which one? Your parent's house or my uncle's shack in the woods?"

"No… when we finally ran away for those days in Big Sur?"

"Neptune, nepples, nipples… something like that. It meant something like naked or nude in Greek. Why?"

Ruth flushed. "Nothing really. I was just telling Thorny about that shrimp dish we had."

Charlie remembered Thorny telling him about the first shrimp she had experienced this last winter. The difference between the tasty, succulent shrimp and the crawdads they ate out at Fish Slough was the difference between looking at a full harvest moon and a picture a five-year-old had drawn. He smirked. "Shrimp… you mean like crawdads?"

Thorny cupped both hands and shot a wake of water across the pool. Both men laughed. The story had made the rounds.

Ruth rolled her eyes as she turned back to Thorny. "It was romantic and wonderful. We packed nothing. I had made the comment about going to a nudist camp, and Stan found one. There was a row of benches along the cliff to watch the sunset. Every evening they were full. The rocks also."

Thorny's brow was arched as she pointed across the pool. "Mr. Stuffed Shirt?"

Ruth's laugh was more of tinkle of pixie bells. "One morning, I came out of the bathroom to find him standing in front of the closet. I watched. His eyes slowly traced from one end of the small closet to the other and back. Just before I asked him what he was doing, he scratched at his chin and said 'Pink, yes pink... I think I'll wear the pink one this morning to breakfast.' He turned, and sure enough, he was wearing his pink birthday suit."

Laughing, Thorny put out her claw to Ruth's shoulder. "Wait. To breakfast. You went to breakfast nude?"

"We were naked from just after we checked in to just before we checked out."

"What about the waiters?"

Ruth harrumphed. "California state law says they have to wear long pants. So they did." The smile was slow to grow, but it was there.

On the hike down, in the full of the moon, Ruth marveled at the light across the valley floor. The size of the harvest moon was almost the brightness of a late evening. "I truly see why you love this valley so much. Even as most of it is dry and a desert, it still gleams with a harsh beauty."

Thorny listened to the vista of what she had seen all her life, but now through fresh eyes. Her eyes caught the twinkle of a car's headlights in the distance, coming in on Highway 6 from the east.

One of the headlights slowed and stopped. The other continued, and then slowed and turned around. I finally registered she was watching Roy and Mace practicing after midnight.

Stan and Charlie's low conversation stopped as they walked up to the two stopped women. Charlie stood next to Thorny. She could still feel the heat she knew he wouldn't bleed off for another few hours. His low rumbling was reassuring. "Hemma hubbu, lizard?" He asked what was wrong in Paiute. It wasn't duplicity, but the shorthand they had used since childhood.

She didn't look at him. There was no need. She pointed at the two tiny lights in the far distance. "Roy and Mace."

"Hmm, in the middle of the night..."

Stan tried to see what they were talking about. Thorny could sense his head moving as he scanned the length of ten miles of the valley but still had no idea what he was looking at. She realized almost everything would look the same as last night, the last full moon, or even years ago. It was the one thing out of place, and therefore stood out.

She shifted her weight to the foot nearest the FBI agent. "When are you planning to go back?"

"We had planned to stay a few days... but, when do we need to go back?"

"How about after breakfast?"

Ruth had backed up as she listened. She turned. "How early is breakfast?"

"May could rustle up some grub around eight..." Thorny watched the couple exchange glances. "Or maybe closer to ten if you two want to sleep in. Heck, at ten, I'm sure we can get breakfast there at the dude ranch with Danny."

Ruth smiled at the understanding of the other woman. "It would be wonderful to see Danny again."

Thorny nodded. "I'll meet you there at ten."

Stan snorted softly. "Now what is really going on?"

Thorny twitched her head toward the distant scene. "I need to see a couple of people down in Los Angeles. But I don't want it to be common knowledge I'm gone."

Charlie rumbled a chuffed laugh. "That's easy. From Danny's, they're used to hiding people in the trunk of cars. Well… bodies at least."

Thorny kept her face stoic, which with the two of them was the same as a belly laugh. She patted his chest with her claw. "Just remember I know where bodies are buried—and better places to hide new ones."

Stan snorted at the line she had used on him two years before. Ruth watched her husband and Thorny. He had told her about what Thorny said at their first meeting, but now knowing more about Thorny, she wasn't so certain it was an idle joke.

Thorny scowled at the two chuckling men as she started to walk. She took Ruth by the arm, and they interlocked like two scheming schoolgirls. She leaned in so their heads touched as they walked. "You do have a nice cocktail gown, yes?"

"Of course. We go out dancing, dressed to the nines, every weekend." She looked over at Thorny's serious face. "Oh crud, you were serious. I can find or borrow something. Just don't ask me to wear a diamond tiara."

Thorny snorted. "Why not? Stan has the starter stone."

The two snuggled and stumbled in the night. As they reached the car, Thorny opened the back door and slid in next to Ruth—the men were in the front. "I need to run by the barn for a few items."

Stan looked in the mirror. "Now or in the morning?"

Thorny thought about the two motorcyclists and where they were practicing. "It's fine, Stan. I'll take the Model T and run out tonight. I'll be back at the dude ranch for brunch. I also need Danny to call his father."

"Good morning, race fans. This is Tom Holloway, reporting from a chilly predawn in the Mojave Desert in Mojave, California. Two men are racing up the California Owens Valley. They are racing motorcycles built by Harley Davidson Motorcycle Company and American Indian Motorcycle Company. These two men are close friends and business partners in a motorcycle repair shop in Bishop, California—the town they expect to pass through shortly after five o'clock later this morning.

"The racecourse today is four hundred miles of some of the most grueling highway conditions from the small town of Mojave, California, to Carson City, Nevada. The elevation here in Mojave is just under one thousand feet. Before they cross the finish line in Carson City, at forty-eight hundred feet, they will have traveled up and down through three passes as high as eight thousand feet and higher. They will each burn over thirty gallons of high-test gasoline and turn the new tires on both motorcycles to trash. The highways and roadways between here and Carson City will be asphalt, rolled macadam, oiled and rolled macadam, oiled dirt, and just plain dirt made from granite and volcanic ash. They're expected to hit speeds over a hundred and as slow through Dead Man's Curve as only fifteen miles an hour. The curve is where one bad slip could result in a trip over the edge and down a six-hundred-foot cliff.

"But folks, we are getting the signal, and we have Flash Kaminski on the phone at the old stagecoach station of Aberdeen. Good morning, Flash Kaminski. What can you tell us?"

"Good morning, Tom. Just seconds ago, our spotter on top of the water tower yelled down to us he could see some headlights. As we look down the valley, we can see only one, but it's coming fast, and they are earlier than expected."

"Is there any way to tell who it is, Flash?"

"No, Tom, it's still dark here... but... Wait a moment, Tom... It's both of them, and they are gripping each other's arm. Obviously, one is out of gas. Yes, we can see their..."

"Flash? Are you there, Flash? Folks, I think we perhaps are having some technical—"

"Sorry, Tom, but we saw the one headlight wink out, and there was some confusion. They are both gliding in—out of fuel. Wow! Look at the time, Tom. They have trimmed nine more minutes off their race time."

"Can you ask them what speeds they have been hitting or maintaining, Flash?"

"Roy, you two came in with no more vapors left in the tanks. Can you tell our listeners how fast you have been riding on this last leg?"

"There was a good patch back there around the Manzanar internment camp where they have been oiling and rolling the highway. We kept the needle over the hundred for several miles, but you could see what it almost cost us. Mace ran out of fuel about a mile back, and if it hadn't been for the slight downgrade at the end, we might have had to push."

"Well, the officials have filled and capped the tanks, so we'll let you go. We hear the folks in Bishop can't wait to see you."

"Tell them we'll see them in thirty-five minutes or so."

"Will do, boys. Tom, they are pushing their motorcycles in what is called a running bump-start. This was the way they learned to start their motorcycles in France during the Great War. Tom, this is something to see. They are no spring chickens, but this race has their blood pumping like they were young bucks again."

"Flash, from what you say, I'm not sure if running out of fuel and having to push a few miles would even cut their time much. This truly is the Race of the Century. Folks, this is Tom Holloway in Mojave, California, and Flash Kaminski with Motor Sports Today at Aberdeen Station, bringing you the Race of the Century. And we will be right back after these words from Burma Shave and Diamond Tires."

"It pulls on my shoulder wrong. If we do this for more than a mile, I'm either going to have my shoulder ripped off or you're going to pull me and the motor down." The man had his left hand on his right shoulder as he worked the right arm in a slow circle. His fist clenched and unclenched in a subconscious reflex—mirroring the sore muscle.

"Look, this is the only way we are both going to get across the finish line. We can't alter the gas tanks—they'd get found out, and then the questions would come." The rope flaccidly flopped in the air by the other man.

Mace grimaced. "What about if we feed the loop this way and have it pull the right shoulder from the front, and have the line come across my back, and then over my left shoulder and out to you?" He wound the rope around his back and demonstrated where it would go.

Roy glanced up and down Line Street. The early morning even precluded the barber from being open. With the war on, the town seemed to sleep in later and later more often than not. Just the day in and day out of nothing changing wore a being down.

"Okay, let's try that. For right now, I'll tie a knot, but if it works, I'll braid it back into the rope to make it smooth."

Mace slid his arm through the loop and worked it around. It holstered snug around his shoulder. "Yeah, that's big enough. Now for you, we could make a larger loop you could fit over your head and shoulder, so the loop is across your chest."

"Like this?"

"Yeah, I think it'll work. How does it feel?"

"A little tight, but we can adjust it later. Let's give it a try."

The tiny puff of a warm breeze lifted Bill's white hair from his head. His chin rested lightly on his overlapping hands. The hands and forearms rested on the rail forty feet from the street and forty more above. The deep overhang of the roof cast a hard shadow camouflaging the small head and arms—if anyone ever looked up.

His official white helmet lay on the floor, next to his knees.

The two men straightened out the rope between them as they mounted their motorcycles. Only the man with the red motorcycle jumped on the pedal to start it. The black motorcycle remained silent. Soon, the red motorcycle eased away, and the rope became tight. The silent black motorcycle eased away from the curb, towed up West Line Street. Bill's eyes tracked as he watched the two racers practice a new skill.

The sound of the single-engine faded. The watchman didn't move. His pupils were cocked in the sides of his eyes—shaded by his furrowed eyebrows. Every word was being digested. Each phrase had a meaning of something underlying. Bill hadn't needed a stopwatch to check the paths the two had been taking. The varied speeds, the testing, the practice—all had been watched, noted, and digested by the watchman in his tower. Even in the middle of the night, when they thought nobody would see or notice, they had been practicing something. Bill understood racing—open the throttle, run with the wind, and leave the devil in the dust. But these two were always side by side, same as in France. This was no race; it was a finely choreographed dance. Bill just needed to figure out the music.

Several minutes later, the single-engine returned. At the last minute, the black motorcycle chuffed and started as it came alongside the red motorcycle. The talk was low as they shrugged out of the rope. The one man hanked the rope and laid it across his handlebars behind the light. He nodded, and they rode off.

Bill slowly stood, pushing on the small of his back. His eyes were still focused on where the two motorcycles and riders had stopped. He knew he wouldn't be getting much sleep that night. Even warmed milk with a shot of whiskey in it wasn't going to stop his mind from trying to work out the puzzle.

Three blocks over, the two pigeons returned to their nest atop the old grange store. Bill had been watching them with his binoculars when they started building the nest, but now only watched the two dots in the sky. The one circled overhead as the other fluttered into the nest to feed the chewed nightcrawler to the chicks.

Bill thought about France. The same had always held true—even with humans and airplanes. When the watchtower rang the bell upon sighting the returning wave of planes, two more scrambled into the air. As the others landed or tried to control their crashes, the two fighters above stood watch.

Bill sipped from his canteen as he glanced down the street to the corner of Main Street bisecting Line Street. The Locomobile truck slowed to a crawl as the gravedigger turned east onto Line Street. The mound under the age-grayed canvas tarpaulin reminded Bill it was Tuesday. Mr. Mortenson, his five children, and four grandchildren would be burying his wife of forty-one years. The Methodist choir would be singing "Shall We Gather at the River" graveside at one o'clock.

Bill, distractedly, screwed the cap back on the canteen. Squinting toward the tallest steeple in town, he mussed how Ester Mortenson's rhubarb pie, Tollhouse cookies, and her tinkling laugh will be missed at the church socials and the county fair in the fall.

21 RACE – INDEPENDENCE

"For those who have just joined us and following along at home. This is Tom Holloway with Motor Sports Reporting, bringing you the Race of the Century in California. I'm reporting from a chilly morning here in the Mojave Desert in Mojave, California. But we go now to Independence, California, about one hundred and seventy miles away. Bob Stubbs with Race Forum Weekly. Are you there, Bob?"

"I'm here, Tom."

"Bob, I hear it's been kind of cold there this morning?"

"It's not what we expected for the Fourth of July, Tom. The mercury dipped down close to thirty-eight degrees this morning around three. The advance guys said to wear my woolies, but I didn't listen. The high desert here is pressed in by mountains on both sides. Mount Whitney is to my west and rises in a majestic crag of fifteen-thousand-feet and then some. Only a few miles to my east stands the softly muted slope of the older White Mountains. They separate us from Death Valley, but we're not feeling any of the fabled heat yet. The weatherman is calling for close to one hundred and eleven this afternoon."

"My guess is by then, Bob, you'll be glad you weren't wearing those woolies. The temperature swing in the desert is one of the challenges facing our two men today."

"You're right, Tom. When Mace and Roy started this morning, the temperature there in Mojave was downright cold. As the sun comes up, they will shed some of the layers they are wearing now, or they will overheat. But the big engines on their motorcycles can't take off a wool shirt to get cooler, so they will be affected as the temperature rises.

"Somewhere between here in Independence and Bishop, the sun will peek over the White Mountains and begin to heat the day. At first, they will be warmed from the bitter cold they have suffered these last couple of hours. But within the next hour, the other torture will begin. By the time they make the second of only three turns in this race, there at Benton Station, the temperature is expected to be over ninety degrees. The sun reflects off the desert, and it feels more like over one hundred."

"Bob, our producer just gave me the signal. Any minute now, you should at least hear the motors."

"Tom, one of the younger guys just stood up. They are looking down the valley into the gloom... hold on. There is a light just rounding the bend. Yes, I see one of the motorcycles, and boy, is he coming fast. They know this is the last of the cool morning, and they need to make as much time as they can. The engines run better on the chilly air... Tom, the pit crew is holding up two fingers now. I don't see the other headlight, but I trust their younger eyes."

"Bob, one of the other pit stops reported one of the motorcycles had run out of gas. It could have happened again."

"Tom, I'm sorry. I couldn't hear what you just said. There is quite a hubbub with the pit crew. They say the one motorcycle is towing the other. If this is true, this is the screwiest race... Wait, Tom... yes. I can see the shadow of a motorcycle right behind the other. Tom, it appears one has run out of gas and whoever is still running is towing the other somehow."

"Bob, can you hear me now?"

"Yes, Tom. Go ahead."

"I was just saying, they are pushing hard, and one ran out before. I think it was Mace."

"Yes. They just went past a car parked down there with its lights on, and it is Roy on the red Indian towing Mace on the Harley. Where do you find a hank of rope in the desert? Boy, this is some… Wait! Tom. Roy's headlight just went out. They are two blocks or so away and from the silence, I think they are both out of gas. These boys are pushing those motorcycles to the limit. They are coasting in now. I'll see if they can talk while they reload the gas."

"I hope you have a long enough cord on your phone."

"Tom, the phone guys said I could only have fifty-feet, so we'll only get one of them… looks like Mace."

"Mace. Mace. How far back did you run out of fuel? And you boys must be frozen."

"She choked just down from the large sweeper. I switched it off before she was completely dry so it will start easier."

"You must be frozen."

"I've been trying to run just downwind of Roy's talking about how much better the Indian is. The hot air helps on a morning like this. But I wish he'd talk toward my feet."

"You two are jokers. I wish you both luck and a momentous day. Tom, they are all fueled, and the pit crew is push starting them. And… there they go. Two tiny red dots and getting smaller. Tom, they just disappeared around the curve a mile past the other end of town. Those are two tremendously fast machines. Next stop will be just after their hometown of Bishop. Tom, back to you in Mojave, this has been Bob Stubbs with Racing Forum Weekly. Tom?"

"Thank you, Bob Stubbs in Independence, California. So, once again, Mace has pushed a tiny bit harder and run out of gas… or he has a small engine problem he will need to figure out on the fly. This is Tom Holloway with Motor Sports Reporting from Mojave, California. We will check back in with you in roughly thirty minutes."

Thorny was still chuckling to herself as she twitched the steering wheel right. The Model T rattled onto Highway 6 as if it was on tracks. She smirked. *If I fell asleep, I think it would still know how to get home.* Her knowledge of every walked yard of the six miles to her ranch was written on the soles of her bare feet. She remembered the first time she had walked home after the sun went down. A friend thought she should see a talkie, and so they gave her a dime for the afternoon movie and some popcorn. She found the movie to be off-putting and left shortly after the first movie started. The theater owner was convinced the young girl was just feeling ill, and so he returned her money. She walked the few blocks to the county library and spent the afternoon reading. The librarian, asking her if she wasn't expected home for dinner, was her first indication the sun had gone down. Her feet had gotten cold from the cool dirt road, but she had worked up a hearty appetite for some late dinner. Pops laughed when she told him she eschewed the Marx Brothers for some time with Mark Twain.

The hooded headlights left the highway little more lit than the night twenty years before. The fence posts were gray ghost sentinels lining the track as if she was a parade. The light wind of the slow-moving car fluttered her shirtsleeve resting in the open window. The presence of the durable Sierra Nevada Mountains eight miles away was a feeling of soft downy fluff. But the White Mountains, with their alluvial fans of granite turned sand, were only a few miles away and pressed on her with firmness like the muscles of a young hunting dog. The firmness was covered with the softness of his hide and fur. She was getting used to the two mountain ranges making their presences known to her, but it was still worrisome as she wasn't sure what it was they wanted from her. If it was something they wanted at all.

Her reflexes jerked the wheel left as she threw the car out and around the elderly man walking in the road. She chided herself for not paying attention. The white helmet should have warned her.

She stomped on the brakes and the car shuttered as it slowed. She swore air as she remembered to also push the clutch in. The engine recovered as she shifted the stick into neutral. Throwing her arm over the back of the seat, she turned and looked back. The helmet glowed pink from the brake light.

The man didn't hurry. The years of grabbing at time were for those of a younger man.

Bill eased up to the door of the T. Opening it, he peeked in. "Do ya got a few minutes there, Thorny?"

"Bill, it's after one o'clock in the morning. What are you doing out here?"

He adjusted himself and slid into the car and onto the seat. He looked out the front window. His eyes blinked as if they were matching his heartbeat. "Well, I couldn't sleep. I haven't slept much for the last three nights." He looked at her as if she might have the answer.

Thorny blinked and forced her eyes open at him in exasperation. "Have you tried warm milk?"

He chuffed, and the smile crept up his face. "Have ya ever tried warm milk with a slug of moonshine in it?"

Thorny fell back laughing softly. "No. No, Bill, I have not."

He bobbed his head only once. "Yes'um, it tastes just as nasty as it sounds. But I ran out of rum and scotch about two years ago."

Thorny washed her face with her hand. "It still doesn't explain what you're doing way out here, Bill."

He leaned back against the seat and looked forward into the dark of night. "Well, no… no it don't. But the truth of the matter is I was coming out to talk to you."

"At one in the morning? You do know my ranch is still another five miles down the road, don't you?"

"Yes'um. Eustis's old place. The Ferguson kids live in the house. She makes great peach cobbler." He snuck a peek to confirm his information. She nodded.

She turned in the seat, her foot still pressed lightly on the brake. There was always the one in a million chance someone might take a drive in the middle of the night, headed out to Chalfant Valley or over into Nevada. She didn't want to risk an accident while she waited for the man in his own time.

"I've been thinking on many things I have been hearing and seeing lately. And all them things haven't made sense, until tonight." He turned with large eyes glowing from reflecting the lit speedometer and soft light of the hooded headlights on the road.

"What sort of things, Bill?"

"Well, you know there is gonna be a big race come this Fourth of July…"

She nodded. The hunting dog of the White Mountains pushed harder against her.

"Well, unless you're blind or deef… ya done seen Roy and Mace out riding them motors of theirs—a lot." He furled in his lower lip as his head bobbed up and down in his self-confirmation. "I've heard them practicing in the middle of the night when they thought nobody was watching. They ride out this way during the days when they should have business to work on. From the tower, I can hear them riding out the lane toward the dump." He crooked his mouth and followed with his head and rolling eyes. "I thought they was taking the back road home for lunch, but ten minutes later, they are riding back. It just didn't make sense."

"Until tonight…"

"Right. But that was just all the work up for over a month or so. But two days ago, they done stopped across the street from the tower. Right there in front of the little kid's school."

"The elementary school?"

He looked at her like she wasn't listening. "Yes, the school all the little children go to." He waved his hand at imaginary flies. "Any who, they was stopped. And they was talking. All the while, they had about twenty feet or so of rope. As they talked and I watched, they tied two loops in the ends of the rope. Then they done the dangedist thing with it. They put the loops over each of their one shoulders. And then the one pulled the other."

Thorny shied her head sideways and furrowed her brow. "Pulled?"

The man pecked his head forward. "Yes'um, just like pulling another car. They done took off up West Line and about twenty minutes later they done comed back. They talked about it a bit and then left."

"One was still towing the other?"

"No, they done took the rope off like they didn't want anyone to know. When they was talking, they kept looking up and down Line Street to make sure nobody was going to see them."

Thorny smirked at the joke he and she shared. "Except the man whose job it is to watch."

He chuckled. "But nobody looks up."

Thorny waited as the man got sidetracked by his own joke. Finally, she nudged him. "So, you put it all together?"

The man's tongue curled in and over his teeth and lower lip. "Shore 'nuff. Slick as a whistle too. With all the running here and running there… nobody is paying attention to what is in front of them. There ain't no race."

"Then what's going to happen on the Fourth?"

"Oh, them two are going to make the drive. But it ain't what people think. Them two is going to drive knee-to-knee for four hundred miles. Then they are going to split the winnings or whatever they done worked out. But there won't be no race."

"Why do you say that?"

"What kind of race is it if you know one of them is going to be running out of gas?"

Thorny started to explain the race was about beating the time, but also keeping the speed down as to not burn too much fuel… But her mouth froze in an open position. Her eyes searched the man's face as he gently turned to face her and leaned against the door. Her mouth stayed open as her forehead started to frown in confusion. She could feel the old mountains pushing harder and the younger ones joining. The valley was squeezing her. The Model T engine idled a soft chortled slow beat in the dark.

The man's hand came up as he pointed at her. "Yup, thet is exactly the look I've been having for the last few days."

"So what did you figure out?"

"All of the runnin' around. They've been trying to figure out how to *not* run out of gasoline. But they also know, for some reason, Mace is going to run out."

"How do you know it's Mace?"

"Pat him on the right shoulder on the front. Watch if he winces."

"But if he's the one being towed, wouldn't it hurt on the back? And why the right shoulder?"

"Because they are going to have to tow him for miles. So the way to do it is pass it under his left arm and come around to the front of his right. If'n ya catch him with his shirt off, I'll bet his left side is rubbed raw too."

"So, you think it's not a matter of if he runs out of gas, but more like he is definitely going to?"

"Not just once either." The man's mouth worked as he thought. "My guess is, it's going to be more often than not."

"I know you aren't a mechanic per se, but aren't the two motorcycles supposed to be almost equal?"

The man smiled. "That's the point of the race. For years, the Indian people have been singing a little song. Harley Davidson made of tin, drive 'em out and push 'em in."

Thorny laughed. "What do they sing about Indians?"

"Nothing."

"Why?"

"Because there's nothing wrong with 'em. Ain't nothing wrong with the Harley either. They just love teasing each other."

"So now we have a race."

"Yup. Supposed to prove once and for all who the better one is. But it ain't gonna be so."

"Because they're rigging the race."

"Ain't so much about rigging the race, but something else is going on."

"Maybe it's—"

"Nope... whatever you was gonna say... it ain't." The man drew his knee up onto the seat so he could square across from Thorny. "I ain't a mechanic, but I do know my way around specs on things. Both motorcycles have the same tires. The gearboxes are slightly different, but the ratio to the back tires are the same. Both engines are within four cubic centimeters of the other." He held his hand up with less than a pea's worth separating the thumb and finger. "I think the Indian is the bigger engine by less than a fly's fart on a Thursday. Any who, their carburetors could have come off the same design table. The same holds true with the engines. The difference between the two is as big as one was built on Tuesday and the other on Thursday. The spread of the steering bars is exactly the same. In fact, I think the same company makes them for both companies. The brakes on both are made by Acme Abrasives in Akron, Ohio. The same exact shoes on this car. Everyone borrows things thet be already made. It's cheaper thet way"

"They don't make their own?"

"You think they make their own tires and inner tubes?"

Thorny closed her eyes and shook her head. "No, I guess not. So, what you're saying is, they should both run out of gas at the same time, yet Roy is going to end up towing Mace."

The man smiled and nodded as he turned to open the door. "Yup, thet was all I needed to tell ya. So now I can go home and get some sleep." The door complained as it opened.

Thorny held out her hand. "Wait."

He turned, but she was still trying to digest it all. She finally looked up and frowned. "You came all the way out here… just for that? Why did you tell this to me?"

The man turned in the doorway. He closed one eye and looked with the open one. "You know for an educated lawyer type… you're kind of slow like a bummer lamb."

Thorny's mouth froze in an oval. Her mind wasn't progressing much better.

"Because you're the police chief."

He closed the door and started walking back toward Bishop. Thorny turned and watched the white helmet darken in the night's gloom.

She called out her window. "You want a ride back home?"

"Nope… I need the walk. I've got some things to figure on. Thank you anyway. I'll see you when you get back from your trip."

"Good night, Bill."

It was almost two miles later she stopped again and looked back. The mountains were pushing, but she was wondering how the man in the tower could know she was sneaking out of town to go to Los Angeles.

THE MORNING LIGHT was bright through the large windows of the dude ranch's restaurant. Thorny stared at the small glass of orange juice. Her mind was still on the conversation with Bill. The waiter poured coffee in two cups. Thorny looked up and then glanced to her right. Danny walked the last few feet and slipped into the seat next to her.

He leaned over as if kissing her on the neck. His breath was warm but still. "Don't slap me. I moved the small bag and the garment bag into the trunk of Stan's car. I parked it in the maintenance garage next to your car. I'll go park the T in its usual place later tonight."

Thorny giggled dramatically and shied away as if he, in fact, had kissed her neck. She grabbed at his chin with her claw, exerting just enough pressure to show a warning. "Oh, you silly boy. What kind of woman do you think I am?" She leaned in and growled low. "Don't you dare answer." She turned and drew her napkin across her lap and reached for a miniature Danish roll.

Danny harrumphed as he muttered, "I assume when I call my father later, he is to make reservations for dinner tomorrow?"

Still playing the ditzy flapper, Thorny gushed. "Oh, you are so sweet. Why of course you may."

The head of brunette curls leaned over next to her other ear. "Either we have missed something or Danny is next to get invited up the hill."

Thorny shook as she silently laughed. She reached back and drew Ruth around. "You haven't missed anything, and I don't think the other would ever happen, but we can discuss it later. How did you two sleep last night?"

As THEY PASSED SOUTH of Big Pine, shortly after eleven, Stan cocked his head. "You can get up now."

Thorny crawled up onto the rear seat next to Ruth. The two rolled their eyes. "Is this the sneaky clandestine maneuvers they teach you at FBI school?"

Ruth mirrored Thorny's earlier behavior. Pressing her hands to both sides of her cheeks and batting her eyes. "Why, oh heavens no. Those skills would be the OSS training."

"OSS?"

Stan sneered back over his shoulder as he drove. "Oh, Shit Services."

Ruth's eyes drooped leadenly as her head lowered. "Ignore him. He's just being a naughty boy because he's grumpy about having to drive first. The Operations Support Services is our spy service behind enemy lines. They are the people who are working with the undergrounds to get information back to our military. Information about where to bomb or safer places to insert troops."

"And they have a school for all of this?"

Ruth stuck her hand up and pushed her finger into her husband's cheek as he was about to say something again. She rolled her eyes at Thorny. "They're working on it. I think it's somewhere back east near Washington DC, but I'm not exactly sure."

"Hmm… sounds like little boys grew up and couldn't play cowboys and Indians anymore." Thorny leaned back into the corner of the seat and door. She rested her head on the back roll of the seat. Her eyes closed behind the dark green of her glasses. Three heartbeats later, she was asleep. The pressure from the mountains had changed to more of a comfortable blanket.

<hr>

THE TWO WOMEN stood in the middle of the highway. The stretch of road dropped away between two ancient volcanic cinder cones to the south. Their focus was on the incoming flock of ducks landing on the narrow lake only yards from the highway.

"They're called mud hens."

"Do people eat them?"

Thorny snorted. "I did once. I spent an hour hunting for bird-shot among the bones to get the five small mouthfuls of meat. The roasted potatoes and squash were more satisfying. I find watching them float peacefully on the water, chasing the little ducklings around, to be more filling than the meal ever was."

"Do you raise turkeys on your farm?"

"Turkeys are filthy to raise. There's a couple up the valley who have Indian peafowl that they let run around their truck farm eating all the grubs and bugs. Come Thanksgiving, nothing beats Mrs. Ferguson's roasted peacock."

Ruth hung her hand on Thorny's arm. "Wait, you mean the bird with the huge beautiful tail that spreads into a fan? You eat those?"

Thorny laughed. "You thought those guys were just for looking pretty?" Thorny looked back at the car where she knew an exhausted Stan was sleeping in the backseat. "Like Stan?"

The two laughed. They both knew there was more to Stan than looking pretty.

Later, Ruth pulled the Chevrolet out onto the road and drove toward the red cinder cone in the distance. She squinted over at Thorny. "So, explain why you're coming down to Los Angeles… oh, and about Danny."

Thorny chuffed. "Danny is easy, but I could be wrong. I think he would go up the hill, and he might even take his shoes off, but I don't think he would go any further. Even in school, he was known for scheduling his physical education class as the last class of the day. He would change in one of the stalls of a boy's bathroom. When school was over, he gathered his clothes and left school still in his gym shorts and jumper. Even during the heat of the summer, when other men have stripped down to their undershirts, Danny is still wearing his long-sleeved shirt. I don't know if he's just shy about his body or is hiding something, but I do know it's none of my business."

"So, you just don't invite him up to the best soaking pool in the world."

Thorny furled her lips and raised one eyebrow as she twitched her head to watch the lower hills drift past. "I guess."

"You two have a… different friendship."

Thorny snorted as she lazily looked out the open window. The wind across her face felt good. She muttered to herself. "Try figuring out my connection with frog and the mountains."

She turned back. "As for coming down here, I need to talk to Danny's father, Mike Rambino. There is a big race coming up, running from down here in Mojave, all the way up to Carson City, Nevada. There are only two racers and it's a motorcycle race."

"Are you planning to place a bet with Mr. Rambino?"

Thorny laughed. "I'm sure he could give me the odds on the race, but I think I have information that would affect those odds. No, I need some information he might have on the racers. It might concern Stan's investigation."

"The diamonds?"

Thorny nodded. "I think the race may be a cover for moving the diamonds in plain sight."

23 RACE – BISHOP

"As dawn slices the black heaven from the cold dark earth, we are shivering here in the Mojave Desert of California. Good morning, race fans. This is Tom Holloway bringing you the race of the century between a single Harley Davidson motorcycle and an Indian Motorcycle.

"Three hours ago, we watched as Mace Gilbert, racing for Harley Davidson Motorcycle Company, and Roy Tollofson, racing on his traditional red Indian Motorcycle, released by the Southern Pacific Railroad's lighted guard arm, start one of the longest motorcycle races in the United States. These two men are the best of friends and are also business partners in a motorcycle repair shop in Bishop, California—the town they expect to pass through in just a few minutes. The end of this grueling four-hundred-mile race is at the far end of Carson City, Nevada.

"The race is not a flat-out run where the fastest takes the prize. Each motorcycle only holds a little more than three gallons of gas. If they were motoring at the forty-five mile-an-hour speed limit, the three gallons would take them about seventy-miles. But the faster they push the motors, the more fuel they burn. The pit stops are spaced about forty-five miles apart, but it seems that Mace has been burning fuel faster and has twice ended short. His partner and best friend has had to tow him the remaining short way to the next pit stop. But, as the desert heats up, they will burn more fuel or will be forced to slow down until they get to the cooler mountains.

"At stake for the race is the winner walks away with his motorcycle and a check for one thousand dollars. But the big winner today will be the Northern Inyo County Hospital there in Bishop. This race is raising money to build a new wing for surgery, recovery, and an X-ray machine. The hospital services a large area, and they have needed a modern facility for a long time. At the start of the race, I was told the donations were just short of the two-hundred-thousand dollars needed. Folks, what a day for a great race and for an even greater cause.

"I'm getting the signal from my engineer. We have Mitz 'The Flash' Steinman, best known for his race across Bonneville Salt Flats at over two hundred and twenty-seven miles an hour. Flash, how are you this morning?"

"I'm doing great this fine morning, Tom. I'm standing on the sidewalk in front of Monte Geronimo's barbershop at the corner of Main Street and Line Street. As I look down Main Street in the early morning gray, I can see nothing but children lining the street. Everyone is holding an American flag. I even see a few French flags. Those are in recognition of where our two racers met and became fast friends. It is also where they rode their first motorcycles, which they had liberated from the Germans, I might add."

"Flash, you're not actually at the pit stop, are you?"

"No, Tom. The pit stop is right next to Mace and Roy's motor shop at the other end of town. They will turn off Highway 395 at that point and continue along Highway 6. At the next pit stop, they will turn left off Highway 6 and take the connection road back over to Highway 395. They will get what we call a booster tan at a tiny town named Dog Town on the south shore of Mono Lake. It's only two-gallons… but needed to make it to the next full pit stop in Lee Vining. A few miles later, they will meet back up with 395 and make their last turn to the right—just before Dead Man's Curve and their pit stop in Lee Vining. That section will probably be the most dangerous for the two riders. It is all soft, loose volcanic dust which hasn't been packed down by rain in the last couple of months. For safety reasons, the Mono County sheriff will be following them in his car through this section."

"Well, our thoughts and prayers are with the two men when they traverse that section. Unfortunately, the best we will have for notice of them making the pit stop in Benton is a shortwave radio the local Civil Defense has set up."

"Tom, I can hear the pistol from the lookout at the city limits. We should see the men in the next few minutes… Yes, I see a light… but there is only one…"

"I wonder if Mace ran ou—"

"I've got two lights. As they get close, I can see they are pressed against each other, knee-to-knee. But they are moving fast. Tom, I think they are… Yes, they are climbing on top of their seats. This is the same trick they do every parade here in Bishop. Why would they come through the town that loves them and not give them a show?"

"Are they riding standing up?"

"Tom, they are standing on their seats. Slowly, the motorcycles are moving apart as they extend their arms. Their hands are clasping onto the other's wrist. Their arms are outright in the form of a cross. They call this their Iron Cross of Friendship. Tom, it is a glorious sight. They just roared past us here, and the children and parents are waving their flags. This is truly a glorious Fourth of July, Tom. Two men, standing on moving motorcycles, a whole town turning out to watch them, and cheering them on. This is the best there is about our country. May all of our boys fighting in the Pacific and Europe be home soon to enjoy this too."

"Yes, Mitz, it's a wonderful day."

"I'm sorry, Tom, but… I'm signing off."

"There you have it, folks. Mitz 'The Flash' Steinman, overcome by emotion, in Bishop, California. Folks, the sun has now crested over the mountains. The heat will be coming on in earnest as we track our racers through the last of the desert as they will begin their rise through the eastern side of the majestic Sierra Nevada Mountains.

"This is Tom Holloway with the Great Race of the Century. We'll be back in about thirty minutes."

"Honey?" Stan fumbled with his bow tie as he walked. "Are we meeting Mr. Rambino there, or is he..." He stopped at the door. His mouth was half open but whatever he was saying was lost in the two women standing in the guest bedroom. His wife was wearing the formal black dress he had only seen when they attended funerals. The tiny dot of light just below her neck was the one-carat diamond pendant his mother had given to Ruth for their first anniversary. The thin platinum wedding ring had belonged to his father's mother. Something old and something borrowed came in spades in his family. His stockings with garters had been the same pair his father had gotten married in—twice. His first wife had died in childbirth of what would have been their first child.

"Holy moley..." With the summer heat, Thorny had opted for a black lace chemise of Ruth's, under her black satin pair of what looked like bib overalls. As she looked over her shoulder, she was the twin of the aeronaut Amelia Earhart.

Ruth giggled and then remembered. "Oh, I forgot... You were brain addled when you saw her special bib overalls before. You were almost bed-bound at the time."

Stan stepped into the room. His eyes were fixated on her left hand, arm, and shoulder. "I... I guess..." His mind simply stopped.

Thorny looked at him. "Too daring?"

He kept forcing his eyes open into his raised eyebrows. Both women could tell he was having trouble processing the reveal of the entire scarred arm and shoulder. The exposed chemise was racy and even flirty, but the scarring pushed the look into the realm of exotic.

"I think this is the longest I've ever seen my husband completely speechless. I can only imagine what you're going to do to an entire restaurant."

Thorny frowned. "Maybe I should wear the blouse..."

Ruth turned Thorny to face her as she addressed her husband. "Stanley, you have ten seconds to figure out what to say." She looked Thorny in the eyes. "Honey, this is who you are. I think I know you enough to know you can walk this into the Brown Derby or any place else, and nobody can tell you it's wrong. Some people have gotten old and gray and haven't lived half as much as you have in the last couple of years. The bullet wound in your right arm is your badge of honor. You show it any time you want. There isn't anyone who has earned the right to say otherwise. Besides, it's too hot for the velvet bolero." She turned. "Isn't that right, mister? Also 'Shot Up' FBI?"

Stan's mouth closed slowly. His eyes blinked wide one last time. He looked at his wife. "Can you get one of those bib overalls too?"

Ruth's face raised back as she pulled the square velveteen jewelry box off the bed. "Sure, as long as you also give me one of these." She snapped open the jewelry box to disclose the string of matching pearls.

THE FOURSOME, stepping out from the back of the dark gray Diamond Rio limousine in front of Mousso and Franks, drew only the doorman's attention. This was Hollywood. The driver offered his gloved hand to help the ladies step out. They did not need any, but it was the proper order of etiquette. As Mr. Rambino was the last to step out, he quietly said something to the driver who saluted him with two fingers from the brim of his perfectly placed hat. As the foursome walked to the restaurant door, the driver silently closed the car door.

From the polished cut crystal in the front doors to their booth in the back corner, and even after they were seated, the Maître d'hôtel and staff fussed over the party. Thorny silently noted not one person ever gave her left arm or hand a second's look.

She leaned over and quietly confided in Mr. Rambino. "Mike, if I thought this is what dating was really like, I might consider it."

He stared at the small piece of bread he was breaking in two. "I don't know what we would call this, but I'd like to believe my late wife would approve of whatever it is." He rolled his head sideways to look at her. "It does my heart good to see how well you're doing. Danny and I talk every Sunday now… I'd like to think it was your friendship, not business, that gave me a friend and the man my son has become. But I also know this isn't just about you needing a place to wear an elegant pair of bib overalls or my being a cute face."

She leaned into his shoulder and rested her hand on his arm. "Let's leave the business until after we enjoy what this establishment has for you to introduce me to."

"Fair enough." He looked up at the waiter who had been standing to one side. "Good evening, Gino. You look the picture of health tonight."

"Good evening, Mr. Rambino, and thank you. I think my new wife has put the spring in my step but may have to put a new hole in my belt as well."

Mike stage-whispered to Thorny. "Gino and I go back for years. His new bride is home babysitting their new grandson. If you play your hand right, he will show you a photo they had taken with his mother holding her great-grandson."

The man reached behind himself as if to produce his wallet. The table laughed.

"Are there any specials tonight, Gino?"

The man rolled his eyes and flipped his one hand in the air. "Oh yes. Sir and ladies…" He paused and winked at his old friend. "Oh, and you too, Mike. We have a very rare special. We have… let me look at my notes so I don't get this wrong… We have crawdads, fresh from the exotic local of Fish Slough. These plump delicacies are hand-caught and come served on a fragrant bed of steamed prairie grass." The man had to stop as Thorny squirmed with laughter as she grabbed onto Mike's upper arm.

"Oh no, you do not want to serve those." She squealed, and Mike couldn't hold his serious face. The other two laughed just to see Thorny teased.

"Well played, Gino. Well played." Mike gave him a quiet clap. A few other tables glanced over to see who was getting such special treatment. After all, it was Hollywood.

Gino bowed to Thorny. "Welcome to Mousso and Franks, Miss Wallace. I hope it's not the only time."

Thorny smiled. "It's starting out right, Gino. But we are all starving. What is the real special tonight?"

"Well, Mike told me about your last visit to our fine city. We don't want to ruin your memories of the lobster at the Hotel Bel Aire, so I would suggest the shrimp and Scallop Scampi. Then you can also steal bites of Mike's Oso Bucco. The butter lime sauce of your scampi will cut the salty taste of his Bucco." He turned to Ruth and Stan. "I also have a line-caught wild trout stuffed with huckleberries and black rice, or there is, of course, the best prime rib on the west coast or linguini with lemon garlic clam sauce."

Ruth made eyes at Thorny. "I want what you're having." She looked back at the waiter. "But I know my husband… he would like the prime rib cooked so a good veterinarian could still get it back on its feet."

"Very good. Then we will dispense with menus. Would anyone like an appetizer or a salad?"

Mike circled his hand pointing his finger at the table. "Why don't you have Franco make us all up a small antipasto platter. And for the wine, Thomas can pull us a couple of bottles."

"Very good, sir." He bowed slightly and disappeared.

The dinner progressed leisurely and with humorous retelling about the crawdads. Thorny was only sorry Danny wasn't there to hit again for never telling her shrimp tasted much sweeter and were superior in the tenderness. She thought about the innocence of their growing up and chasing the crawdads in the tiny stream with their pant legs rolled up.

"Thorny?"

She blinked. She realized the plate had been removed. Then she looked up. The other three were looking at her. She hurriedly dabbed at her lips with her napkin. "Do I have something on my face?"

One eyebrow on Ruth's face slowly rose as her head cocked slightly to the other side. "Egg?"

Thorny froze. "Excuse me?"

Mike gently guided her hands back to her lap. "You drifted off from the table, my dear. You missed the dancing bear with the pink violinist on the unicycle."

Thorny's face contorted and then furrowed into a twisted frown. Her head ground around. "I what?"

Ruth laughed at Mike's attempt to call the woman back to the table. "Honey, one minute you were in the conversation, and then the next, you were gone. This was the fourth time tonight. Are you all right?"

Thorny sat back. "Mike, you two, I'm sorry. Physically, I'm fine. Well, maybe a little tired, but it's this whole thing." She turned. "Mike, we need to talk."

The man smiled slightly and drew his napkin to his lips. "King Solomon used to throw great parties. As everyone was eating and having a great time, he would have his spies sit with him, and they would discuss their reports."

One of Thorny's eyelids drifted closed as her face clamped down.

Ruth came to the rescue. "He did it because nobody suspected he would discuss secrets in front of a large crowd. The more important the secret, the larger the crowd."

"Stan, you married extremely well." Mike winked.

Turning to Thorny, he captured her claw in his hand. "You have been patient tonight. But the only items left tonight are desert, coffee, and whatever you wanted to talk to me about."

Thorny's mouth froze slightly open. Now, when the chance was here, she didn't know where to start. It didn't make sense to start in the middle, but it was all she could think to do. "Do you know Mace Gilbert and Roy Tollofson?"

The napkin froze halfway to his mouth. His eyes fixed on the table. Slowly his hand and napkin sank powerlessly to his lap. The man who had championed an empire now sat thinking.

Looking up, he quietly called out. "Gino?"

The ever-present but unnoticed man turned. "Yes, Mr. Rambino?"

"We're about to conduct some highly delicate business. I think it is going to require some of those stale chocolate torts they've been kicking around the kitchen and some coffee. The kids can have anything their hearts desire."

The man listened and nodded. "Four chocolate torts and coffee. Very good." He bowed slightly and then backed away.

The four relaxed and waited until all were served. Gino bowed slightly as he made one last check. "If you four are good, I'm going to go in the back to test some new dinner the chef wants to try. I'll be gone for about thirty minutes or so. I'll leave the carafe with more coffee if you need it."

"That will be perfect, Gino. Thanks."

The man bowed and left.

They all took a bite of the dark confection. If something still warm from the oven was ever stale, it was not the light confection before them. The warm chocolate cream in the center oozed onto the plates.

"What do you need to know?"

Thorny led. "So you know them." He nodded. "Have they ever done work for you or your organization—other than mechanical work?"

"Now you're sounding like a lawyer, and interrogating?"

Stan cleared his throat. "Mike, this isn't about you or anything that may or may not have happened in the past, but it could help us with something that may or may not be happening soon."

The man thought about who he was sitting with but more about who they were asking about. "They're both fine men. When the French needed help, back in the Great War as we called it, they were some of the first to rush to help. They didn't know the first iota about flying or killing for that matter. They just knew there was a bad side and a good side, and the good side needed their help."

Thorny waited the man out as she watched him take tiny bites of the desert and then asked, "It must have taken a lot of courage."

The napkin was quick to his mouth as he stifled a cough. From behind his napkin, and with a flushed face, he looked sideways at her. "Courage, hell, it was crazy foolishness."

"You're talking about stepping onto a ship and going to a foreign country to help fight someone else's war. But I'm asking about when they came back."

Mike put his fork down, took a sip of coffee, and pushed it all forward an inch. Dabbing lightly at his mouth, he thought about the years.

"They must be in their, what? Late forties or early fifties, now? It all seems like a lifetime ago." He relaxed against the booth's padding. The high back of the booth provided support for his head. The white hair stood out against the deep red of the leather. His eyelids drifted shut as he watched the moving picture of his and their past. "They were so young. They had gone to war, had airplanes shot out from under them, and… cleared the sky of others." His voice was wet. Even with his background, his respect for the men was obvious. "They had returned having proven they were bulletproof. They were fearless."

His eyes opened, and he rolled forward. His forearms rested against the edge of the table. "Did they do some work for us? Sure. But it was nothing… Well, let's just say… Oh heck. Occasionally, there were small packages that needed transporting, either down here or to go up there. Sometimes it was in an envelope. Other times they could just stick it in a bag or their belt and go. They rode like the wind. I didn't have a single driver who could drive a car between here and there any faster, and most times, my fellas were much slower. Mace and Roy moved important small items for us."

"So this race wasn't a surprise to you."

"It makes perfect sense. If anyone can run four hundred miles across the desert and up the mountains in under nine hours, they can. I heard Barney Oldfield just took a run at it with a stripped-down Stutz or something, so he never had to stop. Rumor has it he did it in nine hours and twenty minutes. He's the fastest man in the world, and they must beat his time on motorcycles. I wouldn't take the job."

"Do you think they can do it?"

"I've got five large riding on them. But this isn't about the race. What do you want to know?"

Thorny nodded and looked over at the man on her right. "Stan?"

"Somewhere in Los Angeles, we have reason to believe, there are twenty-four pounds of uncut diamonds. We think they are headed for Nevada to be cut."

The man's low whistle said it all—the conversation just went from uncomfortable to business in thousands of carats flat. It had his attention and his assurance the problem did not have anything to do with him or his organization. He squeezed his eyes shut—thinking. "How many carats is that?"

"About fifty-two thousand."

He sat silent for almost a full minute. "I'm assuming they are high-grade and will cut down to at least half the weight… so we are talking in the ballpark of…?"

"An estimated twenty-million dollars or more wholesale, depending on the final grades. Well north of two-hundred-thousand when set for retail."

His eyes fluttered open. "How big is that?"

Ruth couldn't help herself. "It would take eight to twenty armored trucks to haul it."

The man caught the joke and laughed. "But the diamonds?"

"Uncut? About a quart and a half."

The man spidered his hands just larger than a mason jar. He looked at it and then looked to Thorny and then Stan. "It's not so large."

"So, something in the range of what they know how to do?"

"Oh, most certainly."

Thorny's smile drew back on one side. "When I was in college, a friend took me out to Santa Anita to watch the horse races. Her uncle was a jockey. We sat with him while he got ready for the race. Someone was watching him the entire time he was dressing. They examined every piece of equipment and clothing."

Mike was nodding. "Fairly standard with any serious race. You want to make sure the jockey or driver doesn't stick a pistol down his pants so he can shoot his competition. But you have a point?"

Thorny nodded. "If I know I'm going to be searched, where do I hide something this big?" Her hands matched the sizing he had just made.

Mike's thumb and forefinger pinched and released his upper lip as he thought. "In the tires? I don't know, do you?"

"I have reason to believe in the gas tank."

"It makes sense… but during a race?"

Thorny shrugged her face. Too big to smuggle in the light, and on a motorcycle, there isn't a trunk. From what the man at the Harley Davidson dealer told me this afternoon, they will probably be sitting on a paper-thin piece of leather glued to the metal seat. No cushion to hide some extra stones in. But I also have an expert who says he figured it out. They have gas tanks large enough to hold enough fuel to drive about seventy-miles if they stay at the speed limit of forty-five. But when they are racing at seventy and eighty miles an hour or more, they burn the fuel faster, and the fuel runs out close to the fifty-miles between the fuel stops."

Mike's head had been gently bobbing. "But remove a quart or more, and you run out of fuel and lose the race."

"Unless it's not a race. And your competitor has a rope to tow you."

"But if you're getting searched or watched…"

Thorny smiled and leaned back against Stan's shoulder. "It's a big desert. If it's big enough to hide bodies in, it's big enough to hide a coil of rope."

———

Mike and Thorny stood next to the car. Stan and Ruth had said goodnight and gone into the house. The driver had returned to his position in the front. Mike held Thorny's hands in his.

"I don't want you to get the wrong idea about me and what I'm about to ask. You know who my friends are, and you need to be mindful of our affiliation, not the business I was in."

"I won't break the law, Mr. Rambino."

His chest deflated as he sighed through his nose. "I'd rather keep this more between Mike and Thorny than Mr. Rambino and Miss Wallace. But I also need for Police Chief Wallace to also be listening."

Thorny cribbed at her lower lip. Smoothing it with the smallest of the tip of her tongue, she dipped her head once. "Okay, Mike."

"Mace and Roy are good men. They work hard, and so do their wives. The path they chose was never one leading to financial wealth and security in their golden years. At best, their golden years will still smell like engine grease and gasoline, but they are happy doing what they do well."

"What are you asking, Mike?"

"If you arrest them, I will provide the best counsel I can buy. I want them to know so from the start. Before you question them, they need to know I will help them."

"If they have broken the law… It is their right to counsel. If you want to provide them with said counsel, it is within your legal rights."

"No, that's not what I'm asking here. I want you to tell them that I will provide all the legal defense they will ever need. I want you to make it clear to them up front if I can't be there."

"Interrogation works a lot different from what you are asking. From what I understand, making them aware of how tough a bind they are in—"

"I'm not asking for interrogation. I'm making their plea bargain now—ahead of the crime."

Thorny furrowed her brow and squinted one eye.

"I'm asking, if you can find a way, please help them. I'll back them, but I want them to help you and Stan. If what you say is going on with these diamonds, this goes far beyond the shenanigans my fellas use to pull. This isn't about running a still, or driving the moonshine, or making book, or any of those little crimes. This is about two nations with an agreement, and someone got in the middle. I love my country, but it's a war, and we're helping the other country. Stealing from these two countries is beyond the pale, and if I have anything to say about it, I want to help to bring the real criminals to justice."

Thorny weighed the offer. There was nothing illegal, just unusual. She patted his hand a couple of beats. "Let's see how this plays out, Mike. I like Mace and Roy. So does most of Bishop. The hospital is getting what the region has needed for a long time. If this can all be resolved without tainting the good—all the better." Her soft smile turned into a crooked smirk. "As for justice—there's plenty of desert between here and Carson City."

His face broke into a smile. "In the hot desert, you don't have to dig as deep."

"It is already over eighty-degrees here, Tom. Over."

"Folks, we are talking to Mono County sheriff, Cecil Thorington, over shortwave radio. He will be following Mace and Roy as they make their way across the most treacherous stretch of road in this race. Until now, they have been racing on asphalt, macadam, and hard-rolled dirt highways. But at Benton Station, they will refill their gas tanks, eat some food, and drink a quart of water before they head west on Highway 120. But the word highway is a misnomer here. This stretch is pure slippery silt.

"They will ride the first few miles to Benton Hot Springs, and then turn in a northerly direction and cross twelve miles of pure glass dust. This is the neighborhood of the Mono Craters or old volcanos. The pumice, over the last thousands of years, has been beaten into glass dust. If you can think of a couple of glass shards and how easily they slip across one another, then you can imagine what it is like to race a motorcycle across all this slippery dust. Sheriff, what other preparations will they need to make to successfully cross this piece of Hades? Over."

"Mr. Holloway, I didn't catch all of that. Can you repeat? Over."

"Sheriff, other than taking on fuel, food, and water... what else will they need to make sure they get to Lee Vining? Over."

"Yes, sir. They should have enough gas, as they can't drive the bikes hard through the dust. We have large bandanas here that they'll wet down to stop from breathing the fine glass dust. We follow them from about a mile or more, so we don't breathe their dust either. They are experts at riding next to each other, but if they are close, and one slips and goes down... it could take the other with them. Over."

"Sheriff, I'd like to extend our thanks for helping out today. This is a special stretch of road that you have intimate knowledge of. It means a lot to have you with us today. Over"

"Thank you, Tom. On behalf of the entire Mono County, we are proud of our neighbors as they raise the money to provide a more modern medical center in Bishop. As you know, Crater Flats is where I crashed a car and was transported to Bishop for treatment. The folks at the Northern Inyo Hospital will always have my gratitude for the five weeks I was their guest. Over."

"Folks, as we wait for the racers to arrive, we need to keep the lights on. This broadcast of the Greatest Race of the Century is being brought to you by the fine folks at Burma Shave. Our boys in the Pacific and throughout Europe are getting a closer, smoother shave with Burma Shave. And, by the fine folks at General Mills, who bring you whole goodness at your breakfast table in the box with champions on the front, Wheaties, the breakfast of champions."

"Tom... Mr. Holloway, we can see the racers across the flats. From here it looks like only a couple of motorcycles without riders. They are lying flat and making time as best they can. This part of the highway is almost flat and hard-packed oiled macadam. I can't tell for sure, but my guess is they are hitting a speed well over the legal speed limit. Over"

"Do you think you will be writing them a speeding ticket, Sheriff? Over."

"Not today, Tom. Not today. I just looked at the thermometer we have here in the shade. It is now ninety-one. The heat reflected at them from the road is well over a hundred. By lying low across their motorcycles, they are shaded from much of the road heat. They also aren't being heated by the air. For this hour, heat and dust will be their two biggest threats. Over."

"Sheriff, we can hear they just pulled up. How are they doing? Over."

"Tom, in the time it took for them to open the gas caps on each side of their tanks, both men swallowed a quart of water and stripped their wool shirts off. Both have put their protective leather jackets back on and are now eating sandwiches made with peanut butter and local honey. These were made last night to let the honey soak into the bread. They're messy, but this is the only energy they will get between here and Carson City. This fuel stop is critical for the motorcycles and the men.

"The pit crew has checked the oil levels, and both are taking a quart. As they pour the oil in, you can see the smoke coming out of the hole from the hot oil. This isn't a usual race, but these boys are pushing these machines hard. Over."

"Sheriff, we are looking over the route plan and let them know it appears they are about seven minutes ahead. Over."

"Men, Tom just told me you are seven minutes ahead of plan. Good luck and we're right… Tom, as you can hear, they just roared off and are now turning left onto Highway 120. We are going to fire up the truck and follow. This is Sheriff Cecil Thorington of the Mono County Sheriff Department signing off from Benton Station at the corner of Highway 6 and Highway 121. We'll talk later, Tom. Over."

"Wow. Already ninety degrees, and it's not even seven-thirty in the morning. The heat comes early in the high desert. Folks, many of you have already eaten your Wheaties this morning and gotten a smooth shave with Burma Shave, same as our boys overseas. This is the Greatest Race of the Century between American Indian and

Harley Davidson. Two great motorcycles and two best friends, Mace and Roy, are now entering the most dangerous forty-seven miles of this race. This is Tom Holloway, and we'll be back in roughly one hour."

Elijah Jacobs ran the pencil under the figures. His mind thought about the numbers. The numbers spoke to him, but his heart also had its own conversation. The bank was the lifeblood of the community. It was as true in 1943 as it had been in 1893 when his grandfather and father opened the bank. But when the new century took hold, and his father was bouncing Eli on his knee in the backroom office, there were two large safes and a strongbox. One safe for gold, one for silver, and the strongbox for the occasional mix of Confederate and Union bills. When Eli was twelve, the strongbox only had United States currency and had become the third safe in the room.

The rough-hewn timber building burned down on Eli's thirteenth birthday. The Bishop Volunteer Fire Department had shown off their new fire truck. It was also the official retirement for the two mules who, for years, had drawn the old pump wagon. The school band played in the small parade, the open field across from Main Street was turned into a large picnic and potluck luncheon. For years, Eli's grandfather was convinced the town had thrown a massive party to celebrate his grandson's Bar Mitzva. He had returned to his synagogue in New York and sung the praises of the nice people in California who not only accepted his Jewish family but held great celebrations for his grandson becoming a man.

Eli and his father never had the heart to tell him how, the closest to God they ever got was the Christmas Eve mass at the Catholic Church. For years, the many denominations in the small town worked hard to present a competent choir to sing Handel's *Messiah*. Eli's mother usually sang the voice of the angel.

Eli put the pencil down and leaned back in his chair. He removed the glasses he needed for the seemingly smaller and smaller numbers. He clutched the glasses as he closed his eyes to think. There was more to the balance of making a loan than just the numbers.

The knock on the doorjamb was soft. The older woman was not one to be hard or loud. The silver locket hung just below the soft white doily made into a collar and onto the field of age muted flowers of her dress.

Eli didn't open his eyes. The woman had worked for his father. She may have even started in the old wooden bank for all he knew. "Yes, Ethel?"

"Sir, the mayor and chief of police are here to see you."

The man smiled. Thorny was one of the few people in town he could joke with. "Good, tell her we're broke, and I need to get a loan from her."

Thorny winked at the older woman. "I'm amazed he doesn't have his feet up on the desk. But then the holes in the soles would show."

The woman's head rose in mock propriety and then leaned over in conspiracy. "Get him to walk out from behind the desk. I'll bet he has his boots off." The woman looked down at the mayor's bare feet and smiled. With a wink, she had turned and was gone.

"How much do you need, and in which metal?"

Placing his glasses on the desk, the man rose and stood with his hand out. Thorny took one step into the office and stopped.

Propriety would force the man to step around the end of his desk and cross to Thorny.

He chuckled. "I never could fool Ethel." He walked around the desk. As advised, the man was in his stocking feet.

They shook, and then Thorny turned back, softly closing the door. "I think talking to you here is better than hauling you down to the station."

He returned to his chair as his brow rose on one side. "Am I in trouble?"

Thorny's face was all business. "I don't think you need to call your lawyer…"

"Good. The only lawyer I would want is already here. What can I help you with?"

Thorny sat and edged her forearms on the desk. What she needed to discuss, she didn't want to go beyond the desk, much less beyond the door. The current bank may have been built of bricks and cement, but some walls seemed to have ears on one day and a wagging tongue the next. Small towns are the worst, and Bishop was no exception.

"Is there such a pact as the client-lawyer privilege in banking?"

Eli's eyes flittered back and forth across her face. "For the most part, yes. Is it a written law such as in the legal community? No. But if a banker was to be indiscreet and his customers were to find out…"

She nodded with a slow blink. "Point taken. What we discuss will never go beyond this desk. It has no need to, and it will only back up other information I already have in my possession."

He leaned in and folded his forearms one on top of the other. "Understood." They held each other's gaze. The conditions and respect were shared. Thorny was very aware of the largest safety deposit box in the man's vault. It was there for her and her alone and yet assigned to no one—and therefore not collecting rent. It hadn't collected rent since 1918. The condition of its dispensation was covered by nothing more than a word and a handshake.

"Mace Gilbert and Roy Tollofson."

In the two minutes of silence, Thorny counted the man blinking only three times. She was wondering if she needed to feel his wrist for a pulse.

"Personally, the business, or their homes?"

Thorny thought of her former boss's daughter. The woman was barely older than she was. She was an efficient worker and an asset to her father's office. Her comeliness could be distracting, and she was known to use the advantage on occasion, but her business manner could stop even the most ardent Lothario at the opening of his mouth. When she was at the office, she was the perfection of the profession. When she was home, she could be her father's little girl —all giggles and curls. But when the sun went down, and her gloved hand was in the bend of a gentleman's elbow or naked between his sheets, she was there to make the man feel every bit of the hundred dollars an hour she was charging him. There was a vast divide between the person, their business persona, and who they were at home.

"Let's take the real estate first."

The man thought. His eyes didn't move. His face was calm and evocative as concrete. Even his one thumbnail digging into and underneath its opposite was unmoving. Thorny was certain she could hear the man's pocket watch ticking.

"I should have—a year ago."

Thorny's brow furrowed in confusion.

"Taken it. If I start foreclosure on their business and homes now, it will be a race to the three-year mark when the county can foreclose and sell them for past taxes. Now, sometimes, they have been tolerant, and some people have died still owing a decade or more in unpaid property taxes. Then there are those they have filed papers the day they hit the three-year deadline. For a banker, it's a crapshoot."

"So, they are not financially secure?"

"As much as you look like Amelia Earhart—I still wouldn't trust you enough for us to go flying."

Thorny smiled softly to one side. "I'd like to learn how to fly… but I see your point." Appearances were not always enough—or even what they appeared to be.

The man leaned back into his chair. His cheeks puffed as he slowly let out his breath through his pursed lips. His breath reminded Thorny of the sound of mountain wind coming down the canyons through early spring grass. Soft and steady, with only the tips of the grass rubbing against each other.

"Look, bankers aren't the scoundrels the silent movies liked to make us out to be. We never tied young damsels to the tracks of the Slim Princess. We need to stay in business, but we also have to live here. Half the town knows where I live, and the other half goes to school on Line Street. The boys scraped through the depression by teeth and claw. Some days, I had a note on the calendar to go talk to them. Then, they would walk in and pay everything up. They would have a couple of big jobs, and all the money came here. I take my car there, and the payment for any work stays here. The same goes for Ethel and my staff. It's not like the big city where I can reach out for more customers. The ones we have are all we will get. The rest have their money where they can sleep on it or it has crumbs from the cookies."

"And the personal…"

His mouth fought with his face. He started to talk a few times, but the war was bigger. Finally, he leaned forward. "In the winter of 1929, Mildred took sick. The crash had taken most of our reserves. People just took everything out and buried it in their backyard. We had to borrow a pot from the neighbor for something to piss in. We had a used 1920 Studebaker someone had given us to pay off part of their debt. We didn't drive much, but time and something else had taken its toll. The boys were looking at it, but the engine and transmission were shot. If I remember right, they handed me the hood ornament and told me at least it was in decent shape."

"Ouch."

"Ouch wasn't the half of it. We had an old Army doctor back then. He was a pretty smart fella. But he couldn't do miracles, and Mildred needed one. Only trouble was, it was three hundred miles away in Los Angeles. The Slim Princess could get us down to Owens Lake, but the hundred and eighty miles left would be a long walk."

The man stopped and sighed. His attention drifted to the small silver photo frame on his desk. The frame was a travel frame. It was two frames with a hinge in the middle, and a clasp to hold it shut on the other. Thorny knew one picture was of his wife, the other of their wedding day. The man was in his navy cracker jacks, the young bride in a plain sheath dress, gathered in the middle to take in the volume of fabric on the borrowed dress.

"The mayor had a two-year-old sedan his in-laws had given them for a wedding present. They had taken their smaller car with a heater and driven to San Diego to visit her parents. Nobody expected them back until the snow was gone from the valley floor. And to kill two birds with one stone, they had left the sedan with the boys for a tuneup and to look after while they were gone."

Thorny saw where this was going. "So they loaned you the car."

"They also found us some extra blankets to keep warm. The wind just whistled through the sedan like there were no windows. It was the coldest I had ever been."

"Did your wife find her miracle?"

The tongue curled on his lips, barely moving. The lower eyelids filled until he dabbed them with his pocket handkerchief and then blew his nose. He held the cloth in place on his nose as he closed his eyes. She could see his chest shudder gently. His head finally ground slightly right and then left.

He swiped at his eyes, folded the cloth, and stuck it back in his pocket as he sniffed deeply. "Yes and no. She was dying of consumption. The cold ride was probably a blessing for her. I thought she had finally drifted off to sleep. When I stopped in Mojave for gas, I realized she was gone."

He took a long breath and let it out softly. "I turned around right then and drove back. I took her straight away to Seth Turner's. It was the middle of the night, so I went to his house. I didn't know what else to do. I woke him up, and we laid her out on their spring porch in the back. I'm sure she was frozen solid by morning, but she was in good hands. He and I came to Bishop the same year —right out of the navy. We were the best of friends—the banker and the mortician. Taxes and death."

"Mace and Roy?"

Eli swallowed and waved his hand at an invisible fly. "They felt so bad, they took some old tin and welded her up a metal coffin. They knew she loved pink, so they mixed some whitewash and red-oxide barn paint together and painted it a real pretty pink. Nobody cared it wasn't wood."

He cleared his throat and smiled weakly.

"Ol' Seth was going to give me a great discount on a plot down in the boggy side of the cemetery. But I guess his Eunice made him sleep on the couch or something because, before the funeral, the plot was up in the sunny, dry part, and it was free. I think she and Millie were as fast of friends as Seth and I were."

Thorny slowly drew the middle finger of her claw along the side of her face as she thought. She could hear her grandfather's grumpy voice about stories and facts. She was old enough to know it was up to her to root out the meaningful facts from the story. And, the facts remained, the goodness was still the important fact. The rest was just the story. A story she would have to find elsewhere.

She stood. The man was lost in his memory. She quietly stepped out and closed the door behind her.

"We don't know at this time, Tom. As of now, they are seventeen minutes behind schedule—based on the last report from Benton."

"Have they sent anyone back down the highway, Ralph?"

"A deputy left from his station at Dog Town, which is on the southern tip of Mono Lake. It's about fifteen minutes from here, but we haven't heard anything since."

"Well, Ralph, we have been saying all along, this section of the course is the most treacherous. Between the slippery glass dust on the road to ruts cut in the summer heat to even the occasional deer or wild sheep. These forty-eight miles could just be the undoing of one or both of the men."

"Tom, I drove the track yesterday. There were no ruts cut to cause them any problems, but there was deep silt dust. It's been a bone-dry year, and the usual hard-pack of the road has become soft and slippery. If there has been any problem, I suspect it would be from the motorcycle sliding out from under a rider in one of the curves."

"They shouldn't have been trying to make up time on this

stretch, Ralph. So they had expected to not really have any problems. They left Benton Station with eighteen minutes to the good, so if they show up—"

"Tom? Tom. We've just seen a green Very Pistol flare. We can see across the southern flats of Mono Lake, and they have shot the green flare to let us know both riders have passed Dog Town. We should see them in just a few minutes if they are moving right along… Nope. They aren't that slow, Tom. They just rounded the curve at the south end of town, and they are lying flat-out on their tanks."

"They have time to make up, Ralph. Like the racers they are, this is exactly what—"

"They're just pulling up to their fuelers. Each racer has taken one of their special sandwiches. My gosh, Tom. I don't think they even chewed. Each man is draining their canister of water… the fuel has splashed out of the tanks. They are topped off. The pitmen screw on all four caps, and the others begin the push. As they move forward, both men are pulling their bandanas up over their noses. They jammed their motors into second gear and let up the clutch as they applied the gas. Three of the pushers were caught off guard and are down on the road. Tom, they are already past the end of town, and I think we just heard them shift into fourth gear."

"Their next stop is forty-six miles away in Bridgeport, Ralph. What do you think? Are they going to make up time?"

"Tom, they are hell-bent and splitting the wind. If anything, my guess is they will push hard to make up and gain some time. Once they get to the top of the pass, it is all downhill to Bridgeport. It's a snake whip of curves, but it was oiled and rolled last week. They know the curves in the tight canyon along the Walker River will be their next leg. They will have a wall of stone on their left and rocks and water on their right. There will be no forgiving space or grace on that section. So this is where they will have to make some serious time."

"Ralph, do we know what held them up down the track?"

"Tom, the sheriff just drove up. Sheriff Thorington, Ralph Ramstein with Motor Sports Today. What can you tell us about the men being slow coming in just now?"

"Ralph, we came around the last knee of the craters to find the valley full of sheep. Roy had laid down the Indian, but Mace had made a safe stop. The two were hauling up the Indian, and after they checked it out, they made sure it would start. The shepherd was trying to clear his flock to the north side and up into the tree line, but it was slow going. Finally, we all joined in shooing them—but you know how sheep are."

"Well, Sheriff, luckily, we don't have sheep to worry about on the George Washington Bridge in New York, but we get the picture. So the motorcycles are going to be okay?"

"It would appear so. The road was about two inches of soft silt at that point, so it was a soft landing for both the Indian and Roy. Once we got the road cleared, they took off like there was no time left. I don't know if they fluttered in Dead Man's Curve or not, but there were some large drift marks. Those boys really know how to ride in the worst of conditions."

"Thanks, Sheriff. We appreciate everything you did to help here today. And I understand you are up for reelection this fall. May everyone in your county grace you with their vote."

"Thanks, Ralph, it was our pleasure having this race come through our fine county. And, also, there is a check for a little over four thousand dollars we have raised through bake sales, concerts, and metal drives. It all goes to the new annex of the hospital down in Bishop. It may be Inyo County, but it is sometimes the closest for our citizens."

"That's a great gesture, Sheriff. I'm sure the people of Bishop will welcome you and that check with open arms. Folks, that's all for me. This is Ralph Ramstein with Motor Sports Today coming to you from Lee Vining, California, on the shores of the magnificent Mono Lake and eastern gateway to the beautiful national park Yosemite. Tom, back to you."

"Exciting episode, Ralph. I think my heart is still racing. Folks, for Ralph Ramstein, and this is Tom Holloway with the Race of the Century. We're going to pay some bills here and will check back in with you in about thirty minutes."

28 STEW

"John?" The officer turned slightly in his chair. His movements were conservative in the summer heat. The wood of the desk chair groaned with a tenor but just shy of a squeal. His head lain heavily on his right shoulder. He waited for either the beckoning or the rest of the question. He liked working for the young woman.

She was straightforward and simple. She didn't dance a complex rumba. She moved more in a standard four-step waltz. By the second dance, he knew how to follow.

"It's three o'clock on a warm afternoon. Where would I most likely find our deputy sheriff?"

The chair moaned slightly throatier as the man rocked back. The toe of his right shoe pushed gently on the desk leg. His eyes fluttered shut and then looked at the clock for answers. "It's Wednesday."

It was now her turn to wait.

"He was already at his desk when I walked by this morning."

He watched the longhand on the clock push past the line at the two. His breathing was slow—calm.

The long arm passed the next line and the next.

His head flopped to the other side, and he looked at the thermometer just outside the window, set high enough to stay in the shade of the overhanging eaves, but where he could see how hot the day was.

"The temperature is only one-oh-six…"

He waited.

He heard the soft movement of her chair. She oiled the mechanicals.

Thorny's head appeared in the office doorway. She leaned against the jamb with her arms crossed. Her focus was on the wall separating the police station from the small sheriff's office. "Nap?"

The man pushed his lower lip out. His blinks were slow and moist. "Maybe." His eyes drooped closed as his head softly rocked shoulder to shoulder in a muted metronome. His head slowed to a halt, hovering over his left shoulder as his eyes floated open. "But I'd guess he might have taken them carrots he had in his car down to your mule."

Her head broke focus as she turned to the man. Her eyes narrowed. "How did you know I had a mule?"

He harrumphed little more than a twitch. It was too hot to exert himself. "Anyone who can fog a mirror and carry a pulse knows about you and Heather. Who else would have gotten Flapjack's mule?"

"Where is she at?"

He ran the small of his hand along the back of his right ear. She rarely saw the man sweat. "Across the river from the second artesian well. She likes the deep shade of the twisted cottonwood."

She watched the man through the side of her eyes. "You go down there?"

"Not this month. I didn't have any extra carrots."

Thorny's smile grew a single pull as she shook her head loosely. "I'm going to have to figure you out one day."

His arms rose into the air as he yawned. His fingers knit together as he put his hands behind his head. "You're certainly welcome to try, boss. Lord knows the missus has been trying neigh on forty years now."

Thorny bumped her hip against the door frame and pushed off. Sticking her hands in her pockets, she thought and then headed for the door. "I need some soup in this heat."

As she neared the open front door, the man yawn and stretched. "Say hi to Heather for me."

She stopped. Her hand rested on the door frame. The middle finger—slightly curled, tapped the fingernail—a slow heartbeat. "Call the chief for me, would you? Tell him I want stew for dessert." Her eyes studied the peeling paint on the Feed and Seed store across the small street. The whitewash paint was grained with long runs of blisters. Nothing escaped the heat. Her voice was washed out with the same heat. "And, John… I won't be in until late tomorrow." She pulled the dark glasses down over her eyes and was gone.

The man thought about dinner and then stew for dessert. Drawing a cold bath sounded better.

His hand reached over and lifted the black cast-metal handpiece of the telephone. He heard the voice of his second cousin. She never even identified herself as the operator like the other three did. She was straight to the point. Gossip. His eyelids gave up. The smooth tone of her voice wouldn't keep him awake, but the gossip was always accurate and delivered in grid. She started at the north end. She would finish four minutes later in the south—before she would allow him to speak.

———

IN THE EAST GRID, across the river from the second artesian well, the shadow under the giant snarled cottonwood tree, the slender hand rested on the gray hair of the mule. The fingers drowsily raked in and out. The two bunches of overgrown carrots were long gone. The dull silver badge shown warm in a thin ray secreting between the leaves. The khaki shirt sagged from the large knurl of a former limb, the collar—neatly smoothed out—taking the shape of the head-sized burl.

The long fuzzy ear twitched and turned slightly. Sensing.

"Heather heard your car as you tried to sneak across the bridge."

The tall sun-seared grass whispered against her pants. The knapsack swung heavily from her claw. The bottom rubbed and bent only the tips of the soft newer green.

Thorny stopped on the cooler grass. Her toes scrunched in the blades. Green would stain between her toes most of the summer. The manicured lawns of the town were not the same. This grass was clumpy—wild. There were stories of a fist-sized bunch here, a hand splat of desert dirt, a single bouquet of tiny yellow flowers floating an inch from the dirt, and then more grass. Ever changing stories—written and then rewritten on the desert floor.

She thought of Ulysses's weathered face. The pocks, the scars, the creases, and lines. Stories.

Her vision drifted out over the desert to the north. There were few trees to break the expanse of sun-battered brush. She would never find Heather north of East Line Street. No shade, no sweet grass, and no deputy to lie in the summer heat with while he fed juicy carrots into the soft fuzzy lips.

The man's single acknowledgment to the heat was removing his uniform shirt. Thorny noted the worn soles on the crossed boots. She didn't look for any evidence of wear on his thin-strapped undershirt. There were too many thin soles and edged undershirts these days.

She stepped into the deep shadow of the tree. The heat-lowered river churned mud and sun-sparkle mere yards away. "I stopped at the Bib. The elk stew sounded good."

Peter stretched, yawned, and unhurriedly curled as he sat up. His elbows grabbed around his rising knees. "So, we're not calling it coyote gumbo anymore?"

"May ran out of the gumbo file. It's just root vegetables and meat." Thorny crossed and folded her legs as she shrunk to the ground next to the bag. Her claw reached out and scratched between the two large fuzzy ears. They dipped and stood at the calming touch. "I guess you could call it poachers potage, but then the vegetables were freely given."

As the deputy opened the jar, he could smell the rich earthy aroma. "Let's just call it good eaten."

Only the occasional tinkle of the spoon against the glass jars broke the silence of the desert buzz. The desert cricket can rub their legs together upwards of twice a second. Thorny softly chewed as she counted and then added thirty-seven to her number. The number was close to one-ten. If it gets hotter, the crickets either die or hide underground until it cools off. She figured it would soon be very quiet.

The heat and crickets brought back memories of her grandfather and Charlie's grandfather, the original Piute chief and tribe's shaman. She had only been about eight when they taught her about the crickets. She could hear their wise voices as she ran the tip of her spoon around the bottom of the jar. She knew she was full but still yearned for an extra jar of the stew. She also yearned for the wisdom of the two old voices.

She put the jar aside as she looked across the mile of desert. Her eyes slowly rose as they passed along the knees and humps of the foothills of the ancient White Mountains. A soft sigh passed more through her nose than her lips.

Peter stopped trying to dig one last lick of stew out of the glass. He gently put it near the basket. "That sigh has all the weight of the world in it."

She thought, and her right shoulder twitched a small roll.

"Have you ever faced a conundrum of doing the right thing and doing right?"

"They sound like the same thing."

"Let's say you nab a man for stealing an apple. The law says you're to arrest him." She turned and rolled down onto her stomach. Her hands spread-fingered in the short grass. "But you know the apple isn't for him. He's only stealing the apple for his child who is starving."

The deputy yawned his eyelids in an exaggerated blink. "All right. The law is the right thing…"

She looked over her glasses out of the corner of her eye. "Following the edict of the law is doing right."

"Then what is doing the right thing?"

"I'm not sure…"

"But you have some idea."

Her lower lip rolled in at the left corner. Her teeth eased down as her head bobbed once. "It has something to do with letting him go… but I'm not sure how."

His hand pulled three blades of grass. He held them up. Slowly he tugged at the first one. "This is why I became a police officer. My job is to follow the law and arrest those who do not." He pulled the first blade and dropped it.

His forefinger and thumb took hold of the second blade of grass.

"The lawyer's jobs are to defend him or prosecute him. Their jobs are to debate the legality of the law and how it applies or doesn't apply to the case."

The second blade fluttered to the ground.

"As for whether to let him go free…" He held up the final blade and then let it flutter down. "That is the job of the judge."

She crossed her arms and laid her head down on her wrist. "And there is the Gordian Knot. In this case, I'm all three."

"What is the crime?"

"That is the other problem. It hasn't happened—yet."

<hr>

"WHAT DID HE SAY?"

"That he was glad he wasn't me or in my bare feet."

Charlie snorted. Thorny cupped her hands at the surface of the pool and sent a fountain of water across. It was met with another larger wave coming from the hulking man. They both laughed.

Among the trees, the deep thrumming of the tiny tree frogs filled the narrow valley. The two old friends floated in the warmish water—stewing.

MORNING in the desert comes slowly as the light creeps like a wary lizard from bush to bush. It flows slowly across bone-dry river washes as glacial as the torpor beetles racing against the warming sunlight to reach shade before the same sunlight turns into a deadly blast furnace—cooking them from the inside out, boiling their soft interiors in the hard oven of their own carapaces.

Morning in the mountains is more of frozen full light. The sky becomes day, but the valleys remain night cold until the sun peeks down to the bottom. The Aspen leaves—still, as if they're frozen in mid-rustle. Waiting for the movement granting warmth of the sunshine, filtering down from leaf to leaf.

The pool and its place in the narrow valley were granted both breaks of day. From her seat on her favorite rock, Thorny watched the pink light creep back down the mountain toward the large valley floor. The heat would come later to the Aspens of the slot valley. The thin ghost of smoke, from the meager fire, curled like carded lamb's wool into the reaches of the trees and then was lost. The smell of the burning hard locust, with the chill of the morning, combined to encourage her senses. With her eyes resting closed, she could feel the energy of her grandfather holding his coffee mug. His left middle finger inside the handle with the rest of the fingers gripping over the chipped enamel, his right palm and three fingers resting along the warm side, the chief with the handle pointed out and away from him, his hands flat with the handle sandwiched between his fingertips as if he were praying. Ulysses splayed on the ground, leaning his upper back and head against the side of

Thorny's rock. His mug, rising and falling with his breathing, resting center on his chest.

Thorny had never thought about how the men presented themselves, or how they held their coffee. But, with clarity, she knew their spirits.

The lieutenant, clutching to life. Tortured by death. Now the farmer and rancher with family.

The spiritual one. Able to walk the fine path between here and the other. Grateful for the blessing of both.

The engineer whose mind and sole had become consumed with the power of nature. His world understanding was only a book or touch of the ground away.

Thorny could feel the three all around her. The bendable hard strength of the Aspens, the mystical, there-but-not-there, of the smoke, and now the cradling nurture of the mountains she had come to accept as being part of her as much as she was a part of them. She had come to understand the bones she had burned in the shack were only bones. Ulysses had long before seeped into the mountains he was always a part of. For as long as she needed, she was surrounded and filled with her family.

"You feel them too."

Thorny grunted in her best imitation of Charlie at age twelve. Shortly after, his voice fell down a well, and when it echoed back from hitting the dry bottom, it stayed. The eighth grade he had passed the six-foot mark and towered above every teacher. The next year, at the start of high school, he had been reminded he was also a Piute. He hid his braids under a straw hat. Thorny had dressed down the principal. The fear of being scalped was lifted. Thorny wore the straw hat for the rest of the year.

"They're strong this morning."

"I think it's me." She looked up around the blanket draped over her head and back. "My question. My problem."

As the eyes stayed fixed on the fire, the large head slowly floated up and then down. He sipped. "Thoughts?"

"I think I need to go down to Los Angeles—talk to Stan... and perhaps his boss." She sipped and quirked her pursed lips to one side. "Maybe even my old boss."

Thorny felt the large boulder rumble. Thorny wasn't sure if it was the mountain or Charlie.

Finally, Charlie rolled forward and reached out to the enamel pot. Pouring more coffee, he leaned back, and his coal black eyes locked on hers. "Sounds weighty."

The lawyer, police chief, judge, mayor, and county supervisor nodded.

29 RACE – BRIDGEPORT

"Hello?"

"Hello. Tom Holloway here. Who's this speaking?"

"Deputy District Attorney Edward Denton. How can I help you?"

"We are broadcasting the Race of the Century. We were expecting to find Charles Duryea so he could report on the racers as they made their pit stop there in Bridgeport. I did call Bridgeport, California, didn't I?"

"Yes. You reached Bridgeport. But the two motorcycles have already come and gone. You missed them by maybe only six or seven minutes. It was quite the show. The entire town was out on the sidewalk."

"How did they look?"

"Well, pretty much like they usually do. Just because it's the Fourth of July doesn't mean work stops around here. Molly from the Bridgeport Café does seem to be braiding her hair different now, but everyone else looked the same. This is a small town, but people here work to survive. What do they do where you come from? Where are you calling from anyway?"

"I'm calling from Mojave. You may have heard of it. It's in the desert about three hundred miles south of you."

"Yes, I grew up near there. A tiny mining town named Red Mountain. On good years, there were upwards of twenty of us. What can I do for you… What was your name again?"

"Tom Holloway, sir. I'm with Motor Sports. Do you see a tall gentleman with a long beard around there anywhere?"

"Sir, this is Bridgeport. There is a war on. We take saving resources very seriously—even if there is a strange telephone on a crate, sitting out on the sidewalk. Curious. But there are a lot of men around who have abstained from a clean-shaved face. Maybe you can describe him a bit better?"

"How many tall men with beards are wearing bowler hats?"

"Umm… I see three."

"Do you know any of them?"

"Of course, I'm the Deputy District Attorney. It's my job to know everyone."

"Who are the three men wearing bowler hats?"

"To the south of me is Mike Adams, the butcher. I've never seen the top of his head. He wears his hat even in church. His wife cuts his hair, so even our local barber has never seen his head."

"Sir?"

"Yes?"

"This is long-distance, and about twenty million listeners are hanging from every syllable of your words."

"Oh. Oh my."

"The other two men?"

"Oh yes. Tim the blacksmith, and the man I don't recognize is walking toward me with his hand out. I think this may be your man."

"Tom? Tom Holloway?"

"Charles? What happened?"

"Tom, the boys caused quite a stir here, sir. We were all set up for them to be here, and we even checked the phone by calling the

New York office. But when the motors came roaring around the south curve… Well, sir, every bit of decorum was thrown out the window. Everyone dropped what they were doing and rush out onto the street. As you can imagine, this event is a big cause for celebration and excitement."

"But you didn't call."

"I'm sincerely sorry, Tom. We tried. But with all three of the operators standing out on the sidewalk, no phone calls were going through. But it was the most excitement this town has seen since the original stables burned down in ninety-seven. Everyone wanted to be able to tell their grandchildren they had seen the Greatest Race of the Century and the two racers."

"How did they look?"

"They are tired, Tom. Sorely tired. They pushed it hard enough for one of them to run out of fuel about two miles back. They found a rope and the other towed him in. The damnedest thing in a race I'd ever seen."

"Charles, it wasn't the first time. Mace has had trouble with his Harley Davidson."

"Well, about a hundred yards from the pit, the red motor coughed and died… They coasted in. The pit crew was good. Caps-off to caps-on wasn't even two minutes. They just had time for a bottle of water, a bite to eat, and they were being pushed to start. They ran through their gears before they hit the sharp curve at the end of the main street here. We could hear them roaring up the hill, headed for the hot springs. But no stopping for a soothing soak today."

"They have a treacherous pass ahead of them, Charles."

"Yes, we came through the narrow canyon yesterday. I don't know which would be worse to run off the road and into. The wall on the west side is at most six feet from the edge of the road and all rough blasted granite. The river on the east side is still a wild torrent tossing about through the massive boulders. Either one would be certain death at high speed."

"Our thoughts are with them as they race for Walker—their next stop."

"Good talking to you, Tom."

"Thank you, Charles Duryea, for coming out of retirement to help us with this broadcast. Have a safe trip back to Detroit."

"It was my pleasure and thank you for thinking of me. Goodbye."

"Well, there you have it, folks. The men are now approximately three-quarters of the way through the race. Roy had laid his motorcycle down in the glass silt, and Mace is still plagued with his motor's fuel adjustment running too rich. As we watch their time and miles left, we can only guess at the outcome. Remember, the winner still must cross the finish line by the strike of high noon at the far end of Carson City. If they don't cross, they forfeit, and the companies take the motorcycles back, and there is no payday for the race. The clock is still ticking on this race, ladies and gentlemen. This is Tom Holloway, and we'll be back in just under thirty-five minutes."

D anny Rambino held the cast-iron phone loosely in his hand. He held the handpiece rocked out from his ear and under his chin. "She's looking for him. He's probably taking an evening swim to cool down."

Thorny nodded as if she understood.

She imagined Danny's father possibly lived in some palatial manor in Beverly Hills, but the image didn't fit the man she knew. He was a sharp, detailed dresser, may or may not have hired the limousine they had last gone to dinner in, and enjoyed gourmet food in fancy restaurants. But he also had a reserved nature about him. One that didn't lend itself to expansive swimming pools, maids, butlers, chauffeurs, or any other personal staff.

Danny started. "Dad, Amelia Earhart is here. She has a request."

Thorny could hear the barked laughter as her friend held out the phone. His smirk was one of humor but also understood the nature of the phone call.

She raised the phone to her head as she thought. "Is this the man who only bet on two Golden Glove fights because he was too drunk to remember the third?"

The silence roared in her ear. The man was quick on his feet, and she could sense him dancing for the right answer.

"If you have the air, would you fly or crawl like a lobster?" He alluded to their first dinner at the Hotel Bel Aire. The night's dinner introduced her to Lobster Thermador.

She looked at Danny who nodded with his eyelids. "My copilot says we can fly."

"Is this a threesome?"

"Let's include the boxer and the other."

"Put your copilot on for me."

She handed the phone over.

"Si, Beno?"

"Si, the slaughterhouse. My guess is the cock will be surprised." He hung up the phone and stared at Thorny.

Her one eye clenched closed as she watched him silently. The phone rang once, and then, silent.

Danny nodded. "Still tapped."

Thorny pulled at her left ear. Her index finger and thumb slid from the leather to the lobe. "Do we know where?"

"The check is done here. So the extra line is somewhere down there."

"If it's not formal dress, I'm ready to go."

He pointed at her bare feet. "Maybe we can find you some shoes?"

"We'll stop by Charlie's. My old boots are there just in case."

"How old?"

"I left them there when we graduated. They still fit, and he keeps them polished and oiled."

Danny laughed as he pulled a couple of windbreaker jackets from the closet.

"Just in case."

THE DINER'S counter is the length of the original train car, except for access alleys at each end. The once-freight car had been pushed on to a dead rail and left to rot. An enterprising couple of men, fresh out of the navy, converted it into a dining car with windows where the busted boards had been. Three years later, the depression had settled down around them. Short-order cooking had become more of soup being ladled out by the gallons. Those who had passed through the line never forgot the men or the soup.

"The Car" was a fixture of the industrial neighborhood, and occasionally, those who sought an inconspicuous place for early morning meetings. The first shifts, for many of the factories, started at five in the morning. The hour before was frenzied with stuffing lunch pails full of standing orders from men living in boardinghouses or nowhere to make a lunch. Every pail got a sandwich, a piece of fruit, and a tin of soup with a screw lid. Yesterday's tin and waxed cloth sandwich wrap were removed and replaced with fresh food. Only on Sunday was The Car as silent as the factories.

Thorny's fine fingers touched just beyond her knees. The tips played softly along the marks carved in the softwood. Counter to floor, the boards in the kick-space mirrored the marks of respect and thanks in the rail boards on the wall under the windows. In the hard times and beyond, work-weathered hands, with pocket, jack, or carpet knife, incised marks, initials, and screeds of thanks. There was little room left in the fifty feet of car. Even the ceiling hadn't been spared.

Danny's eyebrow raised in question.

"So many men…" She nodded at the wall under the row of dark windows. Her gaze then floated toward the ceiling.

"During the depression, Dad would bring me down from Bishop. This is where we ate. I don't remember if there was a menu or not, but I remember the food was good. As we left, Dad would pull the stuffing out of the money clip in his pocket. Pressing it into the owner's hands, they would shake. I think many of the men who still had money during the depression ate here and paid the same."

The door at the one end opened. Three men in light shirts and open collars stepped into the car. In passing, Mike Rambino leaned over and shook the cook's hand. Thorny could see there was more in the handshake than skin. Taking care of the neighborhood had never stopped.

Danny moved down a few stools. Mike took the stool on the far side of Danny, leaving the two other men to bracket Thorny. And giving them privacy.

Thorny's old boss and district attorney for one of the largest populations in the United States sat on her left. His right hand gently gave her arm a friendly squeeze. "I'll be Frick, and he'll be Frack."

Thorny smiled at the term Frick and Frack, made famous for two people tied together through their work or association. The term came from two ice-skaters who escaped Germany and joined the Ice Follies in 1937. The two were skaters as well as physical comedians, who always seemed connected at the hip. "I'll just stick with Amelia." The two men nodded.

Three mugs of coffee appeared in front of them. As Thorny didn't see any menu in evidence, she suspected the breakfast would be whatever appeared before her.

She sipped and slowly put the mug down. Turning, she looked at her old boss. "I need a judge. We can't pay much, but we have a house for him to live in. I think we can even take care of the utilities. I'd like another lawyer, but I'm not sure there is enough work. But if you can lend me one..."

"How's the fishing up that way?"

She nudged her chin at Danny. "The kid can tell you. But I hear it's good enough... as long as you don't try to fish the holes showing signs of being dynamited."

The man chuckled. "When should I take some vacation time?"

"I'll be needing both on the sixth."

He chewed on his lower lip in the right corner. "I thought you were the lawyer and judge?"

"I'm also the arresting police officer, mayor, and county commissioner." She closed her eyes a moment. "I think that's it. I haven't heard of being elected to any other position."

The other older man coughed. "Sounds busy."

She smirked as her head ground around. "Speaking of busy—I need to borrow Douglas Fairbanks."

"When?"

"Today. He'll need to go back with us. I need him for juris-diction."

"The FBI can only investigate. He can't make an arrest. You'll need someone with jurisdiction."

She turned. "Frick? If the perpetration was planned and agreed upon in Bishop...?"

"You would have jurisdiction."

She smiled. "Even across state lines?"

"As a local law enforcement officer, your jurisdiction ends at the border of the United States of America. Don't let them run for the border."

"Okay." She looked at the large plate as it quietly landed in front of her. She looked up at the smiling face and asked. "Shrimp or Crayfish?"

The cook chuckled as he nodded toward Danny and his father. "The gentleman only brought me shrimp. My guess is an hour before, they were scurrying around some tank at the market."

The other two plates were the same. She looked down at the father and son. Mike raised his fork and shrimp in a toast. She nodded and took the first bite.

She patted at her mouth and placed the napkin on the counter. "So, as long as they roll over...?"

Her former boss leaned back on the stool. "I'll make it stick with Sacramento. They can work it out with Nevada. But my guess is the sheriff of Ormsby County will probably want to wash his hands of this mess as fast as you can hit the boundary."

Frack cleared his throat as he pushed his empty cup out for a refill. He was aware of the soft light filtering through the windows and knew it would be a long day for all of them. "If there is any pushing or shoving over jurisdiction, I'll add my weight to the fray. This started with us, and it will end with us. Only we'd like for you to handle certain factors as it were."

"Thank you." She nodded her head. "With Frick's help, I think we can handle our end. But any extension or extenuating circum-stances…"

"We'll take over that with whoever needs to handle them. And as for Mr. Fairbanks, I'll go make a phone call." He squeezed her shoulder as he got up to leave. "You just take care of yourself. I'd like to know I have a guide to take me and the missus fishing this fall. Without any bullet holes in her."

Thorny clapped her hand on his. "I'll take care of the bullet holes. You just make sure you get up there this fall."

As he walked past, he waved the other two back down in their seats. "I just need to go wake up a sleeping giant."

Frack turned on his stool to face Thorny. The two had talked strategy in the district attorney's office. He never had the latitude to let her prosecute in court, but he had always valued her talent for seeing the tactics needed for a successful result. "What now?"

"We go back. In the morning, they will be leaving to get down to the start. If what I expect happens, the wives will be packed and headed north. We'll just invite them to leave their belongings and ride up with us."

He smiled at the coercive nature of the plan. "I'll have you a judge and a lawyer on the sixth. Just be safe."

Thorny swung her legs back and stood as Danny did. She stepped back one step and took Danny by the arm and patted his chest with her claw. "Why, sir, I'm just a frail little woman. I have this big strong man to look out for me."

Mike snorted from behind them. "Excuse me." He turned and quick-stepped to the door.

Danny closed one eye as he looked at her. "Can this lamb ask what kind of slaughter you're setting me up for?"

Thorny smiled. "You get to drive back."

He rolled his eyes into the upper right of his lids. "It will take longer. But it will be safer."

"Or we can let the FBI do the driving."

Danny's eyes got big. "Oh no. I've ridden with him."

Thorny laughed. "His wife is faster."

As they walked out to the cars, Frick joined them. "Tinkerbell says Peter Pan will be ready when you swing by. He's grumpy but by no means a dwarf."

Thorny's smile pulled to one side. "And she's no Snow White."

"We are back for the last pit stop in the Greatest Race of the Century. Good morning from California. This is Tom Holloway with Motor Sports News. I'm broadcasting from the hot Mojave Desert, in the town of Mojave, California. The local time is eleven-twenty-one. The two racers have driven three hundred and sixty miles since three o'clock this morning. In the black of night, with only the moon to help them, the Southern Pacific Railroad guard arm rose, and they disappeared into the desert. Since then, we have checked in on their progress at each of their pit stops, thanks to our friends at Ma Bell. At one of the stops, Benton Station, we checked in with the Sheriff of Mono County, Cecil Thorington, over shortwave radio. Our deepest gratitude to the fine volunteer members of the new arm of the Army Air Corp—the Civil Air Patrol. It was their radios there at Benton Station and here in Mojave that gave us the connection. Men, if this was a test, you passed it with flying colors."

"Hello? Tom?"

"Folks, I believe we have the distinguished gentleman all the way from England—Mister Bill Boddy, Senior Editor of the Motor Sport Magazine. Bill, how do you like the wild west?"

"Tom, I've covered many races in many parts of the world, but the grandeur of your west is something I was not expecting. Your mountains are enormous, and the trout in your lakes and streams make me regret not bringing my fishing gear."

"And, to top it all off, Bill, you get to report from the last pit stop in the greatest motorcycle race in this century."

"It is a privilege and exciting day to be here, Tom. We just saw the green flare from the Very Pistol down at the bottom of the grade. We expect to see the boys any second now. This grade is a fast three miles, and yes, they just flew through the large curve. They are in the shadow of the mountain for a one-mile series of chicanes… and yes. There. They. Are. Tom, they are both lying flat on their petrol tanks. Those motors are roaring. I would guess you can hear them, Tom."

"They sound great, Bill. Give them our best. They have forty-three miles of almost flat fresh macadam ahead of them and then two miles of asphalt to the finish line."

"Slow down, boys. There is plenty of water where that came from. The pit crews are fueling both sides of the split tanks at the same time so they have proven full tanks. A wee splash-out and capped off. The team is pushing, the leavers are pulled to second gear and… they are off… and gone. Up around the bend, they have gone. We can still hear the engines as they climb the last snaking mile and then they are through the gap. Tom, it was one of the fastest pit stops I have ever watched in road racing. As you know, I have watched amazing road races around the world. This team is the team I want the next time I take on the Paris to Bagdad race. Fueled motors, fueled men, and a quart each for the last blistering run under the blazing sun-washed stretch to the finish line. Tom, this is one exciting race. I want to thank you personally and from Motor Sport magazine."

"It was our pleasure, Bill Boddy. Motor racing started in your neck of the globe, but we are excited to have you here to experience some of our finest. We're happy you chose to give up watching the

Indianapolis 500, for coming and reporting an import stop in our race."

"Tom, I wouldn't trade these few moments, and a chance to be part of this magnificent event, for even the finest seat at a giant race like the 500. Maybe one day, the 500 will entice me back to hold the checkered flag. But, for today, this has been a highlight of my career. As you can imagine, it was a long trip to get here. But this is the ninety seconds I will trade dinners for and recount to my grandchildren until they have race stories of their own."

"Well, Bill, you're young, and I expect remarkable things in your career. Even being the flagman at the Indianapolis 500. Folks, for Bill Boddy from England's Motor Sport magazine, this is Tom Holloway with Motor Sports in America. We'll check back in with you in a short twenty minutes."

Stan squinted at the rearview mirror. The man in the starched white shirt splayed across the backseat as if scattered by a shotgun. Even waiting until midnight hadn't tempered the heat in Los Angeles. They had all slept a few hours after an early dinner and then taken turns soaking in a cold bath to drop the body heat. The three had lain in front of every fan Stan and Ruth could get their hands on. Even then, their sleep was fitful.

At eleven-fifteen, Stan had quietly gotten up to go to the bathroom. Not wanting to wake the household, he hadn't flushed. He opened the door to find his wife waiting her turn. Thorny and Danny were sitting at the table waiting for the coffee to brew. Nobody had really slept. It was going to be a long day.

Thorny's head fell slightly to her left. She studied the man she had known since the third-grade. Danny was one of those kids who was quiet in the classroom, quiet at lunch, and just as quiet in the play yard. Thorny had seen him take a baseball to the face—and never cry or even moan. The day the swingset broke, and a nail ripped open his arm, she had only seen him wince when the nurse administered a swab of mercurochrome. She might have been better friends, but he wouldn't talk to her until they were in high school. By then, she mostly only talked to Charlie.

"Did he do the driving down?" Stan's voice was as soft as a hunter drawing a bead on a deer.

She blinked a long blink as her head turned. "Yes." She looked back and then rubbed at her face. "He drove most of the way with the lights off." She pointed at the large glowing speedometer. "He said without the distracting light, the moonlight made a better light to drive by."

"He's right. The white light burns the chemical in our eyes called rhodopsin. The rods need it to see in the dark. The cones are useless without strong light. Red light doesn't destroy the rhodopsin, so when the fighters fly at night, the gauges are lit with only red light. Same goes for the bridge of a ship."

Thorny smirked. "Look at you. Mister medical knowledge man."

His head ground around to smile at her. "It is also why they trained me as a sniper after the war. I hadn't thought of the FBI. Those thoughts came later, but my body absorbs the vitamin A it needs to produce plenty of rhodopsin. It's also why there is a light purplish tint to my eyeballs." He leaned forward and pushed in the white Bakelite knob—quenching the lights.

Thorny watched as he blinked a few times in the dark. She looked out of the side of her eyes to see the large full moon floating over the southern tip of the White Mountains. She sensed the car moving faster. "You waited until now?"

"I needed the moon to be just above the top of the windshield. Otherwise, it would have blinded me worse than the speedometer."

They rode quietly in the dark. Thorny could feel Stan setting the car up for a turn before she could see the turn.

"Have you figured out what to do with them?"

Thorny shifted. "We need the people who are expecting the stones. They are the criminals who are the true threat. Mace and Roy are just the errand boys. The people who hired them, they would dump them like a hot frying pan if it meant saving their skin

—the boys just need to understand they need to save their skin and their wives. I need to give them the chance to do the dropping first."

"How do you plan to get them to talk?"

"Arrest their wives first. Do you still have the one stone?"

She saw him fumble as if he were reaching into his pocket. She reached out. "I don't need to see it now. I just wanted to make sure you have it."

She could see the white smile and eyes. "I was just feeling to make sure I didn't leave them in the other pants."

Thorny watched the gray tableau of the night desert. The road had become clearer as her eyes adjusted. She was thankful for the lack of any cars driving south in the early hours of the morning. "If they think their wives have spilled the beans, and you show them we have corroborating evidence, I think they will give us the one final piece in the puzzle."

"How do you get the wives to talk?" The voice from the back was as much gravel as vocal cords.

Stan glanced in the mirror. "Good morning, sunshine."

The sound of small groans and movement filled the backseat.

Thorney squinted into the gloom. The white shirt only helped by being a light gray blob in the black. "What are you looking for?"

The face and folded arms appeared on the back of the front seat. Danny's face was one of hurt and confusion. The same face Thorny had only witnessed a couple of times from babies filling their diapers. "Did you stop at Little Lake and throw some Mud Hen poop in my mouth?" He smacked his mouth with his tongue sticking in and out.

Stan eased the car to a stop. "The picnic basket is in the trunk."

Thorny pulled the door handle. "I'll get it."

Danny opened his door. "I'll do it. It's the gentlemanly thing to do. Besides…"

Thorny pointed at the other side of the car. "You go do your man stuff with Mister FBI on the other side. This bush says ladies all over it."

Danny looked at the remains of a gnarled, stunted tree. "Hmm… a fur-lined seat, I see."

Thorny looked and then peeled the flattened rabbit from the one limb. The dried carcass sailed past the man as he dodged around the back of the car.

The three stood sipping coffee a few minutes later. Danny took another bite from the coffee cake in his hand. "There is a lot of sugar and butter on this. You must not get this very often, with the rationing and all."

Stan swallowed. "I have learned to never ask where we stand on ration cards. I ran out of gas stamps one day. The next morning, I got an urgent call from the office. I walked home from the gas station to fetch the next card. Ruth had her middle finger on the card, pointing at the date. I had to take the bus for three days. The gas station had rotated my tires and changed the oil by then."

Thorny frowned. "I would think you would pay more attention to the cards."

"Except it was our anniversary. She traded some stamps for other stamps so we could drive up to a small retreat above Santa Barbara. I had almost spoiled the surprise."

Danny chuckled. "Even I know better than to spoil a woman's surprise." He turned to Thorny. "Speaking of surprises. What about the wives? What if they leave before we get there?"

It was Thorny's turn to chuckle. "It would be a challenging endeavor for them to accomplish. I understand a certain little Piute intended to hold a raid in the middle of the night. Cars have a tough time starting without a rotor in their distributor cap."

Stan snorted. "Both cars?"

"He's a big boy. Besides, I don't think they have more than one car. Whenever I've seen them coming to work, they are in the same car. They only live a few hundred yards apart."

Danny grumbled as he grabbed the rear door. "So why are we killing ourselves getting home in the middle of the night?"

Thorny rolled her face at Stan as she walked around the nose of the car. "Because then we have to turn around and drive to Carson City."

The muted moan from the backseat wailed softly. "Today?"

Stan softly closed his door and slumped with his hand on the key. "There is a nap in there somewhere, I hope."

Thorny pulled her jacket over her front and shoulders as she curled against the door and seatback. "We get to sleep in the jail with the girls while Danny and Charlie fuel up the cars. If we leave after dinner, we should have enough sleep. Sundown isn't until after nine-thirty, and by then, we should be at least to Topaz Lake. We just need to be at the sheriff's office in Carson before midnight when they shift change."

Stan started the car and put it in gear. "What happens then?"

"They lock the door and go home."

He eased out the clutch and the car began to pick up speed. Stan looked back at Danny. The man had assumed his spread-eagle sleeping position and was already softly snoring. "What about the police?"

"Nope. Only sheriffs in Nevada. I think it's part of their state constitution. Something about all prosecutions are carried out on the street in front of a saloon at thirty paces."

Stan drove quietly as he thought about the whole state being patrolled by only sheriff's deputies. He finally got around to the joke of an old-fashioned shoot-out in front of a saloon. When he looked over, the light curls were half-buried in the fur collar of a flight jacket. He didn't remember seeing Thorny ever wearing a pilot's prized possession.

As they passed the Olancha Way station, he could see several tents and cars parked in among the trees. He figured the old stagecoach station would be one of the pit stops for the race. As he thought about how many people were at the station, he started multiplying the number of pit stops through the course of the race. The staffing started to add up to a major movement and deployment of troops. He remembered flying over large deployments in France. Even from a thousand feet in the air, he could see the grunts slogging through mud to their ankles. He and his wing of fliers would fly out and bomb a position, shoot up another, and return over the same regiment, seemingly slogging in the same spot.

He glanced at the aurora of the moon glowing behind the rearview mirror. Once again, he was thankful for having been in an airplane instead of marching into battle. He squinted over at the huddled mass wrapped in a pilot's jacket and wondered where she had gotten the jacket. Even if it did seem a bit large for her.

Thorny pulled the door shut. She was fishing for her keys when a throat cleared behind her. Tempering her response to jump, she thought about the throat, and the hour.

"I hope you weren't going to make me go find the key under the third stone by the downspout."

She turned to find her officer standing with his head slightly leaned to one side in question. The smile was only half-warmed at catching her off guard.

"That must have been some meeting in the city. Your chauffeur is FBI, and you have what looks like a dead body in the backseat. Are you planning to kill anymore this morning, or can I safely pass?"

"Jeez, John. What time is it?"

His head rose back as he looked through the window at the large clock on the wall. "Looks like a quarter past seven." His stoic face showed no purpose, nor was he asking for any answers. He was just early for work.

Thorny transferred the manacles and folder to her claw and reached behind her to open the door. "Do I have any messages?"

The man's eyes drifted shut as his eyes rolled up to look at the blackboard of his mind. "Geronimo wanted to make sure you came and woke him as you passed through town."

She sighed. "Anything else?"

"May is expecting you for a late lunch or early dinner. I can call her and let her know how many, what time, and what to pack."

Thorny's eyebrows bounced up only once as she rolled her eyes at his soft smile. "I guess I should have guessed I wouldn't get through this without my posse. I'll call her when we get back in an hour or so. My guess is there will be five of us in the cells. Three will be sleeping, and the other two can do what they want. They won't be driving tonight."

John stepped around her and into the station. "Excellent, Chief." He closed the door to trap the cool of the interior. The two-foot-thick stone walls kept the station cool until well after four. Even on the hottest days.

She turned and looked at the dead body in the backseat. She wanted to shove him over and join him. As she looked at the body in the driver's seat, she realized the night had taken its toll on him as well. She stepped around and knocked on the window to a rummy agent. He slid over as she opened the door.

Thorny passed him the folder and handcuffs. "Make yourself useful. See if there is anything I forgot to threaten them with."

He opened the folder as she started the Cord and pulled away from the curb. At Main Street, she turned right and headed south. "They are a year behind on their mortgages, and three years behind on their property taxes. I figure I can take their properties for the taxes and renegotiate the mortgages. I don't think the bank will have a problem with my paying off the mortgages."

Stan looked up. His face was wrinkled as he ground his head around. "So you would become the lienholder? Why would you do that?"

"Leverage. This town is about to start bartering for goods and services they have all been needing since before the war."

"But you would have to pay for the houses. How will you be bartering?"

She smiled as she tipped her head forward and looked at him out of the corner of his eye. "I want a new roof and indoor plumbing. I want a big claw-footed tub with a standup shower. I'm tired of freezing in an outhouse and getting clean—butwith sand stuck where the sun don't shine."

Stan leaned back against the door with his smile half-cocked open. "When did the mechanics become carpenters and plumbers?"

Danny leaned forward with his arms folded along the back of the front seat. "Don't forget electrical, siding, and roofing. Okay, I'm awake now. How are you going to get there?"

She looked at Danny through the mirror. "Who's the best carpenter in town?"

"Doug Peterman."

"Who builds the best homes?"

"Doug."

"Who needs a new motor in his 1931 Bedford 5-ton truck?"

"How do you know he needs a new motor? I saw him hauling a bunch of lumber in from the steam mill just last week."

She snapped a peek at him as she turned off the highway onto a side lane. "Was it a full load or one small enough not to kill his engine?"

He rolled his lower lip as he licked it. "It was a lot lighter than I would have expected him to haul. But then, I figured he didn't have the jobs he normally would."

She downshifted for the hill. "He's also going through a gallon of oil a day. My source says he's been running on broken rings and burned valves for over a year. But any day, it will seize on him, and then he will have to buy a whole new engine instead of fixing the one he has."

Stan coughed at the dust from the road. "But only one engine doesn't solve the problem. I'm guessing this is a problem that will take years."

Thorny turned left and pulled to a stop. As she rolled down her window, she croaked like a frog. "I'm not the only one who has needs or can barter. This will take the whole town working together to figure out what is what and who can do what."

The large Piute rose out of the bitterbrush. As he walked nearer, he looked down the hill at a few houses along a dirt track. "Ernestine found out the car won't start about half an hour ago. She walked down to Winnie's. I'd expect them to stew over coffee for another hour or so."

Thorny nodded. The two watched the morning desert. She could feel the other two's eyes on them. Her voice dropped to their soft hunting voice speaking Paiute. "Our grandfathers are quiet this morning."

His rumble was more felt than heard. "They know they have no advice for you. This is you, lizard. This is your spirit walk. You will take this walk with many, and you will walk it while you are awake. This is as powerful as the stones in your bag and the hand in your pocket. This is about you becoming the chief this valley needs. It is your time."

He turned his face toward her. She reached out her thumb with the thin white scar. They pressed scars.

Stan shifted. "What did he say?"

Thorny looked back in the car. Stan wanted to know something. Danny continued to look straight out through the windshield—he knew she would not reveal what was said in Paiute.

"He said they are down at the other house. Ernestine tried the car earlier."

She turned back to Charlie. "How about you take Danny home and meet us with the Chevrolet at the Bib at three. May's making a late lunch and packing two picnic baskets. I'll drive with the girls, and you can talk hunting with Stan. Maybe he and Ruth can come up for some elk hunting on the back forty."

Charlie held up his thumb and two fingers. "Three."

THE SUN-BLISTERED DOOR matched the house. The lack of money to paint or maintain a building takes its toll. In the desert, the toll doesn't take long.

Thorny used the back of her knuckle to knock on the loose sun-withered panel of the door. She stood back and turned sideways, looking at Stan. The knob turned hesitantly. The door opened a few inches.

Thorny looked over her green glasses as she turned to look at the darkened face in the crack. "Hello, Winnie."

The word was more of an intake of air than spoken. "Mayor?" The door opened another inch and then was pulled fully open.

Ernestine's reddish-blonde hair was pulled tight against the heat. The woman was more imposing than her shorter friend. The small white scar from a bad bar fight she tried to break up shone on her tanned cheek. "What can we do for you, Mayor?"

Thorny slowed down and removed her glasses with her claw. "Good morning, Ernestine. May we come in?"

"What do you need?"

Thorny drew the handcuffs out of her front pocket only half-way. "Actually, I'm here as Police Chief Wallace this morning. Would you like to invite us in to talk where your neighbors won't be watching... or would you rather I have this fine FBI agent arrest you out here on the stoop?"

Winnie took a sharp breath and reached to paw at the taller woman. The redhead grabbed her hands in only her one. "Arrest us... for what?"

The smaller graying brunette whined at her friend. "Nessie"

"Shush, Winnie." She turned back as Stan held up the single diamond between his thumb and finger. Her eyes grew as she swallowed.

Stan nodded. "Twenty-two pounds of little rocks like these."

Thorny finished the charge. "Mace is transporting them in his gas tank. They take up too much room, and the men have been practicing towing him to the next pit stop because he will be running out of fuel at the speeds they will have to run."

The woman stood as a defiant statue. Her grip on Winnie's hands was turning white. Her silent rage was written on her face. Winnie whimpered as they took a half-step back.

Thorny stepped through the door and stood a few inches from the woman's face. Her voice lowered. Thorny knew the only battle was here and now, and only with this woman. "Ernestine, your men are good men. The times destroyed many good people. Mace and Roy kept fighting any way they knew how. But, this time, they took the job from the wrong people. We don't want your men. We want the people who hired them. There will be a price to pay, but I'm here to help them. But first, I need your help to do it."

The woman's eyes never flinched. She only blinked once. "If you arrest us, how are you going to help them?"

"Do you know Mike Rambino?"

"Sure. Everyone in Bishop knows Big Mike."

Thorny dipped her head. "Your men have done work for him over the years. It was nothing anyone can arrest them for. But Mister Rambino and I spoke yesterday. He wants you and the men to know up front—he will pay for the best defense lawyer money can buy. Up front. He wants you to know it up front—before you or they say a word. Do you understand?"

The woman cocked her head and looked through only one eye. "I... think so..."

"Good. Because I want you four to work with me, and then I can work with the lawyer so we can bring your men home where they belong. Either way, they are going to be arrested in Carson City, just the same as I'm arresting you two now. So you can either talk with me now, or we can wait and all talk tomorrow after the race. Is that okay?"

She looked at Winnie, and the woman took a deep breath and

shrugged her acceptance. The taller redhead stepped back. "You might as well come in. We have a full pot of coffee."

Stan put the diamond in his pocket and followed them in.

The pot was still hot as promised. Thorny took the opportunity and stirred in a spoonful of honey harvested forty-feet away. There was a strange earthy taste to the coffee.

Winnie chuckled at the frowns on Thorny and Stan's faces. "It's the chicory. Well, real chicory don't grow here, so we grow poke. I bring home the used grounds from the restaurant. We dry 'em. Well… with the four of us, it makes the coffee go longer."

Stan frowned and looked at Thorny. "Poke? As in salad greens?"

Thorny shuddered as she shook her head. "Leave it, Stan. You don't want to know."

She looked at Ernestine. The pocked face and drawn look weren't as much a dust bowl or depression look, but generations from the deep south. She didn't have to ask where they were from. Even Winnie carried the same family markings John Steinbeck had made so famous a few years before.

"How much do you know about the diamonds and who they're working for?"

The woman's breaths were like slow heartbeats. Thorny was sure the woman weighed how much to tell and how much she didn't have to reveal.

Winnie squirmed. Her face begged her friend. She reached out, putting her hand on the other's arm. Her voice was only a breath. "Nessie… she's trying to help."

The larger put her hand on her friends' hand. She turned and rested her forehead on Winnie's head. Dealing with your life crumbling before your eyes isn't as hard when it had been visible for so many years.

"I know."

Sighing, she sat up. "Not much. The guy will come and get the diamonds while the bikes are in the warehouse in Carson City tomorrow night. We don't know who he is. We… we were…" It was all too much. A tear slid down her cheek. She wiped at it with the heel of her hand. "It was going to be a new start…"

Thorny sighed. "You were leaving and never coming back." The women nodded. "Where were you going to go?"

Winnie sighed a slow blink. "Probably back to Black Water."

Thorny frowned. "Where's Black Water?"

Ernestine's lower lip rolled with pressure. The tip of her tongue wetted the edge. "Mississippi." Her mouth screwed up as her eyes rolled. "There are places nobody would ever find us."

Stan cleared his throat. "Better than Bishop?"

Both heads paused as they wagged. "The people here are nice. We never wanted to leave, but we're going to lose our houses, and now this."

Thorny reached halfway across the table. "We're going to work everything out. All of Bishop needs to work through this. If we work together, we can all do better than just survive. And nobody needs to go anywhere and get lost."

Ernestine leaned back in her chair as she wiped once more at her cheek and eyes. "What do you want us to do?"

Thorny smiled. It was going to work out. "First, how about you two pack a change of clothes and a toothbrush. We'll be back here the night of the fifth. We all have a court date on the sixth."

34 HEADING NORTH

Thorny's boots crossed under the chair as she relaxed her elbows on the table and cupped her left claw with her right hand.

Smirking, she was highly aware of Monte leaning back in his chair, looking past Pete, at her wearing boots in the house.

Thorny growled without moving. "Pete."

The man hummed a single note. She was sure he had been spending too much time with Charlie. The communication was similar but three octaves higher.

"Reach over and pull Monte's chair back down on all four legs, please."

"Does he have a straight razor on him?"

"I didn't frisk him. That… was your job."

May leaned her head between them, but her mouth was closer to the deputy's ear. "If you're going to live your life afraid of a seventy-year-old man, then you better give up this career." She withdrew and eased Monte and chair back into an acceptable stance. "Legs on the floor, Mr. Geronimo. You're scaring the children, and it's not Sunday."

She turned at the end of the table and filled Stan's coffee cup without asking. She knew who would be driving.

Ernestine looked at the extra people nervously, unsure. "So we're riding up... well... you know? Without the... um..." She rubbed her wrists with her other hands. "Jewelry?"

Thorny looked at her with a firm face. "Did you want to be handcuffed?"

"No... but..."

Thorny put down her fork as she swallowed. She pulled the napkin from her lap with her left claw. She dabbed at her mouth as she studied the woman. "Was your cell locked this afternoon?"

"I don't know."

Thorny leaned back. Her hands relaxed on the sides of her plate. "Didn't you need the toilet?"

Winnie nodded her head. Ernestine dipped her head once. "We called..."

"His name is John. He's the sergeant."

"He came and opened the door. Then he walked us to the toilet." She gulped and peeked Stan's way. Her voice dropped quieter—almost a whisper. "After... he walked us back and closed the door."

Thorny's head leaned slightly. "Did you see him unlock or lock the cell?"

Winnie sunk her head lower into her shoulders. The slower one had figured it out first. The redhead's eyes bounced cautiously from item to item on the table. They stopped and looked up. Thorny could see the realization in the muddy hazel. The woman realized she had been free—but didn't know it. It was like Heather. She knew she was free, but the grass and food in a certain area made having her fenced—unnecessary.

Thorny sighed softly. "What were you going to do? Run away?"

The adjusting in the seat and sitting up more defiant was noticeable. "We might have. While you slept in the other cells. We could have just waltzed right out." Her lower lip moved forward rigidly in defiance.

The movement was only a slight blur. One moment, Thorny's right hand and the white sleeve were in her lap. The next, she had reached into her back pants. The large .45 caliber semi-automatic rested on the table. Her hand was still in a position to use it. The barrel pointed between the two women.

Winnie jumped a few inches away from her friend. "Eep."

Ernestine's eyes opened as wide as her mouth and froze there.

Thorny fixed her glare on the woman. "I don't know how fast you think you can run, but I don't think it's faster than my bullets. If you have even the thought of running while we are driving to Carson City, I want you to know about my eyes, this gun, and what you can trust in." She took a deep, slow breath. Out of the corner of her eye, she could see Monte fidget. "I've been practicing with this here pistol. Last month, May asked me if I knew where some Chukar were. Now the lead in these bullets is about the size of your pinky. If you hit a Chukar in the body, it just explodes. But if you hit those birds in the head or neck, it just takes it off, and you don't have to worry about bleeding them. The secret is getting within a hundred yards or so..."

May's hand on Ernestine's shoulder made the woman jump. May kept her hand there to calm the woman back into her chair. "Those were the best seventeen birds I have had here in a long time. Perfectly bled, and not a scratch on the bodies." Ignoring the truth of Thorny having shot the birds with her grandfather's ancient slick-barrel squirrel gun, she patted the shoulder as she poured the coffee. She leaned over, and with a whisper everyone could hear, she advised the woman. "The best to do is not run."

Winnie kept her eyes on the pistol as she leaned closer. Her hand gave her friend a start, but it was familiar. The older and smaller woman sucked on her teeth and licked at her lower lip. "Nessie, she's trying to help us. If you don't behave, the boys will..." She looked up at Thorny's eyes. "We'll behave. You still help us with the diamonds?"

Thorny nodded as she lifted her shoulder. The large pistol slid back and disappeared. "Mike Rambino and I both promised. I have a new judge coming up here on the fifth. The District Attorney for Los Angeles is my former boss. He is also coming up here to be the prosecutor. We've already planned this. So all the men need to do is help us catch the real criminals. Your job is to convince them of it. The only problem is, you will only have a couple of minutes to convince them it is in theirs and your best interest."

Ernestine's eyes waffled as she let out a soft groan. "How are we going to do that?"

Stan raised his hand. His thumb and finger holding the diamond. "The same way we convinced you. We'll be there the whole time. When they cross the finish line, there will be about ten minutes of madness. Then everyone will be pulled back so the representatives from the motorcycle companies, the mayor of Carson City, maybe the governor, and the administrator of the hospital will all want their pictures with the men and the motorcycles. After that, they will have to let you near your husbands. We will bring you over. It is in those few seconds, when we are alone in the middle of the circus, you and I will show them the way it is now and the way out."

Thorny glanced at the hand-carved clock near the door. The white hands stood collected on the dark locust face at the three. "We'll talk more about this on the way up. You two will ride with Stan and me. Pete will drive the Chevrolet. We'll need the second car when we come back with Mace and Roy."

Winnie shyly raised her hand to about her chin level. "Can I go to the bathroom first?"

May put the coffeepot down. "I'll show you, Winnie. It's through the kitchen this way."

As they walked through the kitchen, Thorny could hear May asking the woman about how many hours she was working at the Copper Kettle in the kitchen, the posse already at work.

THE LONG DRIVE UP drifted from a hard clam mouth redhead in the front seat with her unsure but frightened friend in the back. Even the hardest clam can crack with mile after mile of hot mountain roads.

The tall pine trees were a welcome shade after the hot, slow drive around Crowley Lake. The WPA was working on twenty miles of highway to make it straighter and safer. Thorny's fingers drummed on the yellow Bakelite of the steering wheel. The construction, which the race would avoid the next day, was in full swing. The movement of the unskilled labor reminded her of a desert tortoise—slowly crawling from bush to bush, nibbling at what would eventually be lunch. The heat could strip the vigor out of even the most energetic young man. The difference between those in front of her was the age. The young men were in other heat—plains of Italy, fields of France, deserts of North Africa, or the jungles of the Pacific islands. These were the men who were left. Most had left their energy in the fields of France during the first great war. Now, they were struggling to feed their families, or just stay alive, and feel worthy of the small bit of silver at the end of the month of employment. Thorny held no judgment about the pace of work—sometimes it took more than a small town learning to barter.

The man, with what was once a lighter fedora, limped over to the first of the two lone cars waiting to get through the construction. The woman with the green glasses and tossed short hair seemed familiar. Her arm rested on the edge of the window jamb.

He resisted the urge to remove the only shade he would get all day. "Miss, I'm sorry about the delay. We thought we could have this boulder pulled out of the hole and work the rampart where we needed it to be over an hour ago. It just isn't happening. The steam shovel just blew a hydraulic hose to the chain wheel. They are saying it will be six o'clock tonight before they can fix it even to get it out of the way." He pushed his hat back with his thumb as he wiped his brow with an already soggy handkerchief. His light khaki shirt was a mottled camouflage of light and darker sweat stains.

"Sir, I'm Police Chief Wallace from down in Bishop…"

His smile widened as he snapped his fingers. "That's where I know you from. And here I was thinking about some newsreel about fliers or something." He stuck out his hand. "Jeff Mapes formerly from Chalfant Valley. The folks had the small truck farm just past the Jessup place. I was already working as a civil engineer when you were walking into town barefoot. Your folk's place was just before the curve there at Laws."

"Grandfather. But, yes, I still own it, and I just saw Jessup the other day."

"How the hell are you? I mean… I heard you got shot… and, well, everything turned into a handbasket on the doorstep of Lucifer himself…"

She rolled her shoulder. "Still a bit stiff, but I can still carry a 30-30 long enough to bring home dinner." She started to reach out with her left claw but stopped short. "Look, we need to burn daylight, but, only if we are moving. I would like to get at least through Walker Canyon before it's too dark to see in there. Is there any way around this?"

He stepped back and looked down the construction area. A small dozer was flattening a low hillside mound. Thorny looked back at the machine belching black smoke in the air. She couldn't tell if it was a Massey Ferguson like they used down in Los Angeles or the International the crew had who drilled her well the year before. The orange-brown of uniform rust had long destroyed the distinctive reds or lettering. What mattered was it was running and moving dirt.

Jeff pulled off his hat and curled his thumb and ring finger in his mouth. He kept whistling as he waved his hat over his head. Finally, they saw the dozer stop and the driver raise his hand. Jeff pulled his arm in a large sweep. And then, shoved both hands as if he was pushing dirt. Finally, he pointed at the small hump of desert, brush, and rocks just up from the highway. The dozer turned and started lumbering its way toward them.

As it drew to a stop next to them, Jeff jumped up onto the tracks, explaining what he wanted. His left arm indicated the knoll as his right knifed on edge over his other hand. The driver paddled his hands downhill as he and Jeff both bobbed their heads. To Thorny, it looked a lot like the dance of sung words and hand language of the older Paiute storytellers. It was a story they understood and, hopefully, would result in a way past all the construction.

"I'm probably still yelling. But I can't hear after I'm up on the dozer." Thorny bobbed her head and smiled. Jeff pointed at the dozer already cutting a flat track through the thick brush and knoll. "Just follow him. If you feel your car start to slump with the dirt—stop. We'll come back and tow you with a rope. It's soft up there, but the two of you should make it through."

Thorny fluttered her hand as she started the Cord. The large engine rumbled to life. The man waved as she cautiously pulled over and into the dozer's tracks. She watched the massive machine and figured he was more likely to *slump with the dirt* before she did. The tracks never blurred as they carefully crept around the half mile of construction. The bolder the man had spoken about was more the size of her ranch house. As they moved past, Thorny could feel the mass and weight of the chunk of the mountains. There was only one way they would ever remove it.

The dozer pivoted and nosed uphill. The last few feet back to the highway was clear. A single car sat in the oncoming lane. A man sat on the front bumper of the DeSoto. Thorny guessed the thermos beside him had long run empty. A man in a rough work shirt and dungarees sat in the shade on the running board. Thorny pulled alongside and stopped.

"Do you work with Jeff Mapes?"

The man looked at her with a heat-sapped face. "Yes, ma'am."

"Tell him I looked over the little rock he is having a problem with. My guess is boring some blasting holes on the face and around the back side should allow him to stick about four cases of sixty-percent three-by-eights in there. Blow it all at once and use the gravel as the new underbed."

"Are you one of them new engineers."

Thorny put the car back into gear. "Just tell him what I said. Sixty-percent unless he has eighty." The car rolled as the man saluted her with two fingers. She looked in the mirror. Pete was right behind her.

She glanced over at the slack jaw face of the brunette. "What?"

The woman snapped her mouth shut and then giggled. "If I told my Roy what to do with dynamite, he would think I was plumb crazy. How you know about dynamite?"

Thorny's eyes watched the tracks in the dirt of the highway. The spring oiling had burned off with the heat, and the hard-pack was now more of a medium between packed and just dirt. She thought about how she knew about oiling roads, packing down dirt or macadam, and blowing up large masses of stone. Her memory box blossomed with even the smell of the sulfur in the match as it flared into life. Ulysses had let her light the detonation cord to celebrate her tenth birthday. That was the day she found out she could run faster than the old miner.

"I grew up learning how to blow up holes in the White Mountains. My uncle had a silver mine. You might say, the lessons made a large impression on me." Her glance covered the faces of both women. The dumb-founded slack jaw had spread to the face of the redhead who seemed hard to impress.

Ernestine's voice was soft and lacked her usual edge. "How much did you ever explode at one time?"

Thorny had to think. When she sealed the lower mine, she had used every stick of dynamite she could get her hands on. She hadn't counted what was in the large pile. She only stacked until she had no more to stack. The pile was over a quarter mile back into the mountain. She had to run the last two hundred yards out of the hole. She set up one of the old mine cars to one side. She laid it on its side with the opening pointed away from the mouth of the mine. The dust had taken an hour to settle and covered the entire camp. The iron of the mine car rang like a giant bell. Thorny's hearing was back to normal two days later.

She peeked at Winnie who now bent forward like a child wanting to hear the end of a story. Thorny smiled. "Flapjack was just a small one-man operation. I don't think we ever blew more than a few sticks at a time. Nothing like the carbide mine above Rovana. They probably go through several boxes every day."

Ernestine leaned forward. "Then how would you know about using four boxes. That seems like a lot of explosives."

Thorny thought about how she knew, and what she felt. In many ways, it was the same as what to do with the two racers and their wives.

"As with many problems in life, there is what you really know, and then what your gut tells you to do." She looked over at Mace's wife. The hard defensive surface was gone. She was out of her comfort zone. "Like the men. The law says to arrest them and lock them away for a long stretch of prison. But then, what do I do with you two? Your knowledge about everything beforehand—the law calls conspiracy. Outside of the rest of the charges—even if it's stealing candy from a four-year-old, conspiracy carries a mandatory sentence of twenty years. Everything else gets added to those twenty."

Winnie gasped—sucking her lips tight in around her teeth. "All of us?" Her head snapped back to look at her longtime friend. "We would never steal candy from no child. Thet be evil."

Thorny rocked slowly. "Yes, all of you knew. But here's the point. If you are all gone, what does Bishop do for mechanics?" She pointed at Winnie. "Who works your shift at the Copper Kettle? Or your hours, Ernestine, at the Golden State or the market?"

The red hair fluttered in the open window as the woman leaned out into the air. "But if we are locked up...?"

"Which is why Stan and I don't want the men clamming up. We need them to help us now, so we can help them stay in Bishop, and help me do what I think is best for you and for Bishop."

Winnie smiled, and Thorny noticed the missing teeth. "Thet be why you the mayor. You're like Bishop's mommy. The town is sick, but you know how to cook it some chicken soup and rub bear fat and cayenne pepper on its chest."

Thorny smiled crookedly. "I don't have any bear fat. Do you think Tule elk fat would work?"

35 THE FINE LINE

Mace and Roy had experienced the phenomenon before. The shells had rained through the overcast night sky. Hot steel had splintered overhead, mixing with the gentle cold water falling from the clouds. The water drizzled down from helmets. Occasionally, an icy drop would trace its way down a shuttering spine, blending with the terror of yet another night of never knowing. Only the gray fog of morning would give the count of who lived and who did not. This night. Last night. Every night. The slender crescent moon was nothing more than the smile of the grim reaper himself. The trenches were nothing but the cordwood of God's woodpile, standing upright as best they could. Every man who had only yesterday been a scared boy was now a shattered frightened man. Aged by war. Beaten into worn-out figures by fear they had no idea was possible. The bones break, the muscle bleeds, but the soul and mind shatter.

The bombs dropped, the shells whistled in, the heartbeat matched the crump of distant explosions, the heart skipped with the close ones. The Germans kept steel and explosives in the air night and day. There was no sleep for days, maybe weeks. The keening of the wounded came in waves from all quadrants of the battlefield. Language was never a problem—pain was universal.

It was the heat and gripping cold of December.

To the man, no one could tell you more. Until the middle of the night. The lights flashing often enough to read from—winked out. The swirling fog calmed and hung breathless in the air. Your eyes adjusted to the dark, and you could see your boots at the bottom of the trench. As you stared, you realized the mud you stood inn was nothing more than last week's dead. You looked up. It no longer held horror. Your stomach had stopped churning the second week. Now it was just numb like your ears.

The sudden ending of noise is deafening. You don't know if you can hear or not. You grapple to the ladder. Fumbling in confusion, you grab for a handhold. A second and third try. Finally, you secure your grip and hold to the ladder as if it is the girl you last kissed. You don't remember and don't care. The hiss of your blood returning to the tortured ears sounds like something frying—but even knowing what frying is, it's a faded memory. Boots thud dully on the wood rungs of the mud-slimmed ladders. Four rungs bring eyes level with dirt mounded along the edge. Nothing moves the soft cottony swirls of gray morning fog. The stench of burned cordite, rotting tissue, and rusting hulks of metal had long become the normal odor of the field.

What once had been a spare forest, now looked more like a sandbox for giant children. Mounds of dirt heaped randomly, thrown about from explosions. Bits and pieces of metal and wood. Carts, dead horses, busted cannons, an ambulance with half of a single wheel left. The dark and tattered canvas sides hung as hopeless as the rotting slug of what was once a driver or attendant. Toys, broken and tossed aside—littering the play box. All mirth and childhood abandoned.

The edges of the trenches humped with metal mounds. Helmets. English, French, Spanish, American, those issued, and those found.

The sunken eyes but black shadows under the rims. Two dull rings of lighter death—staring at the silence and utter calm.

In the distance, more trenches. Tiny green trees poked in the mud along the lines of last night's death.

A soft clear note wavered in the air. Followed by two more. A German song. Long translated for English children. French words, Spanish melodies. A universal nod to the tree and family. As the harmonica from the German trench continued, a tinny tone of a penny-whistle joined from across the wasteland. Soon, the words blended from every language.

For a brief moment, Hell held its breath. It was Christmas.

THE TWO FRONT tires rolled forward. The brothers in arms, brothers in their hearts, gripping each other's arms, watched as the two tires rolled across the painted line. The red, white, and blue crepe-paper ribbon slipped from the hands of the two boy scouts. The silence seared into the frying sizzle in their ears.

The crepe-paper fluttered about them as they rolled to a stop. Every eye had turned to the large clock face on the small tower atop the bank building. The hand kicked back and then ticked forward. 11:56.

The noise surged back. But this time it wasn't nine hours and four hundred miles of two motorcycles with straight pipes. It wasn't the warble of eighty inches pounding with two pistons each. It wasn't the war. It was a welcoming.

The two men focused on the metal links binding their women together. Their eyes slid to the woman standing next to them—bracketed by two men. Each had a badge hanging from their belts. The five were not smiling. Only Thorny nodded.

The crowd of hundreds surged forward, surrounding the men. Even if they had gas, there was nowhere to run, no way to escape. Prisoners of their own success.

"Gentlemen." Two men in racing jackets stood with their hands out. "On behalf of Harley Davidson and Indian, we have decided in the case of a dead heat, each of these envelopes contains the owner documents for your respective motorcycles, as well as checks in the amount of the winning purse. Congratulations, gentlemen, on an amazingly run race." The four men shook as they exchanged envelopes.

The men were replaced by a formidable man in a sheriff's uniform. "Mace, Roy, it has come to our attention, since crossing into our fair state an hour ago, you have broken eleven-speed limits. You have refused to yield the highway to a herd of sheep, did not stop at two stop signs in Gardnerville and Minden, ignored the flag raising at the state capital and did not stop to salute. I'm sure there were some other shenanigans we can think of as you serve out your sentence as guests of honor tonight at the Silver Nugget." He handed each of them their tickets.

"But, before you get away." The small man in a light gray linen suit stepped forward with two large gold colored keys. "Roy, Mace, as mayor of this fine city, I welcome you, and with these keys, I hereby make you honorary citizens of Carson City, Nevada." His one hand and thumb jerked back at the sheriff. "And, if he tries to pull any funny stuff, these are your get out of jail free keys." The crowd roared and cheered.

The two men smiled at the cheers and fun, but their eyes were still locked on the three people whose faces were set in stone. Eventually, the two racers knew it would be their turn.

A man with a sport coat and microphone stepped in. "Mace and Roy, Bill Garnett with World Race News. Gentlemen, we have been hanging on every word of every report since the race began in the cold desert at three this morning. First, let me say what a great race it was. And, at times, a downright nail-biter. But I know this next question is on every listener's mind. It was almost freezing this morning, you have raced across four hundred miles, with the wind-chill at eighty miles an hour at times. The temperature right now is standing at a cool one hundred and nine degrees. So, answer us this: Have you warmed up yet?"

Mace smiled and glanced over at his friend. It was an old joke shared among long-distance racers. Turning back, he stood with his motorcycle between his legs. He rubbed his hands up and down on the back of his jeans. "Well, Bill, just now, I stood up. A little bit of cold I had trapped when I sat down nine hours ago is starting to warm up."

"Spoken like a true long-distance racer, Mace." The man held out the microphone to Roy. Roy shook his head and pointed at Mace. He drew back the microphone.

"It looks like Roy is still so cold he can't speak. Mace, tell us about running this long of a distance. Would you do it again?"

Mace sat back down. "I hope I never have to again. There is a reason all the long races are run in cars. I love motorcycles, but there is no padding on these old sittin' bones, and the thin piece of leather on metal stopped being fun before the first pit stop."

"Folks, what Mace is describing is to save weight and lower their bodies out of the wind, the springs under the seats are cut down to half, and the normal padding on the seats have been replaced with a paper-thin layer of rough calf hide glued to the metal pan of the small racing seat. Mace, it doesn't look comfortable."

Roy grumbled with a screwed-up face. Mace nodded. "They weren't."

"We heard Roy laid down the Indian instead of hitting a herd of sheep. Did you have any other near accidents?"

Mace pointed at the ground away rubber on his left handlebar grip. "There was a large rock in the last canyon who wanted to give me a hug."

Thorny turned to face Stan and lowered her face to hide her voice. "How long do you think this will go on?"

Stan rolled his lower lip as he pushed his fedora back on his head. "The guy from the news has to sell the time they are charging their sponsors. But it sounds like he got a full tank of gas before they hit town… so I'd say it's up to you. You're the lead on this." He peeked over at the two wives. Behind Thorny's back, he waved them over. "I think with this posse of two, you have the right to break it up and let the men hit the toilets. I heard they drank a lot of water and got plenty to eat, but did you hear them once get a rest break?"

She looked up and smirked. The power of a good woman is strong, but the power of the need for a toilet can trump even the most verbose reporter. She turned to Winnie and Nessie. "Give me the cuffs." She quietly unlocked the manacles. "We need to wind this show up and get the motorcycles into custody."

Turning, she led the women through the crowd to the racers. "Gentlemen, as much as the world of motorsports needs these men, their wives have been without them for too long. And I think the men might want to use the facilities. It's been a long drive and no rest break. You can talk with them more at tonight's celebration barbeque and fireworks." Turning, he looked at Mace. "Gentlemen, I'm going to exchange you your motorcycles for your wives. We will be storing them for safekeeping. And if you require the use of the closest facility, you can push the motorcycles this way."

She turned and waved a break in the crowd. Most didn't know who she was, but the badge was not to be questioned. Nor was the look on the woman's face. The crowd parted like the Red Sea. Each wife took their husband's arm and talked quietly as they pushed their motorcycles. Both women knew they only have a hundred feet to the bank. And then, it was Thorny's job.

THORNY STOOD QUIETLY with the women as the men were busy in the bank. She looked at Ernestine as she figured Roy would go along with whatever move Mace would make. She knew they couldn't run, but stonewalling would only force all the weight of the law to crash down on them. "Nessie, what do you think? Will Mace help us?"

She bit her lower lip as she snapped her head to one side—looking back down the hill toward town. "Hard to tell with him sometimes. I think he's sitting in there talking things over with Roy. They just raced nine hours thinking one thing, only to find something different."

She looked back at Thorny as Stan came out the door and stood with them. "He wanted to know how you knew about the diamonds. He also asked why Big Mike knew about them doing this." She hung her head and wagged it gently. "I just don't know. Some days he likes beef and other days only trout. He's a strong-willed man."

Stan looked at the black motorcycle. His voice was low. "Do you know which tank they're in?" His finger waved back and forth over the split tanks.

"I think it's the left one. If you open the cap and pull it, the chain and tee to keep it attached so you don't drop it has a thin wire connected to it. The pit crews wouldn't be paying enough attention in the rush so they wouldn't have seen it."

Stan leaned against the tank as his right hand unscrewed the cap. He let it hang on the small chain and felt the crossbar on the tee. The wire was soft and small like the wire braided for a light cord. He pulled gently on the wire. Soon a narrow sock of gauzy fabric appeared in his hand. He let it slide back down into the tank. He left the cap off and hanging by the chain.

The two men stepped out into the sunshine. They looked around. The local sheriff and his deputies were standing in a large circle—keeping any curiosity seekers at bay. The six were alone. Mace stepped up to Thorny. "Mayor? Or should I say Chief?"

"Mace, for right now, I'd rather this be more about Thorny. For this moment, it's more important for you to hear what I have to say, and then we can talk as your lawyer or as the chief."

The man blustered for a second, but when he spied the gas cap, his chest slowly fell with a sigh. "Okay... Thorny?"

"Good. First, I want you to meet Stan. Stan is with the FBI. What we work out, he has the authority to accept it and back it. We have the West Coast Director's word on it. Next, I need you to listen very carefully because it's not anything I've ever dealt with in a court of law."

Mace chewed on a piece of his lower lip. His eyes slid over to Roy and back. "Okay, we're listening."

"Mike Rambino wants you to know he will pay for any attorney you need or want, no matter what you do. And you need to understand his offer is unconditional. So, if you plan to stonewall me, he will still find you a lawyer and pay for appeals up to and including the day you stand in front of a firing squad for treason." She let the weight of the final sentence sink in.

"Transporting stolen goods only carries a sentence—"

She stopped him with her hand. "Do you understand what Mike is offering?"

"Yes." The man shifted his weight from one hip to the other. "But the sentence..."

Her hand rose again. "If you picked up a stolen pistol in Los Angeles, and drove it up here, you would be right. Even with crossing the state line, it would only be three to five. But your wives knew ahead of time. Three people or more, with prior knowledge, makes it a conspiracy, and I don't even need the man who hired you. Conspiracy carries a mandatory twenty on top of the crime. And, because they knew, your wives will be serving time up at the women's prison in Vacaville."

His mouth opened in protest. The look on Thorny's face closed it.

"Good. Now, the crime of transporting is only part of this mess. The fact the stones were stolen from the English government, which was bringing them to pay on their debt to the United States, means it was espionage. And that carries the death penalty before a firing squad. You would be bound over and tried in a federal court for high treason. I don't know if they would make you serve the twenty, then the three-to-five, and then shoot you or not. I also don't know if they would shoot all four of you or just the two of you. All I know is if you help us get the people who hired you, we can work out your sentence and keep it all in Bishop." She raised her green glasses onto the top of her head. "Personally, I think it's in the best interest of you, your wives, and Bishop if we can do it my way. But it's all up to you two.

"What do we have to do?" He looked over at Roy who dipped his head.

"How are you delivering the diamonds?"

"The motors will be held in the High Sierra Motor Transfer warehouse. It's a bonded holding warehouse. During the night, they will come and pull the sock out of the gas tank. We don't have to be there."

"Would it be the people who hired you or one of their goons?"

"Probably a goon. Except the stones are a valuable load, even just a few can be rewarding. Pulling some of the rocks out of the sock wouldn't be hard…"

Thorny wiped her chin in thought as she looked over at the sheriff. She waved with her eyes. Mace looked at the sheriff. Her hand still covered her mouth. "Do you think they have connections?"

Mace's head made very small shifts. "They're here just to get the diamonds cut. They're from out Chicago way. I'm pretty sure, once the diamonds are cut, they will be gone."

Thorny looked up. "What do you think Stan?"

Stan scratched the side of his face. "We have seven of our guys, Pete, and you…" He turned and called to the sheriff. The man kept vigilant but walked over.

"What can I help with?"

Thorny pulled her glasses down and looked back down the street. It was all a gamble. She noticed the four casinos within pistol range of where they stood. If she had to gamble, this was the town for it. "Sheriff, we have a potential problem. Tonight, we think the Motor Transfer warehouse is going to be knocked over. These motorcycles, because of this race, have become the most valuable motorcycles in the country if not the world. To protect them, we need to be able to trust whoever we have help us."

"How many do you think you need?" The man crossed his arms, and his right hand was already stroking his jowls in thought.

"Just you and two others. That way, if you sell us out, I don't have to kill any more people than I have to."

The man froze and then smiled. "I'd add one other, the man who hired me twenty-eight years ago. His brother built the warehouse, and Phil worked on the side helping him. We didn't get paid much in the lean years."

"Deal." She put her hand out, and his hand swallowed hers.

"Do you know who is going to hit the warehouse?"

She turned. "Mace?"

"Hans Clapp, but I don't know if he'll do it personally."

"Where is he staying?"

"Out at the old Babcock Seminary."

The sheriff grimaced. "I know the place. There is only one activity they do there religiously." He turned to Thorny. "If we know what he's driving, we can set up a watch in the bar. If he moves, we can get a call."

Stan wiped his brow. "What if he sends a goon or two instead?"

"I can still pick him up and hold him while we crack the goon."

Thorny clustered her hands at the front of her pants. "How long can you hold him?"

The man smiled. "What are they really trying to steal? These motorcycles are a dime-a-dozen."

Stan cleared his throat. "Very valuable property of the United States government and critical to the war effort?"

"Valuable enough to trigger the espionage act?"

Thorny dipped her head. "More than a few times over."

The man's smile grew. "Well, hell then. This is the wild west, and I'll hold them until the next Indian uprising."

Thorny snorted. "When was the last one?"

"These are Washoe. We never had one. Some of the nicest people you'll ever meet."

Thorny smiled. Charlie would be happy to hear of it. She looked at Mace and Roy. "I bet you boys would like to go get a nap before the big shindig tonight."

Mace smiled. "Which one? The dinner and fireworks or the fireworks after?"

Mace stared out the open window as the desert reversed from the day before. The hot wind on the motorcycle was now a tempered breeze playing with his hair. His eyelids gently bounced from closed to half open in his torpor of exhaustion. He had paced and tried to read until three in the morning when Thorny finally knocked on the hotel room's door.

Even with the good news, he had only slept fitfully. The warm body and soft head of hair under his arm, which usually caused him to calm, had only tempered the vibrating body.

He pulled his eyes open and stretched. He turned and pushed his back against the doorpost and seat. He studied the young woman who seemed to have generations of sense about her. He had seen Thorny smile but never openly laugh. Becoming the towns seven or twelve open jobs, in one short leap, never appeared to disturb her. She woke up one morning as the town's trusted replacement for the police chief she had killed the night before. By lunch, she was also the head of the town council. Dessert came served with a side of keys to the city as mayor, and by naptime, she was streets commissioner, county commissioner, judge, prosecutor, and a few other jobs the town's women had voted her into. The town folk had chuckled, though, and then chuckled more as they swung their heads. Every job made sense. Every job could pay at least a few dollars to a woman who hadn't landed a job since returning home the year before.

He remembered her as a strange scrawny girl with a short mop of hair that looked self-cut, shirts made from flour sakes, and bib overalls turned up above her bare feet. No matter where he drove, the girl was walking. The only people he ever remembered her with were her grandfather, the old miner Flapjack, and the Paiute Chief and his grandson Charlie. Everyone knew her, and if they thought anything about her, it would probably have turned out to be a big ball of wound up nothing.

The woman looked over. The shadows of her eyes barely showed through the green of her glasses. He thought she would say something but, instead, returned her attention to the highway.

"I wanted to tell you how much... what it..." His words froze harder as she squinted over.

She shifted the Cord into top gear. "It was my job."

Mace's breath was only a soft, airy snort. "Which one?"

He watched as the thin smile tugged gently at the side of her mouth. Her eye shifted and looked sideways at him. Her head lightly tossed a yes as it rolled over toward her left shoulder. "I never know. Somedays they all roll into one. Others, they scatter, and I'm only left with the slow runner."

"I would say, last night, you were the police chief helping the FBI."

She peeked over. "I think you would have liked being there. Your phone call was what brought Mr. Clapp out of the seminary. Rounding up his other four crew and partner were unforeseen bonuses." She looked over and held his eyes. "What made you think of his goon cheating him?"

The man pulled his left leg up on the bench seat. He reached under the pant leg and down into the sock—slowly scratching as he thought.

"When we were locking up the motorcycles, I could hear the man in the office talking to his wife or girlfriend. Either way, it was friendly, but there was pressure there. He was making promises of taking her out for a fancy dinner this weekend. I started thinking about a fancy dinner and what that could turn into if the man were corrupt enough to also steal some of the diamonds."

Thorny smirked. "And a hint, with time to think, can turn into a lecture." She looked over and studied the man and his half-smile. There was no satisfaction there. He had betrayed the person who hired him. He had broken confidence. But he had made a stronger contract years before with his country, his honor, and his wife. "You did the right thing. Take honor in what right you did, not in the wrong of a person with no honor."

"I just worry…" He looked in the backseat. Pete and Ernestine had both barely kept awake to the border. Only Thorny and he had seen the herd of deer cross the road at the southern tip of Topaz Lake, headed for higher and cooler ground. The tiny pink tip of his wife's tongue rested on her lower lip like a light shadow. His voice lowered as he continued. "We are so far in arrears on our houses and the shop. I don't know if even our double purse will cover everything—even if we sell both motorcycles."

Thorny pulled the Cord around a small pothole. Her foot never let up on the throttle. "I haven't talked to the bank yet, but by next week, you will have a new lienholder. I hear she can be kind of hard at times. I know for a fact she has some ideas as well as some new rules."

"The winnings?"

Thorny leaned her hair out into the wind stream. The high mountain walls trapped the cold of the rushing river in the narrow canyon. The cool reminded her of the fall winds as they moaned down the canyon to strip the Aspen trees of their leaves and remind the land of the coming winter. A one-handed flip of water was all Charlie needed to reach over and adjust the water flow for heat.

She sat back upright and refreshed. "I think you're going to need some new equipment for rebuilding diesel trucks. I know of one I need to be in top condition before the leaves turn. He's going to need to haul several full loads of lumber from the steam mill."

He nodded. "We've needed better machinery since twenty-six. I've been shaping brake shoes by hand. It works for a while, but the drums need milling to make them true and round, but there isn't a mill or lathe in town. Out of round isn't a big problem for old man Jessup, but if someone is hauling a full five-ton, there's going to be hell to pay when the drums shatter."

"Charlie said you don't have the right tools to work on some of the new cars either. His fuel truck needs a new transmission or something... There is just so much here. People have made do or put off because of no money or rationing. But this war won't be going on forever, and when the men get back home, they need to get back to work, not working at fixing everything."

The man hung his head over into his left hand, his arm bent on the back of the seat. "It all sounds good, but where does the money come from.?"

"I have enough money to put a better kitchen and bathroom on my house. Over it all, I need a new roof. Not patching, but a new roof. Ulysses helped my grandfather hang the old tin in 1902. The rust is the only solid part holding it all together. Mr. Ferguson never complained, but I know he climbed up there and put seven patches on last winter. The patches he made by hammering out soup cans. Heaven knows where he got the cans. I don't even know if the missus even has a real can opener. But the point is, they are in their seventies and need indoor plumbing. The kitchen never was big enough to do all the canning she does every year. But, even if she still wants to do her canning out under the cottonwood, I want it to be her choice, not the kitchen."

He started to explain about him being a mechanic, not a carpenter. She stopped him with her finger.

"The carpenter needs lumber from the steam mill. But making a dozen trips of light loads is going to kill his truck just as sure as hauling a real load. What I'm paying him is more than enough for you to rebuild his engine, fix his harness and reins, and get his mules in a team."

"Horses."

"What?"

"You said mules. Engines are measured in break horsepower—not mules."

Her face was pure stone as it ground around to face the man. "Where do you live?"

He had to think. "Bishop?" She was slipping down a slope he wasn't used to. He thought about all the horses people owned... but most couldn't reproduce. They were mules. He chuckled. "Carry on. So I fix Shaker's truck. He fixes your house, you pay him, and he pays me..."

"And you pay on your mortgage."

The smile puckered out his right cheek. "What other circle have you worked out?"

"What's the condition of the town's fire truck?"

"It was old when they bought it beat-up and broken from Los Angeles."

"So we need a new truck... or at least a better used truck. Do we need a second one? I already know we need an ambulance. Digger's cemetery truck isn't fast enough or clean enough to save lives. I think the police department is getting a car. It will be used, and we'll have to repaint the shield on the door, but we're getting one. What else can you two fix?"

She caught the flash of the man's right hand and finger-pointing back at his wife. "If people don't have a problem with a woman doing a man's work... there sleeps one fine plumber. She knows her way around wiring also. Back in twenty-seven, we did a job and got a long spool of house wire. She pulled the old knob and tube wiring off the outside of our two houses and rewired them. Winnie done helped. She's not the smartest fox in the henhouse, but she follows directions good. They be one heck of a team."

Thorny peeked at the rearview mirror. The two bodies in the back seat hadn't moved since Minden. She harrumphed soft and smiled at the man. "Explain to me what man's work actually is. Or tell me which one of my jobs I should find a man to do."

Mace's smile was soft and to one side as he winked.

"Then my wire and pipe problem just became more payments on the mortgage and bills. See, in just a short forty miles, we have solved next year's problems." She smiled as she looked out the side of her eyes at him. "Now, about the rest of Bishop…"

37 BARGAINS

The two largest tables stood pushed together. Monte fussed about straightening the silverware as May fluffed the hollyhock and dandelion blooms in the low bowl. She knew this meal and the attendees would want unobstructed views of the others.

Monte frowned. "Is there a cake dessert?"

May closed her eyes, realizing they were both getting older. They opened as her head rose and looked at her oldest friend. Her voice was soft with a small hint of remorse. "No. I have three quarts of canned peach slices left."

The man rested one hand on the back of a chair as he rocked back on his heels. "Those will need to last until the canning starts at the end of the month. I think coffee is enough." Without explaining, he started picking up what would have been the small desert forks for a cake. May noticed she was short two. If she had baked a cake, she knew who the two would have turned down any dessert, and she knew how Monte loved his small ration of sweets. But she also knew how driven he was about propriety.

The first warning was a soft knock on the door.

The man stood on the stoop with his gray fedora in his hands. May smiled. "You must be Paul Forte, the, um… let's see…"

"I believe I'm the prosecuting attorney this round. Thorny will be defending." He stepped to one side and motioned toward the young man with him. "This is Jonathan Sullivan, your new judge."

The man stepped up and extended his hand. "If I understand the protocol here, you would be May, and so, please, call me Jon."

"Jon, Paul, pleased to meet you both. Please, come in. You're the first to arrive, but I don't expect our police chief to be late."

The two men stepped in. Turning, they hung their suit coats and hats. Monte stood behind the now large table and watched with interest as the two men quietly toed off their shoes as they looked around. Guiding stockinged feet edged the shoes to one side. Monte toed off his shoes and socks. With practiced skill, he guided the set under the heavily draped side table before walking around.

May turned. "Monte, we have the first of our guests. Paul is Thorny's former boss, and young Jon here is our new judge. Gentlemen, may I present the last of the male guiding lights in Thorny's life, Monte Geronimo. He's still a bit wild with a carving knife, but superior with a straight razor and scissors."

As they were shaking, the door opened. Thorny stepped in and to one side. Winnie hesitated until Ernestine pushed her gently from behind. The men came next, followed by Stan. May smiled as everyone met and migrated toward the table, she noticed Stan stop for a moment to remove his shoes. Word was getting around.

Thorny stood back, watching the group take seats. She was glad to see the seating didn't take on opposing sides. There were four empty seats. Thorny frowned at May in askance. The woman rolled her tongue and then her eyes.

As she stepped back to open the door, she quietly reminded Thorny of the day. "After all, it is Sunday."

Inez and Bertha stood smiling at the door. Their shoes were already in their hands. The four women hugged as the door swung quietly shut. Thorny whispered in the two women's ears as she hugged them. *I'm so glad you're here.*

The conversation started off hesitant and unsure. Thorny had stepped in and stopped the confusion about the nature of the meal. "The plea bargain was struck before the real criminals were caught. Tomorrow is only about making our new judge official, and the formal execution of the bargain. The sentencing is as close to standard as the circumstances allow. I think we have come to some semblance of compromise, between national heroes for unearthing traitors within our borders, and sending Mace, Roy, and all concerned up the river for an extended useless stay in prison. But, that, as I said, is for tomorrow. Today is to enjoy being home, welcoming a new member to our community, and enjoying the first of, I hope, many visits from an old friend."

As the talk flowed from business to observations of those new to Bishop, Paul turned to Inez. "And what is your place in all of this?"

She blushed as she raised her napkin to dab at her mouth. She nodded at Bertha across the table. "Why, sir, I thought it would be obvious. Birdie and I are here merely to temper all the manliness filling the room."

Monte choked and recovered. "Paul, they are here to look pretty. But on any other barefoot Sunday, they are major contributors to the sleuthing of old dead cases we fester out of the bowels of dusty boxes and records."

"So, you're a detective? You ferret out and know the evil men do?"

Thorny covered her mouth and feigned dabbing at her mouth. "More than you can guess, Paul. And they are very professional at it. I would say, these two would be in a class with only one other who is so valuable at her knowledge." Her one eyebrow was arched.

Paul thought about who Thorny and he would know. More importantly, a woman who knew the workings of men. Thorny smiled as she saw the light turn on behind the man's eyes. "My daughter."

Thorny dipped her head. "And, to this table, they are every bit as valuable to me as your daughter is to you. Perhaps even more so. After all, I do have two of them."

Paul digested the information about all three women. He had tried to ignore his daughter's extracurricular evening's pursuits but now understood what it could mean, and what she brought to her job and professionalism during the day in his office.

"I think you have reminded me of just what an asset I have been overlooking. I think I need to have more talks with her when I get back. I also believe I find myself marginally jealous of your advantage of two to my one."

Thorny took in the shy smiles of the two women who were now valued for their expertise of the minds and actions of men. "I think if you treat Inez right, you may find her willing to be available for consultations. I think with a good word, Mike Rambino may see his way clear to provide transport to Los Angeles on occasion."

The man smiled at the rest of the connection. "Her coming to Los Angeles may not work out. On the drive up here, we saw a couple of herds of what looked like large deer or elk." His eyebrows were raised.

Stan snorted. "They are Tule elk. A good buck will yield a quarter ton of fresh meat or a couple hundred in dried jerky. I didn't know you hunted."

As the man bobbed his head, he wiped his mouth and swallowed. "What is the preferred weapon?"

Stan smiled and looked at Thorny. She blushed. "Anything quiet enough to not spook the rest of the herd. We usually like to drop two or three in an evening. A 30-30 at a half mile is good. But I believe Stan may prefer his new rifle he… um… acquired last year."

The man turned with a question on his face. He sensed he was in well over his head. Stan smiled. "It uses a 30-06 slug, but the shell is a necked down Holland and Holland 600 elephant hunting shell. Everything about it is custom. But it's good for a mile or more in calm, cool air."

The man's eyes opened wide and bounced from Thorny to Stan.

"Sounds like a sniper rifle..." And then the man remembered. He leaned in. "How is your shoulder doing?"

Thorny twisted her head in a swing. "About as good as Stan's. But we're both ready for stocking the barn full of drying meat. It might be another long winter, and the town can use some extra food put away. Interested in helping?"

Winnie was squirming and looked at her husband. Thorny caught her movement out of the corner of her eye. "Winnie?"

She jerked. Her eyes were wide as if caught doing something wrong. "What?"

"I know you know cooking. Is there something you wanted to say about the jerky?"

Roy cleared his throat to intercede. Thorny's face turned to stone, and her look stopped him cold. Her voice was lower this time. More insistent and comforting. "Winnie?"

The voice was soft—barely more than a whisper. It was not the voice Thorny could imagine in the busy kitchen at the Copper Kettle. "These past years we done get by with a lot of jerky. But we can't make enough fast enough. We was using a small wood rack from a bunch of sticks. Roy be real good with inventing things." She straightened as she took a deep breath. She was surer, as everyone at the table was intent on what she had to say. "When the coons get in the small house and steal all the meat... well, he done made a metal house. It be a lot faster too. We used to hang the long strips on the fence wire in the sun, but this be even faster."

Monte shifted. "How big?"

Thorny's face softened, and her eyebrows rose as she looked back at Roy. The man was chagrined but also proud of his wife for speaking up. "I made it from most of two panels of corrugated tin roofing. There were a few rusted holes, but it lets the chamber breathe. The secret is you don't want to cook the meat, you just want it to dry out. I figure the sun gets it close to two hundred or so. But it's only about the size of an oven. Its got about a foot and a half depth, but it fits some old oven racks we found at the dump.

We were also thinking about building a brick firebox and run the smoke through it maybe."

"How fast is it on how much meat?"

"We started the end of May, and we have about Winnie's weight in jerky now."

Thorny wrinkled her nose as she thought about Charlie's drying rack still draped in the previous months' kill. It was close but not done. "How much meat do you stick in at a time?"

"About ten pounds."

She was running the numbers, but Bertha's math was faster. "So, you stick in ten pounds tonight, and tomorrow dinner, you take out the jerky and put in the next meat. So it only takes a day?"

Winnie's smile was large enough to show her missing teeth. "We like the thinner jerky, so it don't take so long. But, also it easier to break and make chip in the winter."

Jon's head twitched in a corkscrew of confusion. "Chip?"

May laughed at the young man from the city. "You're going to have to run fast to catch up with living out here in the country. Have you ever had chipped beef on a biscuit or toast?"

"I'm not sure I..."

Paul laughed. "He has. He just didn't know what it was." He turned to the new judge. "Down at the deli, they sell it as creamed beef on a muffin. In the Army, it is exactly what it tastes like SOS."

The four older men laughed. At one time or another, they had all been privy to the most special of military cuisine. Usually, it was bad meat of some kind, disguised as edible.

Ernestine lowered her one eye as she smirked with the men. Turning, she took pity on the young man. "SOS is not about saving anything but rotting meat. You cut off the green stuff, slice the meat thin and then chop it all up. Smother it in a spiced gravy and glop it down on a slice of day old toast. It still tastes like its name: shit on a shingle."

Pointing at Winnie who was now laughing as hard as the men, she made her point. "If you reconstitute jerky made with just the right amount of pepper and salt, you get the heaven Winnie cooks up. Even if the jerky was road-kill, with a little water from the well, some fine ground flour, and in her hands you have a dinner you could invite the minister and his wife to."

The two men had stopped laughing and were now nodding in witness. Mace pulled his lips into his mouth over his teeth. "My guess would be some families went for many nights with less. First the depression, and now this war, it be taking a dirty toll on good people." He flopped his hand in the air toward Thorny. "What she wants to do is help people help themselves. One house might have a hundredweight of flour. It might be a coarse utility, but we can show them how to mill it as fine as you want in a mortar and pestle. Some house might have a boy who can shoot rabbits, another catch fish, and maybe someone has chickens for eggs. If we all bring what we can, we can make a stew or creamed chip out of boiling water and magical stone. But we gots ta work together."

The truck pulled up across the street. Thorny sipped on her second cup of coffee as she watched through the police department's window. She guessed that Winnie must have sat on Roy's lap for the four of them to fit in the cramped cabin of the 1928 Ford truck. Except for the green paint, it was a match for Monte's Model T car. She wondered if they could all fit during the winter when the windows needed to be rolled up.

She stepped over and opened the door. "Good morning. It's still early, and they are still swearing in Jon as the judge. Did any of you want coffee? We just brewed a fresh pot." She smiled as she heard John, her officer, scramble to go refill the pot which was at least half empty.

Mace fiddled with his string tie. Matched with the work shirt and dungarees over his work boots, it was a surprise nod to the convention of getting dressed up for his court date. "We had coffee with breakfast. I think we'll just stand out here in the beautiful morning sun."

Thorny could hear the jingle of keys on John's belt as he stood up straight, listening for confirmation of his reprieve from coffee duty.

Winnie patted Roy's hand and let go. Ernestine bobbed her head and whispered to Mace as she shooed the men toward the front of the building where the small courtroom was.

The women stepped over to Thorny but watched the men until they disappeared around the front of the building. They turned as Winnie massaged her teeth with her rubbery lips. "Can we talk?" She peeked inside to see if John was in earshot.

Thorny sensed the delicate matter and invited them in. "Why don't we talk in my office. It will be more private."

The women nodded and almost ran her over as they followed.

Thorny eased herself down on the desk as she watched the two women take the only two seats. It was almost like watching the bundle of energy of young calves.

"Winnie, how about you just tell me what's on your mind."

"Is this Jon going to be a real judge?"

Thorny's coffee mug froze halfway to her mouth. She lowered it thinking. "That's why they are swearing him in right now. We'll mail the paperwork up to Sacramento later today, but everything he does today will carry the full weight of the law."

"So, he… the other legal… I mean…"

Ernestine put her hand on the arm of the nervous bunny before she jumped out of her skin. "What we want to know is will he also be a justice of the peace… or whatever it is who marries people?"

Winnie popped. "Can he marry us?"

Thorny hadn't expected the question. She started to take a sip of coffee, and then thought better of it and placed it safely on her desk. Her head cocked as she looked sideways at the two women. She pointed her finger in a wave. "You two women?"

"Yeas."

In horror, Ernestine realized what had been asked. "No! I mean yes we want to get married, but me and Mace and them two."

"But you're already married."

The two women blushed. Slowly they shook their heads. "At

first, we couldn't afford to. Then, it was... Well, we were embarrassed that we had been livin' in sin all them years."

"So why now?"

"We done talked it over last night. You makin' our men honest and all, we was thinking maybe they ought to be honest all the way."

Thorny thought she needed to sit down and then remembered she already was. She brought her hands up to her face and washed and rubbed her eyes. As her hands finally fell, she looked at the women. "Are the men agreeing to this?"

"They thunk of it. Well, Roy did after I poked him where it make him giggle."

Thorny closed her eyes and pulled them open—stretching her face. She stood. "Well, let's get to it." Remembering her coffee, she reached and grabbed it. She looked in the mug wishing it was something more than brown water. "And I thought your probation was complicated."

JOHN STOOD straight as the door opened. Only John, Thorny, and the new judge knew it was only a large closet. "All rise. The Honorable Judge Jonathan..." He turned to the man and asked in a whisper. "What is your last name again?"

The young man chuckled. "We're going to get along just fine. It's Sullivan, just like the boxer."

John mulled the information over in his head. "The Honorable Judge John L. Sullivan presiding."

The judge hesitated and smiled. "Good enough."

He took his seat at the standard wooden desk and looked at the small courtroom—now almost half filled by only six people. He waved them down. "Please be seated."

He shuffled four pieces of paper, a folded envelope with notes on it, a tattered old calendar, and a thin folder. "I see by the docket we have a very busy day ahead of us, so let's get right to it."

Thorny rose. "Your Honor, I'd like to request a sidebar."

The young judge blinked and glanced back at the door which might, in a larger court, hide an office. "You do? Um… I mean… Where?"

Thorny's face was passively stone. "In your chambers, I would imagine." She indicated the door.

The judge let out a soft *eep* as the prosecuting and defense attorneys both stood. He rose to match the two attorneys. "Court will be in recess. Counselors, may I see you in my chambers?" He looked for a gavel. Finding none, he used his knuckles.

Paul chuckled softly once the door shut. The room could only hold a few small chairs at best. The rough plaster had never gotten the second coat. Three shades of whitewash covered only parts of the walls. Standing next to the mop in a bucket, broom, and shovel would keep any future sidebars to a minimum amount of time. "I think my first real office was this size. I'm sure you will grow on it."

Jon looked around at the floor. "I seem to have misplaced my desk."

Thorny's mouth was tightly pursed. Her eyes twinkled in mirth. The judge looked up at her one squeak of a chuckle. Quietly, she stuck out her hand in congratulations. "Welcome to the big times."

"Thank you, I think? Now, what about this sidebar?"

Her eyes still carried their mirth. "I guess this office is very fitting." She hung her claw on the end of the mop handle. "You see, there are a couple of things to clean up here."

The man rolled his index finger in the air. "Let's move it along, counselor." She knew he was enjoying his new role.

"It has recently come to light of an ongoing crime being committed. We need you to put an end to it during sentencing. I'm sure it will be condemning them all to life at hard labor, but nothing they haven't been performing already."

"And this came to your attention when?"

"This morning your Honor. Just minutes ago. In my office."

"You have a real office?" He fanned his hand. "Strike that. This crime is…?"

"The two couples are not couples. They have been living in sin for the better part of twenty years. They need you to marry them."

The young judge closed one eye and looked accusingly at his former boss.

Paul put up his hands. "I knew nothing about this. This is all news to me. But, as prosecutor, I would move to have the court render sentencing to the full extent of the law."

The judge rocked slightly. "Any motion for plea?"

Thorny flattened her lips and winked. "I see no reason to prevent them from making honest women out of them."

"Agreed. Now let's go get this dog and pony show on the road."

Thorny stopped him with her hand on his chest. "This is Bishop."

"Yesss…?"

"This town has a few horses—damn few. Most of all the riding animals around here are mules."

He smiled. "So, let's get this dog and mule show on the road."

She patted his black robe and smiled. "You're going to fit right in."

"They met the summer after the fellas returned."

"But never married."

"Sometimes you wait for the right moment. But never see there is no such moment. There are just many moments, pick one. None are right, and none are wrong—they're just moments."

"Old Paiute tell me once there is no right way to walk trail. Only feet in front of feet knows right way. But only one time. Next time trail is not same and feet are new too."

"If they are still my feet, how can they be new?"

The man rose steaming out of the warm water. "If you walk path yesterday, your feet are yesterday's feet. Today, they are one day older. New feet have never walked trail before."

"They did it yesterday."

"No. Those were yesterday's feet."

Her hand found the elk-hide pouch between her breasts. She fingered the lumps. She had sealed the pouch the previous year. The new, third lump, had appeared sometime during the raid in the warehouse. The pouch was fuller, but somehow, she knew it wasn't full yet.

She looked at the wash of stars across the sky. "Have you ever wondered about getting married?"

The dark mass grunted as he moved the gate for cooler water. "Lizard… are you telling me you want to show me your stones?" He splashed back into the water. The wave swelled past her chin and ears.

Her hand dropped the pouch. The leather thong was warm around her neck. "No."

They floated in the warm water. Thorny thought about the mountain that seemed to be quiet or at rest. She wondered if it was because she was in the water and relaxed or if the mountain was relaxed also.

"Frog?"

The answer could have been a true bullfrog farting or croaking.

"When you lie in the pool, is the water different here than say in the hot ditch near the Keogh's spa?"

"Sure. Deeper and hotter." His spray of water hit her's mid-air.

"Smartass."

He was quiet. He had never thought about there being any difference.

"You're quiet, so I know you're thinking about it. But if there is no difference between here, hot ditch, or your bathtub… why is the water in the river different?"

She could hear the deep sigh across the pond.

"You might not understand."

Her wave was two-handed, but she noticed he had not moved. No wave. No rebuttal. No joke.

"I'm as much Paiute as you, brother."

"I've seen your paperwhite butt."

"My blood flows through you as yours flows through me." Her forefinger rubbed along the pad of her thumb. With the water-wrinkled skin, she knew she could feel the scar where they had become blood whatever. "Besides, who did the golden hand choose?"

The pond farted with a muted grunt.

"Hot ditch filters through a white man's tubs and pool first. By the time it gets to the ditch, it's almost dead. There is no Paiute left in the water. Just so much white man pee."

"And here?"

"Did you just pee in the water?"

"No." She groaned. "You are a disgusting child."

"Here, the water is straight out of the rock. This is as pure as it gets." He thought about the question. "Are you closer to the mountain here than at the ditch?"

She pushed herself up to side on the rock edge. "I think so. Either it's being close, or I just always felt better here. It never mattered if I was with Ulysses, Eustis, or just you and your grandfather, the water always felt good. Anything cooked up here was perfect, and whenever I drink coffee, I can feel this pond, the air, the heat, the..." Her voice tapered off.

Charlie fanned his arms and hands softly just below the surface. "The home...?"

Thorny ran her tongue curled along her lower lip as it was pulled tight over her teeth. "Yeah... maybe that's it. I never felt home any place else." She slipped back down into the water. "The mine is like an old pair of bibs, but it's not mine... it's Ulysses's. I know every inch, where metal is, where the best ore car is for frying flatbread on, but it's not home."

"You sleep in the barn."

She laughed. "It smells like grandpa. Whenever I used to hug Eustis, I could smell who he had last fed, or shoed, or wrestled with. The barn is like his old bibs. I'm comfortable there."

She could hear him grunting as he leaned back and around to move the gates. "So now what?" He was heating the water. "Do you build a house up here?"

"Too far from town."

"When did the town ever enter any of your decisions?" You don't even live in town, so what do you care about what happens?"

"When I got pregnant."

The throat took four tries to clear. "Lizard, that is nothing to joke about."

She pushed up out of the hotter water. Even the rock wasn't as cool as it was a few minutes before. "Okay, only a little joke, Charlie. I don't know how else to explain it. Maybe becoming a mother is better than pregnant. I feel like I'm the mother of the whole damn town. Forget mayor, this is caring a lot more than 'will you vote for me again in four years.' This is the mother peeking around the corner to make sure the child gets to school okay. This is feeling the forehead in the middle of the night kind of caring. I don't know anything about being a mother, and now I have the biggest kid ever. And it's not doing well. I don't know how to make chicken soup for a child this big."

The snort laugh sounded more like an elk in rut. "Hell, Thorny, you don't know how to make chicken soup no matter how big the child is. But I'm here, and we'll all figure this out together.

"Thanks." She looked at the stars. They seemed a tiny bit brighter. A small breeze came down the canyon and tinkled through the Aspen. Her smile was loose and relaxed. Her eyes began to droop.

As they curled in their blankets a few minutes later, she rolled over and looked at the large mound of her friend. "By the way, I'm getting your truck a new transmission and something in the axle thing."

She felt the rumble through the ground.

"Thanks. Mace told me."

She rolled onto her back and watched the stars.

A meteor shot across the sky.

She missed it—she was already asleep.

ALSO BY BAER CHARLTON

The Very Littlest Dragon

Stoneheart
(Pulitzer Nominee 2015)

Angel Flights
What About Marsha?
Pirate's Patch

Southside Hooker Series
Death on a Dime – Book One
Night Vision – Book Two
Unbidden Garden – Book Three
Boomtown – Book Four
One Day Under the Grass – Book Five

Thorny Wallace Series
Death in the Valley – Book One
Light to Light – Book Two

BAER CHARLTON

ABOUT THE AUTHOR

Baer Charlton graduated from UC Irvine with a degree in Social Anthropology, monkeyed around for a while, and then proceeded onward with a life of global travel, multi-disciplinary adventure, and meeting the memorable array of characters he would come to describe in his writing. He has ridden things with gears, engines, and sails, and made things with wood, leather, and metal. He has been stitched back together more times than the average hockey team; his long-suffering wife and an assortment of cats and dogs have nursed him back to health after each surgery.

Baer knows a lot about many things in this world. History flows through his veins and pours out of him at the slightest provocation. Do not ask him what you may think is a simple question unless you have the time to hear a fascinating story.

You can find more about Baer at his website.
www.baercharlton.com